Blue Ridge to Bolivia

by

Judith Fournie Helms

Cover Art by *Teddi Black*

The Wild Rose Press, Inc.
PO Box 708
Adams Basin, NY 14410-0708
Visit us at www.thewildrosepress.com

Publishing History
First Edition, 2025
Trade Paperback Print ISBN 978-1-5092-6329-5
Digital ISBN 978-1-5092-6330-1

Published in the United States of America

Dedication

For Lily

Siempre adelante

Chapter 1

I had a rare moment of euphoria thirty minutes before the catastrophe.

Mom had insisted on bringing a picnic lunch, although I told her I was sure we could find a decent diner near the Parkway that would serve just as well and without the bother for her. She liked to bother.

When my husband, Mac, and I picked up my folks, Mom lifted the top of the antique wicker picnic basket to show off the brown bread, still warm from the oven, sliced Granny Smith apples from their backyard tree dusted with cinnamon and sugar, and her signature flourless chocolate cake. The drinks and her homemade chicken salad were under ice in an old, red cola cooler—one of the originals from the fifties. Mac asked me to drive because he'd injured his right foot running. Once the basket and cooler were tucked into the trunk, Mac offered to let my mother ride shotgun so she'd have the better view. Because he enjoyed talking about the latest games with my sports fan father, the seating arrangement suited everyone.

It was an outrageously good year for the colors after a couple of seasons of drab browns and short viewing windows, and once we got to the outskirts of town and started up into the mountains, we were blown away. It wasn't just the vivid oranges, reds, and golds, illuminated from behind to a glow. It was also the majesty of the blue-tinged mountains, rising tall and posing to advantage across the richly patterned valleys. Shadows from clouds peppered the farmers' fields sequentially, deepening the hue of one patch after the other. Views like these never failed to bring me as close to a religious experience as the incense and hymns had done when I was a little girl.

Mom was her usual, gabby self, but her cheerful chatter evaporated once we hit the long views. After that, we were all reduced to the inadequate "amazing," "incredible," and "unbelievable." I'd always thought beauty was like death in that way—there are no words. The experience is the thing. As we would say in a negligence case, res ipsa loquitur. And to quote from my favorite president, "far above our poor power to add or detract."

I rounded a turn to a valley view that literally made my jaw drop. I felt a bump in my chest—exactly as though my heart had taken a little leap. It was a sensation I'd experienced before while driving through the mountains, but in no other place on earth.

I pulled into the next "scenic overlook" so we could all get out to fully absorb what lay before our eyes. A stranger agreed to take our picture on my phone, with heaven as our background. After ten minutes or so, we were all climbing back into the car when Mom pulled me aside and told me she really needed to find a restroom. Actually, she called it "a ladies' powder room," a phrase she applied to all bathrooms, including port-a-potties and gas station arrangements with outdoor entries.

I hadn't seen any signs for trailheads or state park entrances and didn't know of any in the vicinity, so I figured the best course was to pull off at the next opportunity and head east until we hit a town. I consciously kept my speed at the impossibly slow 35 mph limit because I think of all small towns and their environs as speed-traps, and flashing lights pulling up behind me always make my stomach drop. There were only a few stop signs on the winding country road, and I gave each its due—a full and complete stop. Each time, I felt the front of the car tip forward into immobility just before my mid-back was thrust against the seat back. I'd been taking this approach ever since the day a cop pulled me over for not doing a "full and complete." I beat the rap in court, but the shame of being told I hadn't followed the rules stayed with me. Up until recently, I had always been a big rule-follower.

We'd passed a few farmhouses but no gas stations when we reached an area marked 55 mph, and I felt like we were moving again. Still, I didn't tempt fate, and suspected that every outcropping of trees hid a wily cop standing next to an unmarked car, crouching as he gripped a radar gun with both hands.

A sign for a town five miles ahead gave me hope I could get Mom where she needed to be in time. It was a hilly area with an intersection on the horizon. The speed limit went down to forty-five mph—still perceptible movement. The forest was heavy to my right, and I saw no other vehicles around. I cruised along, humming Mom's favorite song, the one with lilies in it. Just as I sailed through the intersection, we exploded.

Chapter 2

When I opened my eyes, it was dark in the room, and the soft ticking and periodic beeping reminded me of the sounds of a TV show hospital room. I glanced to my left and saw a machine with a blood pressure measurement displayed in magenta fluorescent digits with smaller green numbers below. Something was sticking into the top of my right hand, with cellophane holding it in place, and its slim tube led to a metal stand holding a bag of clear fluid. A box that looked like a small computer sat beside it. Another tube had sprouted from my left hand. I ran my right hand up my arm, then gently touched my neck, chin, and nose with my fingertips. All of my parts seemed to be in the right places, but I felt a plastic tube sticking out of my nose. It was unexpected and immediately sickened me.

I closed my eyes to think—to remember who I was and why I was lying in a hospital bed. All I could come up with was that I was me, that Mac and I had picked up Mom and Dad, and we were looking for a bathroom for Mom. I must've been injured, but I felt no pain. I was too disoriented to think to press the button to summon a nurse. I lay still trying to remember more. There was no more. I nodded off.

The next time I opened my eyes, both natural and artificial light flooded the room. A young nurse with very short hair was adjusting the bag of liquid. I cleared my throat before speaking. "Who are you?"

As she turned to look at me, her eyes grew large, and she smiled. "I'm Anna Winston. Can you tell me your name?"

"Of course. I'm Suzanne. Suzanne Summerfield."

"Can you tell me your date of birth, Suzanne?"

"April 3, 1970. Why? What am I doing here?"

"Let me get the doctor." As Anna placed her hand on the door handle, she turned back to me and said, "Do you know what day it is?"

I cleared my throat as I thought for a moment. "I know it's Sunday. I believe it's October 15. You see, we were looking at the leaves."

She nodded and smiled again before passing through the sliding glass door.

A few minutes later, the nurse was back, accompanied by a slight gray-haired woman in a blue cotton lab coat, stethoscope hanging from her neck. She walked up to me and smiled. "Hello. I'm Dr. Mattingly. It's nice to see you awake."

"What do you mean?"

"Can you tell me your name and date of birth?"

"Okay. But I just told Anna."

"I know. I'm sorry to tell you this, but you're going to be asked that by pretty much everyone who walks in here." The doctor smiled.

"All right. I'm Suzanne Summerfield. Date of birth, April 3, 1970."

She glanced down to the screen of a laptop she held. "Good. Do you know why you're here?"

"Not really."

"You were involved in an automobile accident. You've been here since then."

"What do you mean? How long?"

"Nine weeks."

I couldn't comprehend how that was possible. "What?"

"You arrived here by ambulance on October 13th."

"So, not the15th?"

"No." She was as certain as I was confused.

I tried to process it. "Define 'here.' " That came out like a demand, so I added, "Please."

"Charlottesville General."

I took a moment to wrap my head around her answers. Two months in a hospital was insane. "So, where are my husband and my parents?"

"I'm sorry." She shook her head slightly. "They didn't make it."

I thought, *"Didn't make it."*

What does that even mean? Didn't make it here? Went home from the accident?

My face must've conveyed my thoughts. Hers answered my questions. "Oh, my God!"

"I'm so sorry, Ms. Summerfield."

"All three of them?"

She nodded.

The scream came out of me in the shape of the word, "No."

Chapter 3

The feeding tube was removed from my nose that day, and I began exercises to rebuild my muscles. Two days later, on December 29th, my last IV was pulled out and I was discharged. The doctors seemed to be confounded that my only injury had been a closed head trauma resulting in a coma. I had no residual medical issues at all except for the muscle atrophy.

A good friend, and the only other woman partner in our firm, picked me up at the hospital and drove me home. When we arrived at my house, a modern log two-story Mac and I had built, Marilee pulled into the driveway and came to a full-and-complete. When my back hit the seatback, I started weeping. My sobs grew in intensity until I was gasping for air.

Marilee didn't try to comfort me. She just let me go on until there was nothing left, then handed me a full box of tissues she must've realized I'd need. I blew my nose about a hundred times and threw the tissues into a trash bag she held open for me, more evidence that she'd known what was coming. She released her seatbelt, so I un-did mine. She handed me a bottle of water, and I took a long drink.

"What do I do?" I asked.

"You go into your house. I'll be with you."

She got out and came around the front of her car to my side, opened my door, and took me by the elbow. In the hospital I'd been taught to use a cane, and I carried it in my other hand. I swallowed hard several times as we took the slate sidewalk to the front door. Marilee had the key in her hand and quickly unlocked and opened the heavy oak door. I stood in the foyer and looked around. The light poured in through the window wall, and the wide-plank oak floors gleamed. "It's so neat," I said quietly.

"I asked Beth to keep up her weekly cleaning for you."

"But how did you pay her?"

"I just paid her. I felt sure you'd be back, and I wanted your place to be ready for you."

"What about our bills? And all the newspapers?"

Marilee took a step around me so we were face-to-face. She took the cane from me and leaned it against the wall, then took my hands in hers. "I put a vacation hold on the papers." She squinted. "Well, that sounds insensitive, but it's what they call it. And I monitored your mail and paid anything that looked like a bill."

"I'm so sorry you had to do that."

"It's okay. I knew you were good for it."

"Thanks, Marilee." I glanced at the mission oak hallway table to my left in the foyer, and noted something was amiss. My framed photos were gone. One was a picture of my parents, taken at their church, and the other, my favorite, was from my wedding day—Mac and me dancing and laughing at ourselves. I nodded toward the table. "My pictures?"

"I was afraid they might upset you, so I moved them until I could ask you about it." She bit her lower lip. "Was that okay?"

I hesitated because I didn't know the answer. "Yeah.

Thanks. I'll give it some thought. But in case I want them up, where did you hide them?"

"In your pot-holder drawer. I figured it would be a nice, soft resting place so they wouldn't get scratched."

I let out a little whistle. "I'm glad I asked. It might've been a bit of a shock if I were to be greeted by my parents the next time I reached for a pot-holder." I was trying to lighten the heaviness between us, but I couldn't sustain it. "Have you done anything else for me?"

"Yesterday, when you confirmed you'd be released today, I stocked your fridge."

I raised my eyebrows. "Really?"

"Certainly." She dropped my hands and added, "How about I make us a cup of tea?"

I nodded. Marilee was directing the scene as she liked to do, but this time, I appreciated it. She motioned toward the little breakfast booth Mac and I used for meals, an intimate space I'd always loved. The table-top was only two feet wide, so he and I would look into each other's eyes when we spoke. She took my arm to get me there. "How long will you need to use the cane?"

"Not long if I do my exercises every day. Maybe a week or two."

"Good. Does it hurt to walk?"

I smiled at her. "Not at all, Marilee. I'm just rebuilding the muscles."

"Well, that's a relief." She walked up to the island to put the kettle on, then pulled out my tea drawer to grab what she knew we each liked. We said nothing as the water heated and the kettle finally broke the silence with its shrill whistle. In the meantime, Marilee had cut thick slices of a bakery banana bread. Once she'd served us, she slid into the booth across from me. She gave me an incredibly tender smile, for Marilee. Her dark green eyes, the color of wet seaweed, were riveted to mine. She said, "Where would you like to start?"

"Mac and my parents. Where are they? I mean…" I paused. "Well, you know."

"As you know, I have the back-up key to your house."

I nodded, although I really didn't remember giving it to her.

"I found your file cabinet in Mac's music room. So, I rummaged through it until I located your wills, and saw that Mac wanted to be cremated. I also stumbled on a key to your mom and dad's house, so I let myself in there and poked around until I found their wills."

"You did?"

"Of course."

"You had them all cremated?"

"Per their wishes. Well, I worked with the law firm that had drawn up your parents' will. The attorney there, Darren Long, confirmed we were looking at their most recent testaments. He and I figured out who their pastor was, and the priest also knew they wanted to be cremated. He remembered because it was against his advice."

"And Mac?"

"Obviously, our firm has a current copy of Mac's will—and yours. So it was easy to confirm his intention to be cremated, as well."

"I see." I was hearing the information, but it seemed to be bouncing off my ears. I had to concentrate to retain it. "And their ashes are…."

"At my house. I wanted to guard them for you until

you could make your plans about what to do with them."

"Oh." I had to take a moment to process it. Now the people I loved most in the world had been turned into boxes of dust, and Marilee had taken custody of them. My first thought was that she had a lot of nerve. But I forced myself to think it through. In her defense, I hadn't been available to ask, and for all she knew, I might never have returned to consciousness. I gave her a soft smile. "Thanks."

I took several sips of tea from my favorite mug, the one Mom had given me when I was little. My six-year-old face was smiling, with gaps where front teeth would eventually appear, a little girl with no idea what was in store for her. My desire to not ask the next question was almost overwhelming. I took two stabs at it before actually getting it out. Marilee was staring at me, patiently waiting. Finally, I just spat out, "What happened to us?"

"They all died instantly."

"Yes. The doctor mentioned that at the hospital. She seemed to think that would be a great relief to me—that they hadn't suffered."

"Isn't it?"

I thought about it. "I'm glad they felt no pain. But, Marilee, they were alive. Now they're dead."

She said nothing for a moment, and then asked, "Do you want me to tell you how the accident happened?"

I hesitated. The answer was "absolutely not." And, "of course." But what I said was, "I remember it, Marilee. I was driving through an intersection. I didn't have a stop sign or anything."

"You didn't. But you should have."

"What?"

"The night before your accident, some local delinquents removed the stop sign." Marilee shook her head and grimaced. Then she took a sip of tea.

"Why?"

"We don't know for sure. The criminal trial isn't set until April. Of course, their lawyer won't let them talk." Marilee took a deep breath and avoided my eyes.

"But there's more. Right?"

"What do you mean?"

"I know that dumb-dog-look on your face."

She smiled. "So, I'm that transparent. I'd better do all of my settlement negotiations by phone."

I raised my eyebrows.

"Okay. I hired a private investigator. Well, the one the firm uses."

"Harvey."

"Yeah. He says the word on the street is that it was just a prank."

I had my mug halfway to my lips, but froze it there. "As opposed to—what else could it be?"

"Apparently, some kids take them to put the road signs on their dorm room walls."

"But not these kids?"

"No dorm rooms. These three are fifteen-year-olds."

"Ah." I set the mug down to give all my attention to trying to imagine what Marilee was laying out.

"The police found the sign—still on the post—in the trunk of the car they had borrowed from the older brother of one of the boys. She used air-quotes around "borrowed."

"So did they wait in a culvert to watch the carnage?"

"No. They weren't that sadistic. They were a little drunk when they took it. Word is they weren't expecting anything spectacular. Harvey got the feeling they hadn't formed any real idea of consequences at all."

I shook my head at their unbelievable indifference. "Who hit us?"

"Semi driver. He'd taken the route before, and knew your road had a stop sign. I got this from his lawyer at the traffic court hearing. The driver himself was too stunned to talk. It looked to me like he was in shock. Honestly. He couldn't even say his own name."

I thought about it. The driver's reaction seemed completely appropriate to me. "Who's defending him?"

"Insurance defense counsel from the county where it happened. The guy showed up at the first hearing along with the trucker's traffic court lawyer."

"Anybody we know?"

"We know his firm, Yang and Gray."

"May's firm."

"Right."

"But I didn't know the young lawyer who appeared. Never heard of the traffic court lawyer or his firm. I did introduce myself to both of them."

I closed my eyes to think. "You know, Marilee, I'm not sure it was his fault."

She put down her fork and stared at me. "I'll pretend I didn't hear that. I'm sure he was speeding, Suzanne. He had a 55 mile per hour speed limit. It was a clear, dry, late morning with almost no traffic out there. Can you imagine that anyone wouldn't be doing a few miles over the limit?"

I met her gaze. "Yes."

"Ha. Good point. I mean anyone other than you."

"Wait. You're saying I should sue the truck company?"

"It's a big one."

"I don't care about that."

Marilee paused, then patted my hand. "I think you should take some time and think it over. And keep in mind that discovery is the best way to find out exactly what happened."

"Why should I care?" The moment the words came out of my mouth it struck me how callous they sounded. "What I mean is, at this point, does it matter?"

Marilee let out a long sigh. "Let's just say, lest you ever have to deal with any feelings of guilt." She glanced down briefly, then studied me for a moment before speaking. "What I mean is that what happened wasn't even a tiny bit your fault. Get the facts. Satisfy yourself about that."

"I see. I'll think about it."

She leaned back in her seat and changed the subject. "So, Suzanne, do you want me to stay with you tonight?"

"No. I'm okay." I paused. "Wait. Don't I look okay?"

"It's not about how you look. It's just that this will be your first night at home since Mac died. It'll be hard, sweetie."

"Yeah." I stirred what was left in my mug, and watched the brown liquid swirl.

After a couple of moments, Marilee said, "So?"

I shook my head as I travelled back to the present. "Sorry. No, thanks. I have to face this some time."

Marilee shrugged. "Okay. But call me anytime if you want me to come over. My reliable availability is one of the many blessings of being single."

As we hugged at my front door, I knew I wouldn't call her. And I knew the night would be as close to hell as I'd ever come.

Chapter 4

Using my cane, I hobbled through the house, expecting to feel nothing and everything in each room. Because Marilee had paid Beth to come over to clean, there were no dirty dishes in the sink with the remains of Mac's last cup of coffee. I couldn't decide whether I was relieved or grievously disappointed. The entire great room was tidy, as though ready for a real estate showing. I noted that the half-bath was immaculate, then corrected myself—the ladies' powder room.

As I made my way slowly and cautiously up the open staircase, I could see the entire main floor, and nothing was lying around as a reminder of my husband— of the lack of my husband. Upstairs, the two guest bedrooms looked the same as always, no special clues as to what I'd lost. But I knew that entering Mac's music room would be hard, so I inched the door open hesitantly. Three guitars were at the ready, out of their cases, on stands. Sheet music was all over the piano, on top, on the stand, on the bench. And the seat of his ancient, comfy, red leather armchair held several notebooks, and an array of pencils and pens. His desk looked just as messy as it always had.

Mac's hobby was composing. He earned his living as a social worker, but it was creating music that kept him going. It was his therapist, worming out of him his deepest fears, most intense feelings, and hardest childhood memories. As a result, most of his lyrics were dark. Still, every once in a while, he wrote lines that bespoke some joy. Either way, I'd felt honored that all of them were for my ears only. Most wives aren't allowed into their husband's therapy sessions. But mainly, I'd felt fear. I always dreaded hearing that he had been sad, and probably still was, because it forced me to face the fact that I wasn't doing enough to counter it. I left the room without looking through any of his work, drew the door closed, and impulsively resolved not to open it again for a year.

I sat on the floor outside our bedroom. I'd had no clothes with me when it was time to leave the hospital. Apparently, the ones I'd been wearing when I arrived were covered with blood—not mine. Marilee had loaned me leggings, one of her warm tunic tops, a coat, and pull-on microfiber boots for the trip home. All of my clothing was in our master closet, and I wasn't ready to pass through the bedroom door. Marilee's clothes would be fine.

Somehow, I got back downstairs. I clicked on the electric fire and settled in on the couch with our alpaca throw for a blanket. I recalled Mom telling friends with pride that it had come from Bolivia. I slept deeply, but not for nearly long enough. When I awoke at 3:00 a.m., for the first moment it seemed possible that everything was normal. Then, as reality came into focus, I cursed the slumber that had tricked me into thinking I was still alive. I couldn't fall back asleep. I lay, perfectly still, allowing only my eyes to move. I'd left one light on in the foyer, so I was able to make out the shapes and shadows and to connect them with the furniture I remembered.

A half hour later, I forced myself to crawl out from under the warm afghan. My cane and I travelled to the powder room to wash my face, and I was struck by how long it had been since I'd looked in a mirror. My freckles, which I'd despised as a child, did more than add a little color to my face. They, like my hazel eyes, connected me to my mother. I remembered one time I'd rushed into my parents' house, just as Mom was leaving. Face to face so unexpectedly, I saw my future self—just as though I were looking into some magical time machine mirror.

I swallowed hard and reached into a drawer in the vanity where I kept an extra toothbrush and paste. I combed my hair with my fingers. I'd always expected to have at least some red highlights in view of my face full of freckles. But it was jet black, with just a few gray strands poking through. At forty-eight, that was the least I should expect.

I circled the great room—living, dining, kitchen space—and paused to turn on every lamp and overhead can light. My *Hits From the Seventies* CD was ready to go, so I pushed "play" on the remote, and my favorite artists were with me. But not really. I hadn't lived alone for eighteen years.

I went back to the couch, lay down, and fell deeply asleep again. When I awoke around eight o'clock, I went through the same horror. For the tiniest second, between sleep and consciousness, reality could've gone either way. Then, bam! It veered the awful direction—again. It was at that moment I realized my life as I knew it was over. In its place would be something entirely superficial—what doctors and lawyers call "the activities of daily living." For me, it would be the activities of daily dying. My job was just to get through each day until I could join Mac and my parents in oblivion.

Chapter 5

Two weeks into knowing that I'd become a widow and an orphan, I was back at work. Everything I did during the workday was fake. Everything I did at home was real. I accepted condolences, planned and executed a joint memorial service, arranged ash-filled urns on my mantel, spoke with clients, went to court, researched points of law, wrote briefs, bought groceries, had the oil changed, and generally acted as though I were alive.

But at home, I tiptoed through my bedroom like I might waken Mac. I apologized to him and to my parents for not having been a better person with them when I'd had the chance. One day, I found myself standing before the urns on my mantel, quietly studying the brass name plates. I turned away and let out a blood-curdling scream, so loud and so long that it terrified me. Once I'd calmed down, I worried the neighbors would assume I'd been murdered. I knew I would never wail like that. Someone else who lived deep inside me had somehow escaped all the barriers and released her pain with the primal scream. Another time, she took over while I was preparing a salad for dinner and spewed every swear word I knew—and some I didn't—in a fit of rage.

The first week I was home, I had no appetite at all, and tried to fool myself by moving morsels around on my plate before dumping the meal into the garbage disposal. The second week, I ate whatever I could find.

Just ten minutes after I'd finished, I had no idea what I'd consumed as I tried to reconstruct it by studying the empty containers. But I returned to the fridge for another few bites—of anything. By the third week, I was able to moderate my eating, but still without laying down any memory of the particulars.

I folded up and boxed all of Mac's things to give away. The next week, I carried the boxes to the attic so I could keep them. Later, I carried them down and put them in my new, old car, the one that had been my parents'. Then I carried them back into the house, and lugged them back up to the attic.

Mac and I had only had a few close friends because neither of us wanted more. We were hard core introverts, happy with just each other's company, and seeing my folks and our friends periodically. We were both only children, Mac's parents were long dead, and neither his nor mine had any siblings.

We had no children, though not for lack of trying. I learned it takes more than lots of sex to make a baby. Good eggs, decent sperm, a clear path to bring them together, and the pure luck that they stay that way are prerequisites. Mac and I were thirty when we met, thirty-one when we married, and forty-two when we went through our last in vitro fertilization attempt. That, plus two years of trying to adopt, brought us to forty-four, and a decision to let it go and accept that we would be a childless couple. That was four years before I lost Mac forever. As it turned out, the grief of losing out on my dream of motherhood had been good practice. After the accident, the incomprehensible feelings of loss were vaguely familiar.

But what I experienced more and more frequently

was beyond loss. It was guilt—not just the shame I felt about not having done enough for them or having been kind enough with them. I thought of that as normal guilt for a bereaved person. The dreadful self-reproach that engulfed me was about how my choices had killed my family. Of course, I'd chosen the wrong route. Obviously, I should've exceeded the speed limit, like any normal person would have, so that our path and the truck's never would have crossed. And it was undeniable that I should've seen the truck coming by simply pausing at the intersection to look both ways. I'd always been the most cautious driver I knew. How did I fail to take that simple, life-saving step on October 13th? This was the regret that frequently roused me in the middle of the night and gnawed at me until morning's light. I was always exhausted the following day, but in some pathetic way, I relished the deep fatigue because it was part of the penance I deserved.

I preserved the privacy of my real life, the insane one I lived at home, by never having anyone over. Marilee and other colleagues and their spouses from work invited me out, but I always declined. I knew they just wanted me to rejoin the living. But the truth was, my membership had expired and I didn't have the wherewithal to re-up.

I would probably still be living this Jekyll and Hyde existence if Marilee hadn't stormed the gates of my fortress one calm, cold February night.

Chapter 6

Friday evenings were my favorites, but for reasons opposite from most people's. They meant I wouldn't have to put on the act of being alive for two whole days. I'd picked up dinner at a restaurant Mac and I had never visited. I was sitting on a stool at the island, having just taken my last bite, and not remembering what it was. My plan was the same as every night. Put on an old movie or read a boring book to fall asleep, and pray the escape would come quickly and continue all through the night.

So when the doorbell rang, it jolted me, and I instinctively jumped. I worked up the courage to sidle up to the peephole, eyes glued to the locked deadbolt. I held my breath and put my eye to the spot. Marilee. I heard myself say, "Crap."

When I released the lock and opened the door, she walked in without invitation, carrying a pile of slim manila folders. She smiled at me, then headed over to the kitchen island and dropped off the materials. Then she hugged me and I hugged back the way I thought a living human would. This was new. My grief space was being invaded.

She said, "I didn't call first because I knew you'd tell me not to come over."

I nodded.

She flashed a quick look around the kitchen. "Cup of tea?"

I nodded again, not knowing how to get out of the visit.

Like on that first day, she glanced at the booth and I headed for my side. Neither of us spoke until she brought the two mugs over and slid mine across to me.

I tilted my head. "No banana bread?"

"Actually, I have a warm loaf of homemade pumpkin in my car. But I wasn't sure you'd let me in." Marilee jumped up, hurried out the front door, and returned in a minute with the dessert. She grabbed two plates from my cupboard and a couple of forks, and set it all on the table between us.

"That's better." I sliced off two pieces of the bread. "And what do you mean you 'weren't sure I'd let you in?' "

Marilee took a sip of her tea, then leaned forward and placed her arms on the table, hands down. "It's enough, Suzanne."

"Excuse me?"

"It's been a month since you returned to work. People say to me, 'She's not even in there anymore.' I'm tired of them saying it. And I'm tired of it being true."

My pulse quickened at the accusation. "*You* are?"

Marilee placed her chin on her fists as she continued. "Yes. I'm tired of it for you. What you went through was indescribably horrendous. I don't pretend to understand how you must feel."

I said, too loudly, "Yes you do."

"What?"

"You say you're tired of it for me. But you don't even know what the 'it' is."

"Of course I don't, Suzanne. I just said I don't."

I wanted the conversation to end so badly that I was

tempted to say, "Please, leave." But I couldn't do it. I said, "And yet, here you sit."

"Listen for a minute."

I didn't respond. I looked away, my face as neutral as I could make it.

"Please."

She'd been a close friend for a long time. I owed it to her to hear her out. I glanced at her. "Okay."

"I didn't know your folks. But I knew Mac. And there is no way he would've wanted you to isolate yourself with your grief."

I just stared at her for a moment, then looked at my plate. "You say you knew Mac. Good for you. I didn't. And I lived with him for eighteen years. But I would never claim that I really, truly, knew him."

"You know what I mean, Suzanne. You knew him well enough to know he'd want you to be happy."

I was about to take a fork-full of banana bread, but let it drop. We both jumped as the fork clattered against the plate. "Sorry. But that doesn't even make sense. I mean, yeah, I suppose he wanted everyone to 'be happy.' But he wasn't stupid. He understood that sometimes it's just not possible."

Marilee looked out toward the window-wall for a moment, then sighed softly. "You're right. 'Happy' is probably too much to hope for. How about this—he'd want you to be in the world and of the world, at least as much as you were before the accident."

I thought about it. "Probably." I paused. "But, Marilee, his wanting it, or your wanting it, or even my wanting it doesn't make it possible."

She stared at me. "I suppose not. But doesn't the process at least have to start there? I mean, do you really want to live the rest of your life as the walking dead?"

I snorted a laugh. "Actually, I'm only the walking dead out there. Here in my space, I'm quite alive with grief, and anger, and guilt, and…" I hesitated. "And a profound feeling of isolation."

Marilee took my hand above the tabletop. "Oh, sweetie. I'm so sorry."

I let out a long sigh and took my hand back. "Thanks. And thanks for stopping by. I'm feeling really tired all of a sudden. I think I'll go upstairs and lie down, if you don't mind." I stood up, but Marilee simply took another sip of her tea.

"Didn't you hear me?"

She smiled up at me. "But you see, I do mind. I've brought you some things I want to go over with you."

"The folders."

"Yes." She rose and walked over to the stack on the island. She pointed to my stool, where my empty dinner plate sat. "Have a seat. This will take a few minutes."

I joined her and sat heavily, trying to make sure Marilee knew I wasn't happy about it. "So you're basically refusing to leave my house until you show me this stuff."

"Basically. Why? Gonna call the cops?"

I grunted a laugh. "Okay. What's so important that you're willing to camp here until you get your way?"

Marilee pulled papers from the top folder. "This is your Complaint against Toby Thomas, Dean Mitchell, Harry Phillips, Tooley Freight Lines International, and Charlie Bixby."

"Hm. So Toby, Dean, and Harry are the juvenile delinquents who pulled the stop sign?"

"Yep."

"What theories?"

"Two counts against the boys, negligence and reckless disregard. Just negligence against the driver and his company."

"I see." I rolled my eyes to show Marilee my displeasure, but I was vaguely interested—both to learn more about what had happened, and because the proximate cause argument against the boys intrigued me. "What are the other papers?"

"Summonses, interrogatories, document requests, subpoenas, notices for depositions, and a motion to require the truck company not to tamper with the cab until we've had our inspection."

I quietly paged through the pile of documents, then looked up at her. "Marilee, it's been six months. Surely, they've already tampered."

"Harvey says they haven't. The cab of the truck and what's left of your car are being held at the same junkyard."

"Why do you want me to do this?"

"One reason. And unlike with most of my plaintiffs, it isn't money."

"So…"

"So, you need to put the demons to bed."

"Hm."

"It won't be over until you know what happened, and why."

My eyes were resting on the documents, but I jerked my head up to look at her eye-to-eye. "'Be over'?"

"Sorry. I do realize it'll never be over. But I really think knowing the story could help you."

I took a moment to consider it. "Will you represent me?"

"I'll do all the written work." She paused, then added, "But you know we're too close. So, John volunteered to take the depositions and handle any settlement negotiations and the trial."

"John's good."

"Plus, I'll keep my eye on him to make sure he doesn't muck it up."

"John isn't much for mucking things up."

Marilee smiled. "I know."

I pursed my lips as I often do when I think things through. "I'll tell you what. I'll read what you've prepared this weekend. I'll promise to let you know my decision on Monday if you'll agree to stop trespassing." I eyeballed the front door.

She laughed and straightened the piles of papers. "I'm on my way." Just as we reached the door, she turned back to me. "One other thing. Have you taken Mac's things to Goodwill?"

"Yeah. Finally did."

"Good. And what about your folks' house? Are you getting it ready to sell?"

"You said one thing. That's two."

"Okay. I lied. But what about your parents' house?"

"Actually, I've been thinking about it. I need to clean out the personal things, then have an estate sale or something like that."

"Right. Well, Suzanne, I need you to promise me you'll let me be with you when you do."

"Seriously?"

She nodded.

"If I agree, will you finally leave?" I'd been holding the door open the whole time, as though it would help to move her along.

"Yep."

"Fine. I agree."

As I closed and deadbolted the door, I wondered what I could possibly find at Mom and Dad's house that could require me to bring along a caretaker.

Chapter 7

On Monday morning, I walked down to Marilee's office and straight through her open door, leaned against the wall with one hand on my hip. "Fine. File it." She gave me a thumbs up and went back to what she was reading.

Two days later, I texted her to let her know I'd stopped at the hardware store for a half-dozen boxes, some large trash bags, and tons of package sealing tape, and planned to be at my parents' house at 11:00 a.m. on Sunday to clean out the personal stuff. She texted back immediately. *Good. I'll meet you there.*

My parents had both been high school teachers, and they'd still lived in the brick ranch house I'd grown up in, on a street lined with mature trees in a small town about an hour west of where Mac and I built. There was no garage at the end of their neat, paved driveway, and the crawl space was only large enough for the plumber to crawl around in. So, beyond the living areas, there was only the attic to rifle through.

I arrived early so I could have a few minutes alone in the space where I'd spent so much of my life. I pulled open the screen door and let it rest against my hip as I unlocked the sunshine yellow front door with the key I kept in the leather sunflower key case Mom had given me. The first thing my gaze landed on was my mother's cushioned rocker, and I could see her as though she were there, sitting with her ankles crossed, knitting needles clicking away, a dwindling ball of yarn at her feet, another colorful throw pouring out of the needles. I glanced at the small mahogany table with the LP record player, arm at the ready to drop on one of their worn albums of '60s folk music. I had to look away, but was then faced with the dining room table in the room to my left. There was Dad as I'd so often seen him, only yards from Mom, with his arms extended over a yellowed piece of oil cloth as he worked on painting one of his beloved model cars. It hit me that this was going to be harder than I'd thought.

I turned and let myself back out the front door, the screen door slapping shut behind me. I took a seat in one of the two white wooden rockers on the small porch and tried to focus on the tall, bare maple trees, all lightly dusted with snow, and the random appearance of a fat snowflake.

Marilee pulled into the driveway behind my car at exactly eleven o'clock, then stood looking at the house for a moment before she approached. She wore blue jeans, a blue jean shirt, an off-white puffy vest, and work boots. Her auburn hair was pulled back in a high ponytail. As she approached, I pointed at her steel-toe boots. "We're not here to demolish it."

She laughed. "My brother gave me these the year he helped me re-do my kitchen." She looked at the front door, which was wide open with only the screen door keeping non-existent bugs out. "You've already gone in?"

The cold seemed to make her words more pronounced. No one else was out and about, which made me feel lonely in spite of her presence. "Yeah. Big mistake. I'm glad you came, Marilee."

"Sure. Where do you want to start?" she asked, as she held the door open for me.

"I don't know. What do you think?"

Marilee said, "I'd go up in the attic first, and work our way down."

"Suits me."

Marilee walked ahead of me through the stone-quiet, slightly musty-smelling house carrying a large flashlight. She walked straight to the overhead door to the attic, reached up and took down from the wall the flat, eighteen-inch-long piece of wood with a hook at the end, then stretched to slip the hook through the screw-eye on the overhead door.

"How did you…"

"Don't you remember I told you I had to let myself in to look for your parents' wills?"

I'd completely forgotten that she'd been in my folks' house while I was in a coma. "I do. Now that you mention it."

We stood shoulder-to-shoulder staring up at the door. She spoke softly, "The wills weren't all that easy to find, so I pretty much had to scour the whole house. I started my search up here, but everything was covered with dust, so I figured it was more likely they were in a file cabinet or drawer somewhere in the house."

"Where were they?"

"Where I should've looked first. Your mom's underwear drawer."

"Ah."

She yanked on the stick, and the door came screeching down. Then she pulled the bottom half of the built-in stairs until it hit the carpet, while everything metal in it rubbed against everything else metal, and it screamed like a box of alley cats. Marilee probably thought it was best to keep things moving along swiftly, because she sprang up the stairs as though someone were after her. Every tread she stepped on creaked its displeasure at the disturbance. She was standing at the top, looking down at me, before I took my first step.

Once I reached her, and we could hear each other again, Marilee asked, "How could your folks stand the noise? Hadn't your dad heard of WD-40?"

"Yeah. That was awful. As far as I know, Dad only came up here to get the Christmas decorations."

"But still—"

"I don't know. I never really thought about it. He used to hand the boxes down to me. I can't remember actually being up here before."

She turned to stare at me. "You're kidding."

"What?"

"There was a whole floor of the house you grew up in that you never explored?"

"I think I was afraid of the mice."

"There were mice up here?" She looked down and around her.

"I never heard any. But Dad told me so when I was little, so I imagined small armies of them. Now, I just feel stupid, and…" I paused. "Incurious. Is that even a word?"

"I don't think so. Maybe."

Light was coming in through the windows at both ends of the space, so I could make out four overhead lightbulbs with a long string hanging from each. I pulled on the two on one side of the attic, and Marilee made her way across the room to turn on the lights on the other side. With the space well-lit, Marilee walked back to the top of the stairs to set down her flashlight. She looked around slowly. "You know what, Suzanne?"

"What?"

"There aren't any mouse droppings. Then again, maybe the snakes got them."

I jumped and Marilee laughed. "I was kidding." She paused. "It's funny. I never thought of you as gullible before."

I said, "Yeah." But I wondered why Dad would lie about the mice? It wasn't like him to be dishonest with me—unless, of course, Mom had asked him to be. I'd observed from an early age that he was a very compliant kind of husband.

We surveyed the stuff piled around the perimeter of the room: a neat row of boxes and plastic bags marked "Christmas," a couple of trunks, and twenty or so cardboard boxes, spread out along the walls. Marilee pointed at the Christmas pile. "Do you want the holiday stuff?"

"No. We'll leave that here for the estate sale person to deal with."

"Cool. This is really going fast."

I groaned.

We stood, both of us looking around, but there was no obvious place to begin. Marilee said, "Why don't I take the boxes on one side of the room, and you start at the other, and we'll meet in the middle?"

"Good idea." I looked more closely at them, and saw a thick layer of dust and lots of package tape on each. "It looks like they're all pretty well sealed."

"Not to worry. I have two box cutters in my pocket."

Sure enough, she pulled them out of the back pocket

of her jeans. What amazed me was that anything in addition to Marilee could've fit in there. Of course, I knew she was very pretty, but I'd forgotten how shapely she was. I leaned over to cut open my first box. I ripped off the remaining tape and yanked at the cardboard flaps. "Crap."

"What?"

"It's my papers and report cards from grammar school."

"Seriously?"

"I was an only child."

Marilee looked up from across the room. "What are you going to do with it, Suzanne?"

"Are you kidding? Chuck it."

"Are you sure?"

"Yes. What possible reason is there for me to keep this stuff? I mean, who would I show them to?" The space was so quiet that each word seemed to reverberate.

"A couple of things come to mind. It might be helpful if you decide to write your memoirs."

"Not gonna happen." I was already re-taping the box.

"And, if one of your teachers becomes famous, you could sell her signature from your report card. You know, like on E-bay."

"If any of my teachers were going to get famous, don't you think they'd have done so by now?"

There was a long pause, so I assumed she was considering it. She finally said, "Yeah. Probably."

"Marilee, I think I'll pile all the throw-away cartons in one spot. Then I can ask the estate sale person if she'll dispose of them for me."

"Um-hmm."

"So, what's in yours?" I asked, without looking up, while pushing the box of school stuff out of the way.

"Your parents' old pay-stubs, W-2s, tax records." A couple of minutes later, she added, "Nothing later than the nineties. I don't think you need them."

"Right. Can you push it over here to the discard pile?"

Marilee rose and leaned over to slide the box to the spot I'd chosen. It sounded exactly like she was pushing it over gravel, but it was just the decades of dust. We both gave up on bending over after our first boxes, and simply sat on the gritty wood floor to cut them open, go through the contents, and push them where they needed to go.

My parents had amassed quite a collection—old science magazines, dishes, and knick-knacks. One box was all old cookbooks. Another held two silver tea sets, a silver-dipped rose in a vase in a velvet box, a personalized silver wine chiller, and an engraved crystal ice bucket. I remembered the gifts from their 25th anniversary party, and wasn't surprised they hadn't used them. My folks were simple people. More accurately, good people with simple tastes.

Marilee hollered over to me. "High school. A ton of stuff." I looked over and saw that she was up to her elbows in one of the trunks.

"Don't bother. I'll help you scoot it to the throw-away pile."

"You don't want to look at some of this stuff first?"

I walked over and leaned down to help her shove it across the room. "I'd rather you shoot me in the head."

She fake-huffed, "A simple 'no' would've done."

A half-hour in, the remaining boxes were mainly in

the corners. Marilee and I sat kitty-cornered from each other like two boxers before the big fight, but separated by most of the length of the house. My next box had a large "X" in black marker on the top. I ripped through more of the ancient yellowed package tape with the cardboard cutter and pulled out four fat photo albums. I flipped through a page or two of each. "Hey! Guess what?"

Marilee mumbled something.

"I think I've finally found some things I'll keep. I may even be able to look through them some day without killing myself." I laughed, but Marilee didn't respond. I tried again. "Hey! Over there. I thought you appreciated dark humor." Still no response. Evidently, she was engrossed in some bit of my family's ancient history. I pushed the box of albums to the top of the stairs and then resumed my position in the corner.

I stretched to reach the next box, which had no markings on the outside except for a large "A" in faded red marker on the top. The old masking tape peeled right off without the need for the knife. As I folded back the cardboard, I could see that a number of folders were stacked inside. I lifted out the whole pile and set it on the floor beside me, expecting something boring like more old tax returns. But as I scanned the first papers, I shook my head. I mumbled, "What the heck?"

The first page was captioned "*Home study for baby girl Suzanne*." My mom and dad were listed as "the adoptive parents." My tongue immediately swelled, and my ears felt as though someone had taken matches to them. I managed to whisper, "Oh, my God." The next pages were forms filled out by Mom and Dad, their work histories, personal references, church affiliation, and details about our house, our neighborhood, and the schools I'd attend.

Marilee yelled, "What did you say?"

I couldn't respond because my mouth refused to work. I began to breathe rapidly, but I knew I had to slow it down.

She asked loudly, "Have the snakes eaten you?"

I needed water, and I needed to lie down. In a moment, Marilee was standing over me. She said, "I take it you found something interesting."

I managed to nod my head.

"Well, what is it?"

I opened my mouth to speak, but nothing came out.

Marilee knelt beside me. "Listen. You're starting to scare me, Suzanne. Can you just spit it out?" She was staring encouragement at me, but it didn't help. She said, "You've gone pale. Are you okay?"

I forced myself to get up and stumbled to the stairs. As I hurried down, all I could get out was, "Water," which I doubt she heard over the cacophony of the squeaking and groaning of the metal. In the kitchen, I grabbed a glass of water but I still felt faint, my tongue swollen, and my ears still on fire. I lay down on the tile floor and put my feet up on one of the wooden kitchen chairs to get some blood to my head.

In a moment, Marilee was kneeling over me. I waved her away as I managed to whisper, "I need to lie here for a minute." She rose and stepped back, her eyes still glued to me. I took deep, slow breaths for a good couple of minutes until I was feeling a little better.

Once I was able to sit up, I smiled in an effort to reassure Marilee I wasn't actually dying. "It's in those folders I was looking at. Could you bring those down for me?"

Without a word, Marilee headed for the attic stairs, and the screams of the steps assured me she'd gone up. I got myself to the bottom and yelled up at her, too loudly, "Just push the box to the top of the stairs, then you can hand it down to me."

She poked her head over the opening. "You don't have to scream. I'm right here."

"Sorry."

She pushed the box to the top, where I could see it. I stepped up the stairs to the halfway point, and she leaned down to hand the box to me. I moved slowly because, although the box was fairly light, it was obvious that it would be easy to fall off the hidden-stairs contraption. I wasn't ready to kill myself quite yet.

Marilee descended quickly, took the box from me, and set it on the floor. She faced me, her hands on my shoulders. "What's going on, Suzanne?"

I bit my lower lip, hard, before I spoke. "I was adopted. I didn't know."

She shook her head. "Hey. I've seen pictures of your mother. You have her freckles and her exact ski-jump nose. I don't think you were adopted."

I could feel my eyes tear up. "I know. It's unbelievable."

She dropped her arms and bent down to retrieve the box. "Let's just look through this material carefully before you jump to conclusions."

I said, "Okay," but I knew what I'd already seen was pretty clear. We needed some space to lay out the materials. "Kitchen or dining room table?"

"Dining room is bigger," Marilee said as she spread out the folders so we could both see each heading. She stood back and added, "Are you sure you're okay to do this?"

"I've never been less okay." When I realized what I'd said, I added, "Except for every day since I woke up in the hospital." I took a deep breath and sat.

Marilee said nothing for a moment. Then she patted me on the back and said, "It's going to be okay, Suzanne." She paused, then added in a bright voice, "Listen. I've got a gallon of iced tea in the car, and some homemade chicken salad in my little cooler for our lunch. Shall I bring it in?"

I stared at her. "Yes to the tea. No to the chicken salad." I paused. "I'll tell you why later. Maybe."

"Okay," she said. "And by the way, your folks left a pantry full of food. I mean, I cleaned out their fridge right away. But there's still a lot of non-perishables. So, if you get hungry—"

I grimaced. "I don't think I could."

She said, "No. You're right. Maybe you could get the estate sale person to donate the unopened stuff. We should just call for a pizza if we get hungry."

Marilee ran out of the house, screen door slamming behind her. She was back in a flash with the gallon jug of tea, two legal pads and two pens. I grabbed two glasses and filled them with ice from the freezer, then poured the tea. I opened the dining room windows an inch to a blast of refreshing cold air and sat down next to Marilee at the rectangular mahogany table. I glanced at the writing pads and pens and raised my eyebrows.

She said, "You know me. Always prepared." She smiled.

I nodded. "Thanks." I grabbed the folder under the one I'd already seen. It was headed, "Hospital Records."

I opened it, pulled out the papers, and we both stared at the first page.

"What the hell?" said Marilee.

I glanced up at her then back down at the top document. I picked up the rest of the pages and we both quickly looked through them.

"They're all in Spanish," she said.

"Yeah. And several words are blacked out." I looked up at Marilee as though—somehow—she could explain it to me. "I don't understand."

Marilee shrugged. "This is very strange. Can you read any Spanish?"

"No. You?"

"I took two years in high school. Let me try."

She studied the first page for a minute or so, then looked up at me. "Okay. Here's what I make of it. Something about a mother and a baby, and the people's names are all blacked out."

"Helpful."

"Well, let me look through the rest of it."

Marilee studied each page for a moment or two.

"So, what else?" I asked.

"Suzanne, these pages are from a hospital in Bolivia."

"Bolivia?"

"Yeah. For sure."

I was stunned. What did my family have to do with Bolivia? My parents had never taken me out of the country except for a summer vacation trip to Canada and a couple of spring breaks in the Bahamas.

Marilee asked, "Were you ever in Bolivia?"

"Never. I don't understand what's happening." I paused to think, but I couldn't get my head around it. "I guess the first thing we need to do is find out what these medical records say."

"Agreed."

"So, do you have any Hispanic friends?"

"Regrettably, no."

"Crap."

She smacked her palms together. "Wait! I do have a good friend who is fluent."

"Really?"

"She's a high school Spanish teacher. Her name is Polly. Actually, Polycarp."

"What?"

"Never mind."

"Do you think you could take pictures of the pages and text them to Polly to translate for us?" I was already pulling out all the pages that weren't heavily obscured by black-outs.

"Of course. Like I said, she's a good friend. But I think I'd rather just ask her to come over."

I put the papers down. "Do you think she'll come?"

"Probably. Unless she had a late show last night."

I shook my head. "Wait. I thought you said she's a high school teacher."

"She is. But her passion is improv. She's in a company that performs around the area a couple of nights a month. Oh, and her group goes to big events in New York, and Atlanta, sometimes LA. But she hasn't mentioned going out of town."

"Interesting hobby."

"I think it's more than a hobby. Unfortunately, it's impossible for her to pay the rent with just performances and teaching improv. And she'd rather teach Spanish than wait tables for her day job."

"I would think so. So, can you call her now?"

"I think I'll just text her in case she's in the middle of something."

Marilee's fingers flew over her phone, and we moved on to the next folder, the one with the home study, while we awaited a response. By the time we'd read over the last page, my jaw was on the floor. Feeling sick to my stomach again, I pushed back my chair, slid down to the tile floor, laid back on the cool, hard surface, and took deep, slow breaths.

Marilee leaned down toward me from her chair. "Are you sure you're okay? You look really pale again."

I whispered, "It's just that all my stress goes to my stomach and then my blood pressure drops. My tongue swells and my ears start to burn. My doctor calls it vasovagal, and says there's not much I can do about it. I'll be fine in a minute."

"So, you're a delicate flower." She leaned over with my glass of iced tea. "Would a sip help?"

With considerable effort, I managed a smile. "No, thanks. I just have to wait for it to pass." I closed my eyes and a couple of minutes passed in silence. Once I felt almost normal again, I got back up and into my chair. I said, "Sorry about that."

"Nothing to be sorry about." She paused. "But I am wondering. How do you deal with that problem in the courtroom?"

I laughed. "Well, I don't. Actually, work doesn't give me this kind of stress."

"You're so weird." She shook her head and laughed.

"I know. So, have you heard back from Polycarp? You know, your friend's name sounds like a fish."

"It's a Catholic thing. She was born on the feast day

of St. Polycarp, so her parents thought that would be a great name. She always makes a joke about it on stage. And yes, I've heard back." She peeked at her watch. "She'll be here in a couple of minutes."

"So quickly?"

"I just included the address in my text. She already knows all about you."

"How?"

"Number one, the story of your accident was in the papers for about a month—front page for the first week. I just filled her in on the rest."

"Wait." I shook my head trying to follow what she was saying. "You told her about my depression?" I glared at her.

Marilee acted as though she didn't notice my accusatory tone. "It's called grief, Suzanne. Being a sentient human, Polly already figured out that you'd be sad about the fact that your husband and your parents died suddenly in an accident."

"I'm sorry, Marilee, I'm having trouble controlling my emotions lately."

"No kidding. Anyone would, you know."

We were interrupted by the doorbell's two loud tones. Since the front door was already open, Marilee shouted, "Come on in!"

As Polly rounded the corner into the dining room, I could see why she'd be good on stage. She was a petite, cute blonde, probably in her mid-thirties, but she had a huge presence as she sailed into the room. Marilee rose, and they hugged quickly but tightly. Then Polly whipped around, crouched in front of me, and took both of my hands in hers. "Suzanne. I'm Polly. Polycarp Kuharski. I can't tell you how sorry I am for your incomprehensible loss." As she looked directly at me, her pale blue eyes clouded with tears. This woman was either a fountain of empathy or an excellent actress. I immediately felt overwhelmed. Polly was clearly far superior to me at self-expression.

I mumbled, "Thank you."

Polly whipped two deli club sandwiches from her tote and walked over to place one in front of me and one before Marilee.

"Where's yours?" asked Marilee.

Polly smiled as she took the chair beside me and opened an empty notebook. "Oh, I've already eaten."

I said, "Thanks so much. I really was getting hungry." I knew I couldn't risk more than a few bites, but my blood sugar needed that small jolt.

"Me, too," said Marilee. "Suzanne rejected the chicken salad I brought."

I was embarrassed. But Polly jumped in with, "And, no doubt, she had a very good reason."

I nodded, and she patted my right hand. Then she pulled a pen from her tote and said, "Okay. I'm ready to have at it."

Marilee slid the hospital pages over to her. Polly started with the top sheet, quickly eyeballed each page, and then went back to the beginning to read slowly while writing in her notebook, uttering "hmm," "oh my," "um-hmm," and "yep" from time to time. Sometimes she let out a whistle. Other times, she shook her head slightly. She could've been up on a stage doing an impression of a person reviewing an interesting document.

I nibbled at my sandwich and felt better almost immediately in spite of being so anxious that my fingers were tapping the table and my right leg was shaking.

Marilee snarfed hers, probably having been fantasizing that I'd let her bring in the chicken salad. After about twenty minutes, Polly turned over the papers and put down her pen. She leaned back in her chair and sighed. Then she turned to look directly at me.

"Let me summarize all of this for you, Suzanne."

I nodded, and swallowed hard.

"A twenty-two-year-old woman appeared at the emergency room of this hospital—in Bolivia. She was in labor. She arrived there at 9:00 a.m. and delivered the baby at 7:15 that night. Since she was at thirty-seven weeks, the baby was considered later pre-term. The mother was five foot seven inches tall, and one hundred and thirty-five pounds—before she delivered. Her name was in the records, but it's been blocked out by someone. It was April 3, 1970." Marilee and I both flinched, but Polly didn't seem to notice.

"All of the mom's blood-work is included and all of it appears to fall in the normal range. Oh, and the space for the name of the father is also blacked out. But it looks like nothing was actually written under the magic marker, or whatever they used. The mom was doing well, but the baby was transferred to the neonatal unit because she was technically premature. The baby was six pounds, three ounces—so not super tiny."

While Marilee was making notes of everything Polly said, I was simply taking it in—trying to make sense of that baby being me.

"April 3, 1970 is Suzanne's birthday," Marilee told Polly, who turned to me.

"You were that baby girl?"

"It's starting to look that way."

"Wow. Well, there should be more hospital records.

This stuff is all from the day the baby was born. But there should be separate records for the baby—like how she did in the ICU and when she was released. And more on the mom's progress, and when she was released. So, do you have anything else for me to look at for you?"

Marilee said, "No. That's all there is in Spanish—from Bolivia. I mean, we have adoption information from the U.S. and lots of copies of everything, but it's all in English and we've gone through it. Suzanne's folks definitely adopted a baby girl born on April 3, 1970. There's a fair amount of information about the adoptive parents, their histories, references, etc. The only name that's blocked out on the adoption form is the birth-mother's. And the titles on all the stuff in this folder refer to babies born out of wedlock."

Polly turned to me. "Your folks never hinted to you that you're adopted?"

"Never."

She said dramatically, "Hmm."

We all took a moment to process what we'd learned. Polly said, "I don't think it takes an expert to see that you don't look Bolivian."

I shrugged.

She added, "By any chance, do you look like either of your parents?"

Marilee said, "She does."

I shrugged again. "I'll let you judge for yourself." I went to the living room and gazed at my parents' wedding picture. They were both twenty when they married, but they looked much younger. I took a quick picture with my phone so I'd always have them with me, then returned and handed the wedding portrait to Polly.

"Holy moly! Why, you look just like your mom,

except for the hair color." She thought for a moment. "Did either of you dye your hair?"

"No. Our hair color actually was different."

Polly said, "But still. I don't see how you were adopted. You have her hazel eyes, freckles, and her same features."

"I know. But I assume lots of people must have freckles and ski-jump noses."

"I suppose that's true," said Polly. "But what are the chances?" She thought some more and added, "Maybe your folks were travelling in Bolivia when they had you."

Marilee and I just stared at her.

"No. You guys are right. They wouldn't have had to adopt you."

We were all quiet. All flummoxed.

Polly spoke first. "Do you have any aunts or uncles or grandparents you could ask about it?"

"I wish I did. My mom and dad were also only children. And my folks were eighty-two when they died—this past October—so their parents are long gone."

"I have an idea," said Marilee. "Why not track down the three people who gave character references for the adoption?"

"Maybe. But, Marilee, it was almost fifty years ago." Marilee could be pushy, and I'd never loved that quality in her.

But then Polly piled on. "We can help you," she said. "Let's go ahead. Let's do it now."

I felt a little annoyed to be rushed, but I couldn't come up with a reason not to move forward. I turned to Marilee. "Okay. What do your notes say the names are?"

She paged through her legal pad. "Eileen Foster, Martinsville; Stephanie Hudson, Roanoke; and Tom Divers, Charlottesville. She circled each name as she read it aloud.

"I don't mean this to sound pessimistic," Polly said. "But wouldn't it be most efficient to check the obituaries for the towns they lived in? For most people, that little article in their local paper *is* their fifteen seconds of fame."

"I think that's fifteen minutes of fame," said Marilee.

"Maybe," said Polly. "But who spends fifteen minutes reading a stranger's obituary?"

I shrugged. "It's as good a starting place as any. Polly, why don't you take Eileen, I'll take Stephanie, and Marilee, you take Tom."

Chapter 8

We all pulled out our phones and got to work. Because Stephanie Hudson was from Roanoke, I knew I needed to search the archival information for the Roanoke newspaper. Within fifteen minutes, I found her. And her obituary wasn't her only moment of fame. There was one article which concerned her work on the school board, and one about her service as a faculty member at a local women's college. But she was gone, and donations to breast cancer research were encouraged in lieu of flowers.

Ironically, Tom Divers had passed away in November. I was sure I knew what Marilee was thinking when she announced his date of death. If I hadn't been in a coma, and had gotten myself up into my folks' attic shortly after the accident, I might've had a solid clue to pursue.

A little smile crept over Polly's face until it burst into a full-fledged grin. "Mine's alive!"

"And?" I asked.

"There's an announcement from two years ago about Eileen Foster retiring from the Henry County bench. I suppose she may still live in Martinsville."

"That's terrific," said Marilee, turning to me. "Suzanne, you may be about to hear the explanation for all the secrecy."

"It can't be that easy. She probably retired because

she has dementia, and doesn't even know her own name." I exhaled loudly. "Sorry, guys. I don't know why, but I don't feel optimistic."

"Well, the only way to find out is to give her a call," said Marilee.

Polly said, "I've got her phone number. She's listed in the Martinsville directory."

I was feeling hurried again. I said, "So, you guys think I should just ring her up out of the blue?"

Marilee and Polly both nodded. Marilee's was quick and emphatic. Polly's was long, drawn out, and solemn. I laughed out loud.

"What?" said Polly.

"I'm sorry. That was just so dramatic."

Then she guffawed. "Suzanne, I would do it naked on a unicycle to hear you laugh."

I smiled at her. "You're very good, you know."

She instantly displayed a red blush, and said coyly, "Thank you."

"How did you do that?" asked Marilee.

"What?" asked Polly, apparently earnestly.

"Turn red on a dime."

She smiled at each of us. "I can cry on demand, as well. Want to see?"

"No thanks," I said. "But that could come in handy."

"You have no idea," said Polly.

"Okay. So, I'm calling. What's Judge Foster's number?"

As Polly read it to me, I touched the numbers on my cell phone, my hand shaking the whole time.

She answered on the first ring. "Eileen Foster speaking." There was a lovely lilt in her voice and she didn't sound like she had dementia.

"Hello. My name is Suzanne Reynolds Summerfield."

"Yes. I know who you are."

I cleared my throat. "You do?

"I read about the terrible accident in the papers. I'm so sorry."

I'd forgotten about my recent notoriety, so Judge Foster had me flummoxed already. "Well—thank you." I couldn't think how to go on.

"I knew Betty and Ron for many years. Your parents were exceptionally fine people. Good people."

"Yes. They were."

"I've been expecting your call, Suzanne."

"You have?"

"I suppose you found my name in the adoption records."

I could feel my eyes widening, and my face flushing. Marilee and Polly stared at me intently. "I did. Just today. Well, I was clearing out their attic. And the other two adoption references aren't available because they're—well, dead." I felt as inarticulate as I could remember.

"Yes. I believe they used Stephanie and Tom. The world lost two fine people with their passings."

I didn't know how to respond since I hadn't known either of them. "I'm sorry for your loss of your friends."

She said softly, "Well, they weren't close friends. Closer with your parents, I expect. But I knew them well enough to know they were lovely people."

I had no idea how to respond to that. It was as though I'd lost the ability to converse when I dialed her number. What I lamely offered was, "I'm sure."

"I assume you would like me to explain the

circumstances of your adoption."

Her question gave me a quick surge of optimism and I flashed a smile at my friends. I said, "Very much."

"I'm truly sorry. But, I can't."

My smile evaporated. Stunned, I said nothing for a moment. Then I managed, "You can't?"

"I swore to your mother that I wouldn't."

This answer was even more bizarre than the one before. "You swore not to answer my questions?"

"Yes."

"But why?"

"I can't answer that, Suzanne."

Panicking, I sputtered out, "But…But," until I finally got it out. "But surely, since my folks are both dead—Well, my knowing can't possibly hurt my parents now."

"That's true." I knew the tone of voice. It rang of, "Motion denied, counsel."

"What if I drive—I mean, I could come over—" Although I stumbled over my words, she gathered what I was suggesting.

"I would love to meet you, Suzanne. But not under false pretenses. You see, I won't be swayed. I am a hundred percent resolute about this."

"I really don't understand that." I could feel my tongue swell and my ears flush.

"I'll tell you the truth. If this had all happened a year ago, I probably would've shared with you what I know. But—"

"But, what—" My heart raced, so I knew I'd better slow down my breathing or I'd end up on the floor—for the third time.

"It was about a year ago—last August to be

precise—after Stephanie died. Your mother called me out of the blue."

"So you hadn't kept up?"

"Just Christmas and birthday cards. We both had busy lives. And we did live three hours apart. Anyway, she called to tell me that she might not get around to cleaning out her attic. She'd been thinking about me being the last living reference from your adoption. She reminded me of my promise not to divulge anything to you. She said she was thinking about a way to arrange with someone to clear the records out of her attic. But, because she hadn't done it yet, she was just confirming that I wouldn't breach her confidence. Of course, I assured her I would keep my word." Eileen Foster paused for a few moments. "Maybe she ·had a premonition. Or maybe it just hit her that she and Ron were both eighty-two, the age at which her own mother had died."

"I don't really understand any of this, Judge Foster."

"Eileen, please. And I really am sorry, Suzanne. If it had been up to me, I'm not sure I would've kept all that happened a secret. But it was never up to me."

My heart was still beating too rapidly, so I took a deep breath before forcing the words out. "You do realize how difficult it is for me to learn this way that I was adopted." I looked up and Polly was motioning for me to cry. I ignored her and kept talking. "And after losing Mac, and Mom and Dad—to be faced with a secret about who I am. And that the only person who could help me refuses to do so—" I didn't want to burn any bridges by insulting her, so I added, "Of course, I get it. It's a matter of honor for you, Eileen. But, still—" This opened the flood gates, and I was suddenly full-out sobbing. Once I got a grip, I said, "Excuse me," and blew my nose several times into tissues Marilee whipped out for me. I said, "I'm sorry."

She waited a moment until it was clear I wouldn't start bawling again. She said, "Over the years, your mother has told me about you in our long, annual catch-up letters. About who you are—your character, your courage, and your persistence. I do not have an ounce of doubt that you will unravel this mystery yourself. And when you do, you'll know far more than I do. You may even choose to share it with me, which I would absolutely love. God bless you, dear. And I hope you find what you're looking for."

"Thank you." It was strange, because her final words really did leave me feeling encouraged.

"What?" said Marilee and Polly at the same time.

Once I'd filled them in, Polly said, "That's incredibly cruel."

We both stared at her. She added, "I do get the honor thing. She swore an oath to a friend. But since the friend is dead—"

I shrugged.

Marilee said to me, "I think the question is how do *you* feel about what Eileen said to you?"

I took a moment to think and leaned back in my chair. "I feel okay. I respect her. And she's probably right that I'll want to dig deeper than the part she's privy to."

Polly's eyes softened as she looked at me and said, "You're a very understanding woman, Suzanne. I hope we'll become great friends."

I was going to say, "Me too," but Marilee interrupted.

She looked at me, and then at Polly. "There's a good chance of it since we'll be spending a lot of time together on our trip."

"What trip?" asked Polly.

"Bolivia. Obviously. And you're the only one among us who speaks Spanish."

Polly lit up, her ice-blue eyes wide. "Best idea ever. You guys couldn't stop me from joining you if you tried." She smiled as she quickly gathered her notes into a neat pile. "When do we leave?"

"I would absolutely love to take a trip with you guys someday, but I have a couple of other options before we grab seats for South America. I think I should check with the agency that did the home-study. Then if they can't help me, I'll try to find the lawyer my parents used to see if I can wrestle any information out of him or her." I paused to think about making time to fit this in. "I'll work on those two angles tomorrow." As I rose from my chair, I added, "Would you guys be willing to help me finish checking out the rest of the attic boxes while we're here? I'd so love not to have to come back later to visit the scene of my—" I felt my chin quiver as I paused to search for the right word. "—destruction."

"You're not destroyed," said Marilee.

I shot her a look along with, "Really?"

"Of course not," said Polly. "You're exactly the same person you were before you found the documents."

I stared at her for a moment before responding. "Except that I now know that I'm not the offspring of my parents. Which means that all the family medical histories I've given to doctors over my lifetime have been lies. I may even be carrying some rare, inherited disease."

"You're forty-eight," said Marilee.

"So?"

"So any weird, inherited disease probably would've shown up already."

I shook my head as I began replacing the adoption documents into the box.

"I can see why you're worried though," said Polly.

I stopped what I was doing and looked at her. "You can?"

"Yeah. Think about it. Why were your folks so over-the-top paranoid you'd learn your birth story? I mean, these days, adoption isn't usually kept a secret, at least, not for very long. Lots of my friends were adopted. Why the big mystery?"

I stepped back to lean against the wall, and gave her a half-smile. "If you're trying to reassure me, Polly, it's not working."

"What I mean to say is that all the secrecy probably is just making a mundane story tantalizing because your imagination is bound to come up with a more bizarre explanation than the truth."

Because I knew Polly did improv and stand-up work, I assumed she'd be able to dream up scenarios far stranger than what I'd be wondering about in the middle of the night. "Okay. You're on, Polly. What situations can you think of that would justify my birth story being a state secret?"

"How many do you want?"

"Top three."

Polly rose and swung one leg over the chair to straddle it backwards, facing me. Her manner was completely relaxed, as though we'd been visiting like this for years. "Okay. Number one. Your biological parents were murderous but devout Russian spies, living as Bolivian peasants. They didn't want to raise their daughter as a peasant, so they went to a U.S.-based church or adoption agency or something like that, to find good, righteous parents for their infant daughter."

Marilee asked, "Why wouldn't they have wanted Russians to adopt their baby?"

Polly grimaced. "Duh. Because they'd been to Russia."

"Interesting," I said, wondering how much of her was real and how much performance. "What's number two?"

"It's also possible that your father was a highly ranked Bolivian government official who fell in love with the married Minister of Public Morals. They both would have been ruined if word of the woman's pregnancy had gotten out. So they contacted a friend, a high government official in the United States, to help place the baby girl in a good home in any country but Bolivia."

"Plausible," said Marilee.

I shook my head at them. "And scenario number three?"

Polly nodded at me before speaking. "Scenario number three, and the most likely, is that you are the second child of a Chinese couple touring the major Andean cities on their vacation. Because your birth-parents were both government officials in Beijing, they dared not risk defying the one-child rule. Therefore, your mother listed herself as a United States citizen when she was admitted to the maternity ward. After that, the hospital employees looked at the records rather than the patient—"

"That's true. They do that," said Marilee, who remained sitting, still sipping her iced tea.

"Which is why your birth was recorded to show you as the daughter of an American woman, and born in Bolivia."

Marilee sighed. "Polly, perhaps you haven't noticed, but Suzanne doesn't look at all Chinese."

"Of course not. Because her birth-mom's mother was actually a wealthy French woman who fell in love while vacationing in Shanghai, and conceived Suzanne's mother out-of-wedlock in that far away land. Suzanne simply resembles her grandmother. And her straight, black hair is all the proof I need that her birth-father was Chinese."

Marilee laughed as she finished her drink and walked to the kitchen sink to wash our glasses.

I opened my mouth to say something but nothing came out. I shook my head at Polly. "Okay, ladies, back up the stairs to the attic to finish this."

Marilee bounded up the stairs, leading the way, followed by Polly, and then me. Again, the attic stairs reacted as though they were under assault, screaming at the tops of their lungs. Marilee and I had left the lights on, so everything up there was in plain view. Marilee pointed at the spot where the most boxes sat, and said to Polly, "The discard pile." She waved her hand in the other direction, and said, "Christmas stuff, etc. for the estate sale."

"So there's not much left to go through," said Polly.

"Thank goodness," I said.

"Oh, no. I love this old attic," said Polly, as she slowly turned 360 degrees to take it all in. "Fabulous. It's the perfect spot to store shocking journals and passionate love letters, and diaries full of famous names and scandalous details."

"I guess," I said. "But the only shocker we found was the adoption stuff." I surveyed what was left, as Polly spied the box of photo albums. She zipped over to it, fell to her knees, and started rummaging through it. "Oh my God, Suzanne, these are your parents' ancient photo albums. Maybe they'll help explain things."

"I'll tell you what, Polly. Why don't you flip through the pages and see if there's any reference to my adoption, or pictures of me as a baby. But if they're just family photos, I'll hold onto them. Someday, I may even have the strength to look at them."

"Okay. But I'll be dying to know who each picture is of."

"I'm sorry, Polly. I can't."

She said softly, "Understood."

Marilee and I each plopped down beside one unopened box after another, pulling out an odd assortment of objects: carpet pads, a large fondue set, a croquet game, scented candles, a couple of sets of dishes, and two boxes of old, well used pots and pans. I pulled the tape from the last two boxes and found Dad's old suits and Mom's winter dresses and coats. I resealed those in a panic as soon as I realized what they were. Marilee must've been watching. She said, "You found some snakes."

"Pretty much."

She surveyed the room. "I think we've covered everything."

I nodded, then looked over at Polly, who had moved next to a window for better light. I asked, "Almost finished?"

She seemed absorbed in one of the albums, but looked up. "I've flipped through all the books, Suzanne. I'm sorry. I didn't see anything that gives us any clues about your adoption, and no baby pictures at all."

"That's okay. Somehow, I didn't expect there would be." I turned to Marilee. "Would you get the lights over there? And I'll get these two. Polly, can you carry the box of photo albums to the stairs, or is it too heavy?"

"I'll just push it over. Then once you guys start down the stairs, I'll lower it down to you carefully so nothing falls out."

We managed to get ourselves and the box down intact. Once Polly joined us, Marilee and I stared at the stairs. "I guess we have to," she said.

"What?" asked Polly.

"Oh," I said. "It's just that this contraption is a pain to push back up, and really loud."

"Let me do it," said Polly. "I've never seen one of these before."

"Okay. You just push it up with your hands, and then shove it the last couple of inches with the tip of the wooden rod."

"Brilliant."

We endured one more outburst from the metal parts as Polly shoved the bottom section into the top, then thrust it to within a few inches of its recessed position in the ceiling and jabbed the stick against it until the gap was closed.

Marilee carried the box, and helped me get it into the trunk of my car, as Polly watched.

"Sweet car," said Polly.

"Mine was pulverized. This belonged to my folks."

Marilee and Polly watched as I slammed down the

lid of the trunk. I persuaded them to go back in with me to box up all the paintings and photos from the walls and all the papers from the desk my parents had shared. We stuffed all of it into my back seat, and I slammed the car door on what was left of my parents' lives. I thanked Marilee and Polly profusely for saving me from the heartbreak of having to return to the house alone anytime soon, we exchanged quick hugs, and they took off in opposite directions.

I was grateful that part of the process was finished, but fully aware that I might well regret stepping into the minefield of secrets surrounding my birth. I knew exactly why my hands shook and my heart raced all the way home. I was as determined to pursue the truth as I was terrified about what appalling reality unravelling the mystery might reveal.

Chapter 9

The following day at work, I made time to call the adoption agency whose director had signed off on the home study—a Catholic-affiliated, non-profit located near Charlottesville. I explained my situation to the woman who answered the phone, and she gave me false encouragement in return. "One of our adoptees! How wonderful that you found us after so many years. I am so sorry for the loss of your adoptive parents, and the unusual way you became aware that you were adopted. Listen, dear, I'll put you right through to our director, Lorraine. I'm sure she can help you."

I told my story again, this time to Lorraine, who said nothing but "um-hmm" during my recitation. I held my pen above my yellow legal pad, hoping for something worthwhile to jot down. She said, "First of all, Suzanne, I am very sorry for your loss. I read about the terrible accident in the paper. But, of course, I had no idea we had done the adoption home study on the couple who were killed."

"So, you can help me?"

"Maybe. Do you think your birth mother may've signed up on one of the registries?"

"Excuse me?"

"I should explain. There's no reason you would know about this, having just learned you were placed as an infant. You see, there are a number of voluntary registries, the goal of which is to reunite consenting birth parents and biological children."

"I see." Absolutely nothing I'd lcarned suggested she would've done so. I asked, "But what if my birth mother didn't sign up?"

"In that case, there would be very little you could do—at least in Virginia."

" 'Very little' suggests there is something. Right?"

"Well, you certainly have the right to petition a court. Basically, you would explain the nature of your need for medical, psychological, or genetic information. If the court grants your request, an intermediary is generally used to attempt to obtain the information for you."

I scribbled down everything she said. "But what about identifying information about my birth mother?"

"Only with her consent. Well, actually I'm assuming yours was a closed adoption based on the year of birth you gave me."

"Can you check your file?"

"Of course. I'll look for it right now. Give me a half hour to pull it and look it over, then I'll give you a call back. What phone number shall I use, Suzanne?"

It was almost an hour before Lorraine called me back. I'd gotten absolutely nothing done in the interim except reading over the same paragraph of one of my opponent's briefs—about a million times. I still had no idea what it said.

"Suzanne?"

"Speaking."

"Good. I'm sorry. It took longer than I expected to get my hands on your file. 1970 was a busy year for us."

"And?"

"As I anticipated, your adoption was closed. In fact, yours was zipped up extra tightly."

I could feel my ears warming. "What does that mean?"

"We've seen this kind of verbiage before, but only in very rare cases. It concerns how, under no circumstance whatsoever, should anyone be told the identity of the birth mother. In fact, the agreement compels our agency to resist any and all efforts at disclosure. Our director attested that we would not release any information without a court order. Beyond that, she agreed we would fight disclosure in the courts up to the highest court of appeals any petition might reach."

"You're saying all of this is unusual. Right?"

"Definitely. It makes one wonder why secrecy was so important in your case."

"Yes. It certainly does."

Lorraine insisted on taking my contact information in case my birth-mother might "reach out at some point in the future." I almost laughed out loud at that, but disguised it with a cough. I sighed as I hung up, then immediately turned to my computer. Unfortunately, it turned out that Lorraine was essentially correct on her presentation of Virginia law.

For the first time, it occurred to me that I might never solve the mystery. As shocked as I'd been to learn I'd been adopted—from Bolivia—and in spite of what I may've said to others, I'd believed, deep down, that I could unravel what my parents had tied up so tightly. Now, I wasn't sure. And I knew I'd get little work done at the office until I at least tried to pursue my other prospect, my parents' adoption attorneys.

I told Marilee I was taking the rest of the day off, threw several memoranda into my briefcase on the off-chance I might get some work done that night, and moments later pulled out of the parking lot, headed for the law offices of Camp and Long. I'd talked with the son, Darren Long, when he assisted me in winding down my parents' estate. But, according to the invoice in the papers I'd discovered, it had been his father, Bartholomew, who had handled my adoption for Mom and Dad. I knew that Bart had been their lawyer for general things, and that he was a friend. I also knew from my conversation with Darren that his father had passed away a couple of years before. I thought that fact might actually be to my advantage since it was the deceased Long who had been a good friend of my parents, and probably would've felt loyalty to them. The son, however, just might be willing to help me.

Darren was around my age, overweight, with a goatee, and wore no wedding ring. I figured he might be susceptible to whatever charms I had left, so I tried to appear as promising as I could manage without actually promising anything. He knew I was a recent widow, so anything beyond the mildest flirtation would've been grotesquely unseemly. But I was growing desperate.

I was seated across from Darren, with his oversized, mahogany desk between us. I began with, "Darren, your father must've thought very highly of your legal abilities to leave all of his clients in your hands."

"I suppose so. Then again, he was my mentor."

"Well, I'm sure you are doing a fabulous job. You know, my parents absolutely raved about the service they received from your firm."

"That's nice to hear."

I lowered my voice, trying for a serious tone. "It's important work, you know. General practice law is the front line in a lot of ways. Wills, real estate closings for young couples, then eventually planning their estates. Those are the legal issues that directly affect the lives of real people. Some may not think it's as glamorous as trial work, but the truth is, it's the only interaction with the law that most folks have. Ensuring that the process plays out smoothly for them is noble work. I admire what you do." I started to worry I was slicing the baloney too thickly.

Darren looked puzzled. He said, "That's very kind of you."

"Well, it's just obvious." Embarrassingly, this went on for another few minutes before I felt that I'd done as much as I could, in reasonably good conscience, to prime the pump. "So, Darren, the reason I sit here taking up your valuable time is that I recently learned about a secret that my parents kept from me—my entire life. I'm pretty sure it was your father who made the legal arrangements for them."

"A secret?"

"Yes. It turns out I was adopted as an infant—in 1970."

Darren raised his eyebrows.

"From Bolivia."

"Bolivia?"

I nodded. "For some reason, it was kept very hush-hush. Now that I know, and now that my parents could no longer be hurt, I'd like to learn my birth story—the real one."

"That's very strange." He stroked his goatee once, and added, "And how did you learn this?

I told him the about the trip to the attic, and the call to the adoption agency.

His hands were folded on his desk, and he studied them for a moment before speaking. "It's odd because my father never mentioned anything about it. And the fact that we had a new adoption file, or an interesting old one, was never a secret around here. He would've remembered every detail."

"Because it was unusual?"

"He would've told me because it was unusual. He would've remembered because he remembered every detail of all the files. He had a photographic memory."

"That must've come in handy."

"Indeed. Unfortunately, there is no one else living who was with the firm in 1970."

I was disappointed, and aimed to express it on my face. I probably should've gotten tips from Polly. "I understand. And I'm not really surprised. What I was wondering is whether you could find your firm's file on my adoption."

"I can look, Suzanne. Everything we have from that time period is still in paper files. We never converted the old materials to the computer. Depending on what's in there, I may be able to share some of it with you."

"Wonderful." I didn't want to leave without having in-hand whatever was in the file. I lowered my eyes, then looked up at him as plaintively as I could manage. "Could you possibly look for it now?"

He glanced at his watch. "I can make time to do that. If you're comfortable here, I'll just run to the file room. Would you like a cup of coffee or tea—maybe a cola?"

"No, thank you, Darren. I'll just get some work done." I leaned over and grabbed some papers from my briefcase and began staring at them without comprehending. He slipped out the door, which he left wide open. I accomplished nothing but counting the minutes. He was back in fourteen, with a file folder in his hand. I about fell out of my chair trying to read what was written on the side of it. He took his seat, laying the expandable folder on his desk.

"That's it?"

"Yes."

"May I see it?"

"Yes. Under the circumstances."

He handed it to me, and it was so light in my hands that I knew only a few pieces of paper could've lain within. The label on the front said, "Adoption, baby girl, Suzanne Reynolds." I reached my hand inside and felt nothing. I raised it to catch the light from the window and peered in. "Darren, why are there no contents?"

He seemed as puzzled as I was disappointed. "I don't know. This is very strange."

"That it's empty?"

"That it's empty while all the files that sit around it are full of documents."

"Why?"

"I don't know, Suzanne."

"Who had access?"

"Just our two secretaries and my partner, Leon Camp. But Leon doesn't do adoptions or wills." He paused for a moment. "I'll ask all of them about this. But I have an idea about what may've happened."

"What?" I could feel my heart rate shoot up in anticipation of some big revelation.

"My dad had pancreatic cancer. He knew he was dying for almost a year. He easily could have disposed of the contents of the file if he had a reason."

"What reason could there have been?"

"If Dad discarded the materials, it would've been at the direction of a client."

"You're saying my parents asked him to destroy them?"

"Had to be." He took in a deep breath and let out a long sigh. "As you know, the record retention policy of most law firms is much shorter than fifty years. But Dad believed things could come up decades after we closed a file."

"It seems he was right." I grimaced at having reached another dead end.

"Yes." He studied me for a moment, then leaned forward in his chair, hands folded on the desk. "So, what's really going on, Suzanne?"

"Excuse me?"

"All that schmoozing and flattery—"

"Over the top?"

" 'Front line'? Seriously?"

"I'm sorry, Darren. But you were my last hope, so I was trying to get you on my side." I told him about the three references, and how the only living one refused to help me.

"Your parents were orchestrating all the secrecy?"

"It looks like they were."

"Hm. If they put that much effort into guarding your past, they must've had a good reason."

I shrugged.

"But you won't be able to rest until you figure this out. Will you?"

I shook my head.

"I understand. I'd feel the same way." He looked out

his window for what seemed a couple of minutes.

"Darren?"

He turned to me and smiled. "Sorry. I was just thinking. Do you happen to know how your parents chose my dad as their lawyer?"

I laughed. "Actually, that's the one thing I do know. They were friends from church. My dad and Bart were in the men's group together."

"Interesting. Do you suppose your adoption has any connection to the Church?"

"What do you mean?"

"I'm not sure. But back in the fifties, and sixties, and even through the seventies, a lot of Catholic girls gave up babies they had out of wedlock. We have a whole wall of cabinets filled with the files."

"You think my birth-mother was a Catholic girl?"

"Logical?"

"I suppose. But a Catholic girl in Bolivia?" I rolled my eyes.

He nodded. "That part is odd."

I grabbed my briefcase and rose to leave. "Thanks so much for your help, Darren."

He held his hands up and said, "Can you stay for a few minutes?"

"Sure." I sat back down and looked at him, wondering if he might know something more.

"I just wanted to ask how you're doing—after the loss of your husband."

My immediate impulse was to say, "As well as I can," and get out of there as quickly as I could. But there was something so warm and genuine about Darren that instead I spilled my guts. "I feel like I should've done more to help him through his dark days."

"Mac suffered from depression?"

"Lifelong."

"How did it affect you?"

"We were married for almost eighteen years." I looked out the window as I spoke. "At first, he did a pretty good job of hiding it from me. Or at least, minimizing how bad he felt. We did well in that altered reality for a decade. Or, at least, I thought we did well. But as it tormented him more, and he opened up about it to me, I walked the path with him. It was sadder, but more intimate."

"Ah. 'For better or worse…' "

I returned my gaze to Darren. "But we paid a price. I did what I thought I was supposed to do for him. But the truth is, I missed having joy in our life together. I wasn't really frustrated or bitter. It was no one's fault. It was just sad."

"It wore on you?"

I nodded. "I tried to be the good soldier for him. I read everything I could get my hands on to attempt to understand what he was going through. He deserved empathy, not sympathy. I don't know that I ever got there. And I felt guilty that I was too worried about the weight I carried, and not enough about his."

"So, now that he's gone?"

"I think I failed. I clearly didn't save him. I'm not sure I even lightened his load all that much. There were moments of intimacy which reconnected us. Of course, temporarily." I was starting to feel the burn of tears. "But now it's too late."

"Are you saying there's something you didn't do, that you wish you had?"

"Not really. But I always harbored the hope that

he'd get better once he reached retirement and could focus all of his energy on his beloved music. Now, I fear I put too much emphasis on that, and did too little when I had the chance." My tears began to flow, and I reached out for a tissue from a box Darren held out over his desk.

Once I'd stopped crying, he pursed his lips and looked at me as though he were deciding whether or not to say something. "Actually, Suzanne, I think what a partner can do to save a mate from depression is pretty limited."

"You sound sure."

"My ex-wife tried to help me. Now that I've come out of the closet as gay—to myself and to the world—I think she's starting to accept the fact that there was never a lot she could've done for me, under my circumstances. Couples may travel the path together, but they are always two separate people. There are limits to how much each can do for the other."

"I suppose."

"It's hard enough to know ourselves. I'm pretty much resigned to the fact that we can never really know our partner—or anyone else, for that matter. I tell myself stories about other people's feelings, their motivations. But I've come to realize that most of my stories are crap."

"Mine, too."

"My favorite poem concerns exactly this."

I raised my eyebrows.

"It's about an enormously successful fellow, whom everyone admires and envies. He is handsome, rich, educated, and kind. I'll just give you the first and last stanzas." Darren leaned back in his chair and closed his eyes as he recited the poem, which ended with the gifted man shooting himself.

"That poet said a mouthful."

"Beautifully. I'm just one of the people on the pavement, Suzanne."

"Me too." I paused. "Nevertheless, I'd love to hear your flawed theory about why my folks treated my birth story like a state secret."

He laughed, and it was obvious he was an unusually empathetic person. He had cared enough to ask how I was doing, actually expecting an answer. He'd listened with sincere interest as I shared. He said, "I wish I had any kind of theory. It's a complete mystery to me." He actually scratched his head, which was pretty cute.

"Thanks, Darren."

"For what?"

"For caring."

"I do, actually. And you're welcome."

As we walked toward the reception area, he said, "Where will you search next?"

"Bolivia."

He stopped, then nodded. "Ah. Always the last place people think to look."

"I'll let you know if I solve the mystery."

Darren held the door to his office suite open for me. As he followed me through, he said, "Please do. And I'll buy you lunch to thank you for celebrating my front-line work."

I laughed. "You'll never let me forget that, will you?"

At the elevator, as I stuck out my hand to shake, he pulled me in for a quick hug. He said, "Never in a million years."

Just before the elevator doors closed, he added,

"Good luck, chum." And he winked.

I could think of no explanation for why he seemed like an old friend when I'd just met the man. Maybe it was because he was also sad that he'd let his spouse down. Or maybe it was that every word he spoke seemed to come right from his heart. But I left feeling better than when I'd arrived, in spite of not having learned a thing to explain the mystery of my birth.

Chapter 10

I asked Marilee and Polly to go to dinner with me that evening. As had become my practice, I chose a restaurant Mac and I had never been to. Memories could burst on the scene so suddenly, and I hated how readily I could unravel and embarrass myself—and no doubt, my friends.

Tony's was basically an upscale hamburger joint. I knew fine dining would've been wasted on me because my mind was completely occupied by the hot potato my parents had left me holding. I was hoping we could eat on the patio, but it was so cool that evening that the outdoor seating had been roped off. I asked the hostess for a quiet table, and she led us to a booth as far from the noisy bar as we could get. My friends, both wearing skirts and sweaters, walked ahead of me, and I couldn't help but notice they were both turning heads. I looked down at my clothes. I was in jeans and a sweatshirt, and pretty sure no one was craning his neck for a glimpse of me. It had been so long since I'd cared whether other people appreciated my appearance that I'd forgotten how it worked. I wondered if some day I'd care about my looks again.

I embarrassed myself by reflexively thinking that their attractiveness might help me in my quest in Bolivia. I pondered the possible benefits of looking alluring for worming information out of strangers in South America, and decided to add make-up, skirts, and dresses to my packing list for the trip.

We slid into a booth, Marilee and Polly on one side, and me across from them. We ordered beers and Tony's special onion ring appetizers, all of which appeared at our table within minutes. The restaurant so pulsed with indie rock in the bar area, and the rise and fall of conversation and laughter throughout, that it seemed like one giant, undulating organism. Fortunately, we sat just far enough toward the back that we could make out each other's words. I wondered why it felt so odd to me to be there, but it dawned on me that I hadn't eaten in public with other people since before the accident.

I filled in Marilee and Polly on what happened with the adoption agency and with Darren.

Marilee said, "You know, I've spoken on the phone with Darren."

"Really?"

"It was while you were still in the hospital. Darren looked at his copies of your folks' wills for me to confirm they both wanted to be cremated. And he helped me figure out who their pastor was. Nice guy. Very kind."

"Yeah. He is."

After taking a sip of her beer, Polly said, "So, what's interesting to me is that your parents were all over the secrecy thing from the time you were born until they died. This was no whim. No quick decision not to tell you that you were adopted. But why?"

I said, "The three scenarios you gave me are possibilities." Marilee groaned. "And I'll bet you could think of a hundred more."

"I could. No limit, actually." Polly fluttered her

eyelashes, which made me laugh.

"Honestly, I don't care how horrific my birth-parents may've been. I just want to know."

"Anyone would," said Marilee. "Can you think of anything else you can do here, or is it time to plan our trip to South America?" She took a long sip of her beer.

"It's time. But I want to do some research to narrow our focus."

Polly finished an onion ring, then dabbed at her lips with her napkin. "I agree with that. Not knowing the customs or the dialects is bad enough. We'll be digging for facts that are almost fifty years old."

I didn't know how to read that. "So?"

She let out a slow burning smile, revealing her amazingly straight and white teeth. "So, we may have to stretch our imaginations, and possibly our courage."

Marilee set down her beer glass and leaned in. "What do you mean?"

"Bolivia is one of the poorest countries in the Western Hemisphere. I believe we're heading for the poorest part of it."

"What difference does that make?" I asked.

Polly said, "It's just that destitute people are pretty wrapped up in the business of staying alive and making it to the next day. Feeding their kids—that sort of thing. I don't know that they'd have the energy to remember somebody else's business from fifty years ago. We'll have to think of creative ways to dig."

"That's probably true, but I don't think that's limited to poor people," said Marilee. She paused. "And why did you say we'll need courage?"

"I'm not sure." Polly looked at her glass as though the answer were printed on it. "It's a Socialist country with a history of governments that don't appreciate opposition."

"But we won't be doing anything political," said Marilee.

Polly pushed her loosely flowing hair behind her ears. "From their point of view, we'll be three American women, chatting up their citizens, looking for their documents, and visiting their hospitals. We'll look supremely suspicious."

"Oh, great!" I said, actually throwing up my hands. "So the price I need to pay to learn my true identity is that we possibly end up as political prisoners in some damp, adobe prison with mud floors and gruel for dinner."

"Well, yes," said Marilee. "But I think you're leaving out the torture and molestation."

I looked at her. "If you're serious, why would you go with me?"

She took my hand and looked me in the eye. "Because you have a right to know your history. Frankly, it pisses me off that your parents put you in this position. Also, you're my dear friend."

I squeezed her hand, then turned to Polly. "What about you?"

She took a sip of her beer, then set it down and dabbed her lips with a napkin. She looked at me with an earnestness which suggested world events could turn on her answer. "It's a rare opportunity, Suzanne. I get to help a new friend, see a country I've never visited, help to try to solve an interesting mystery, and maybe end up a prisoner in a dank cell."

"Wait. What's positive about jail?"

She smiled, then said in apparent seriousness, "I also

do stand-up. I think I could milk this scenario for at least five minutes of material."

I shook my head. "You do know you're nuts?"

She grinned. "So I've been told."

The waiter came for our dinner order, and we took our time studying the menu and making our selections from among the dozens of specialty burgers—from vegan to juicy, red insides, for which you had to sign a special waiver in case you would get E. coli. As we settled back to await our food, I leaned toward them and said, "What do you guys think our plan of attack should be?"

Marilee said, "We go straight to the hospital with your birth records in hand."

"Then what?"

She tilted her head. "Then, we politely decline to leave until we get some answers."

"What if we don't?" I asked. "I mean, what if they all refuse to talk with us?"

Polly reached into her purse, pulled out her wallet, and spread out a dozen singles like a dealer with cards in Las Vegas.

"Bribes?" asked Marilee.

"Certainly not," said Polly. "Just something for their inconvenience. In local currency. In large volume."

I ran my hand through my hair as I thought about it. "I don't mind spending the money. But if I pay, they may just make stuff up. Like the way torture yields unreliable intel."

"I don't think bribery and torture are the same," said Marilee.

"Well, I'm not recommending that we torture anyone," Polly said. "But money could loosen a tongue or two. Maybe we should tell them they'll get the money only if the information pans out."

"So, more of a reward than a bribe?" asked Marilee.

"Exactly," said Polly.

I took a deep breath, then nodded. "Okay. What else?"

Marilee sighed. "There is nothing else. You have one lead. We'll just have to get the information out of the hospital staff."

"I'm terrified we'll fail," I said.

Polly smiled at me. "We won't fail." She rested her elbows on the edge of the table and leaned in, eyes rivetted to mine. "Think about it, Suzanne. We're three beautiful women, you are willing to spend money, and we have no fear of embarrassing ourselves."

"Are you speaking for all of us?" asked Marilee.

"The way I understand it, I *will* be speaking for all of us. So, we've got my high school teacher language skill, and all the female charm we can muster. I figure, that should about do it."

"Yeah. I tried relying on my charm a few days ago with Darren Long and embarrassed the hell out of myself."

Polly laughed. "Just follow my lead." She tilted her head in exaggerated thought for a moment, then added, "You won't really have much choice. Will you?"

"I couldn't do this without you, Polly," I said.

She winked at me, the second person to have done so in two days. "We'll have fun. I guarantee it." She paused. "I have a feeling you'll get answers to all of your questions, even those you haven't thought of yet, and that they'll bring you great peace and joy."

I loved her over-the-top positivity, which was just

what I needed.

Polly excused herself to visit the restroom, and I used the opportunity to quiz Marilee about her. Once I was sure Polly was out of ear-shot, I asked, "Do you think she's for real?"

She swished her beer before speaking. "I can understand why you might wonder. But, Suzanne, I've known her since third grade. She's always been like this."

I stared at her. "You mean she spoke in superlatives and showed unusually deep concern for others as a child?"

"Yes. And yes. And she was passionate about everything that interested her, and funny. It's just who she is. In fact, her mother is just like her."

"You're kidding."

"No. You're right, Suzanne. Her mother doesn't do improv and stand-up. But she has the same positivity and ebullience. All the neighborhood kids loved to visit Polly's house because her mom was so nice."

"That is interesting. So, it's all sincere."

"Oh, it's sincere all right. I think of it this way. Other people who are kind tell white lies to make others feel better. But Polly finds something truly admirable to comment on. She can act sincere because she is." Marilee checked the door to the restroom before continuing. She lowered her voice. "Of course, her personal life has as many ups and downs as anyone's." She took a sip of her beer before continuing. "This is weird to say, but I think a lot of people find Polly addictive."

I nodded. "Yeah. That's a pretty weird thing to say." As Polly walked toward us with a big smile on her face, and I saw other diners follow her movement, I quickly added, "But I can see it."

Once Polly was seated, I said, "Now, let's set definite dates, and I'll check for thc best airfare. I'll also grab us hotel rooms in Oruro for the duration."

Marilee said, "See if you can get us a suite for three. I'd prefer not to sleep alone in a country where I can't even cry out, 'Help! I'm being murdered!'"

"Wise," I said.

Polly said, "And we should all get prescriptions for altitude sickness medicine. A friend told me about it. You take it over a four-day period and it alleviates the headaches, fatigue, nausea, and dizziness we'd probably get as soon as we step out of the airplane in Oruro. Apparently, our trip is too short for our bodies to acclimatize naturally."

"Thanks, Polly," said Marilee. "I wouldn't have thought of it."

"Me neither," I said. "This is going to be hard enough without migraines and barfing." I knew we couldn't do much else until we firmed up the dates. "Polly, are you definitely clear for Saturday, May 25 through Sunday, June 2?"

"I can make it work," she said. "I have a terrific sub I can call."

"Great. Marilee and I are in the process of getting our files covered for the week."

"Do you think you'll be able to?" said Polly.

"Friends will do whatever they can for me, 'the grieving widow,' and all of my law partners are my friends. Of course, it complicates things that Marilee and I will both be gone since ours is a small firm. We had to promise to take off no more than one full work week."

Marilee's face clouded. She sucked in her breath, then said, "So, how is the grieving going?"

I took a moment to decide whether I wanted to go into it. But, like with Darren Long, it seemed I needed to say the words. "I miss Mac every day and every night. I'm still trying to keep my waking hours to the minimum needed for work and household chores. Sleep continues to be my best friend."

Polly looked at me, forehead wrinkled. "But what about when you wake up?"

"Yeah. That's the problem. I can't figure out how not to wake up. I mean, apart from the obvious. And I'll be damned if I'll leave this world without finding out the truth about how I entered it. So, permanent sleep is out of the question—for the time being."

Polly pursed her lips. "Wait. What happens after you unmask your birth-mom and dad?"

I closed my eyes to think, and took some time before I answered. "I don't know. I really don't know, Polly."

The waiter returned with our tray full of fake burgers and plenty of real fries.

Chapter 11

As I planned our trip to South America, I made sure the dates wouldn't conflict with the discovery dates already set in my court case. John told me he'd arranged for all five deponents to give our testimony on the same day, Tuesday, May 7. John had taken into consideration that it would be best if the criminal cases were already concluded before the three boys sat to give their testimony in my civil suit. That way, they wouldn't be able to take the fifth and avoid answering his questions. As it turned out, each of the boys pled guilty and ended up with a year of supervision, a fine of $1,500, and 300 hours of community service. The bitter part of me assumed that was all the State thought my loved ones were worth.

After working with all three of our calendars, Marilee, Polly and I made definite arrangements to travel to La Paz on Saturday, May 25. We planned to be in Bolivia for the full week because we had no idea what we'd encounter. We scheduled our return for Sunday, June 2, and Marilee and I handled our concern that jet lag might make it hard for us to get into work on Monday morning by making it clear we wouldn't be arriving at the office until noon.

I told John I didn't need him to prepare me for my deposition since I'd taken hundreds of them and knew what to expect. The plan was for me to give my testimony on May 7th at 10:00 a.m., the three young men starting at 1:00 p.m., and finally, the truck driver at 4:00 p.m.

When the day arrived, I walked into the conference room feeling like I was just one of the attorneys. Being sworn in didn't faze me, but when the questioning began, I fully realized I was playing a completely different role—and would be re-traumatized.

Details about me and Mac—education, work histories and incomes, hobbies and interests—felt intrusive, but I was able to keep my emotions in check. When we got to the day of the accident, it was smooth sailing right up to where Mom opened the picnic basket to show off what she'd prepared for us. It was as though someone had pressed "re-play." I was there. I was in those moments again. I gave the whole story—the fall colors, pulling over at the scenic overlook, Mom whispering to me that she needed to visit a ladies' powder room, the route, the care about the speed limits and the stop signs—with tears streaming down my cheeks. Fortunately, John had placed a full box of tissues next to my spot at the table. I explained feeling that we had exploded, and that I had no other memories until I awoke in the hospital nine weeks later.

Counsel for the truck company and driver, May Yang, was an attorney I knew from the Women Lawyers' Association. She had approached me before the deposition to tell me how sorry she was about my terrible loss. I took that as a genuine kindness since I'd sued her client for causing it. She questioned me in a respectful and sensitive way. The lawyer the three boys had hired, however, whom I'd never met before, apparently thought he could crack the case by badgering me.

He insinuated that it was less than credible that I'd been driving within the speed limit. And he seemed to find it extraordinary that, when stop signs were actually in their correct positions, I'd always rewarded them with a full and complete. But it was his last question that really got under my skin. He said, "Ms. Summerfield, isn't it true that as of nine weeks after the accident you were completely fine?"

I laughed out loud. Not only that. I couldn't stop laughing. John suggested we take a break. But the creep lawyer said, "Not between a question and an answer, counsel."

John sighed. "As you wish." My laughing fit was over by the time he turned to me. "Ms. Summerfield, I'll ask the court reporter to read back the question. Then you may go ahead and answer." She read it back. This time, my reaction was the exact opposite.

I said to the boys' lawyer, "Counsel, I will give you the benefit of the doubt and assume that you are merely ignorant, rather than meaning to inflict emotional distress. The answer is that I lost my husband of eighteen years, my mother, and my father in an instant because your clients thought it was a fine idea to remove a stop sign—the very one that stood between life and death for Mac, and Betty, and Ron. We were simply out for a drive—a celebration of life—when the callousness of your clients turned it into a cataclysm. They robbed me of my entire existence—in an instant. Not the instant when we exploded. The instant when they took the stop sign. So, I promise you, that neither I, nor any normal, sane person in the position your clients put me in, will ever be 'completely fine' again."

After I'd finished giving my testimony, I hung

around in my office, waiting for the depositions of the four defendants to begin. Marilee poked her head in. "Hey. Are you sure you want to see the miscreants in person?"

"Yeah."

"I mean, we could just ask the court reporter to expedite the transcripts, and you could read all of it tomorrow morning."

I raised my eyebrows. "I know that."

"So, why do you want to see them?"

"I don't. I want them to see me."

She nodded, then pulled my office door closed behind her.

We used the same conference room for the defendants, and none of them was present for anyone's testimony except his own. Each was sworn in after taking the seat I'd vacated just hours before. But they didn't require the tissue box. That is, the first three didn't.

Toby Thomas went first. John asked the questions and I sat, not ten feet from Toby, at the center of the long side of the rectangular table. Toby didn't look at me until the very end, but my eyes never left him. Small in stature, he wore his lank brown hair in a ponytail, had on a dress shirt, worn jeans, and sneakers. He was an average looking fifteen-year-old. I couldn't have picked him out in a crowd.

After he told us about his education—high school sophomore, and his family situation—an only child, living with his mother, John asked him about the night before the accident.

Toby: "It was a Saturday night, so me and my friends were hanging out at Bennie's Burgers' parking lot."

John: "Who else was present?"

Toby: "My best friends, Dean and Harry, for sure. And a few girls we know. And some other guys."

John: "Their names, please?"

Toby: (Giving girls' and boys' names.)

John: "What time did you arrive at the parking lot?"

Toby: "Around ten o'clock."

John: "Did you, at some point, leave Bennies' and remove a stop sign at the southwest corner of Blackwater Road and Chivens Highway?"

Toby: "Yes. We did."

John: "At what time?"

Toby: "Maybe ten thirty or eleven."

John: "Why were you at that location?"

Toby: "Dean had borrowed his brother's car. So he took us out for a ride. Just us three guys."

John: "Did Dean's brother know he'd borrowed his car?"

Toby: "Doubtful."

John: "Did Dean have a valid driver's license?"

Toby: "No. Learner's permit."

John: "Did you have anything alcoholic to drink between the time you arrived at Bennie's and when you left?"

Toby: "Me? Not much. Maybe two beers."

John: "Did you continue to drink in the car?"

Toby: "Not really. We each just took the beer we were working on. You know. To go."

John: "So you all three did drink beer in the car?"

Toby: "Yeah."

After he covered the route the boys had driven, John got to the specifics about the stop sign.

John: "Who in the car first suggested or mentioned

the idea of removing a stop sign?"

Toby: "It might've been me."

John: "Was it you?"

Toby: "Maybe. Probably."

John: "What do you remember saying?"

Toby closed his eyes for a moment, then quoted himself. "'You know what would be funny?'"

John: "And then?"

Toby: "Then I told them my idea, and we sorta argued about it."

John: "What was the argument about?"

Toby: "Dean didn't want to put a dirty old sign in his brother's car."

John: "And you did?"

Toby: "Sure. See, I thought it would be cool to have a stop sign that we could put up wherever we wanted. But Harry said we'd get caught for sure if we kept it. He didn't see much point in it."

John: "Did the three of you discuss what could happen to the drivers at that intersection if you removed the sign?"

Toby: "No."

John: "Why not?"

Toby: "I never thought about it. I just wanted a stop sign. Maybe Dean or Harry thought about it. But they didn't say anything."

John: "You're saying it didn't enter your mind that someone in a car could be injured by that sign not being in place?"

Toby: "Yeah. I guess so."

John: "So what did you three decide to do?"

Toby: "Take one down and wrap it in an old blanket that was on the floor in the back seat.

Toby explained that there was a chainsaw in the trunk. (Was I the only one who imagined serial murders?) They'd picked the corner at random from among those far enough out in the country that there'd be no witnesses. And it had to be a wood post. Even with the saw, it took them a good five minutes. His friends quickly grew bored with the project, and became irritable. They all lifted the thing, wrapped it on the ground, and tossed it in the trunk. Toby testified that there was no more discussion about the stop sign until they got back to Bennie's parking lot.

But once among a group of friends, Dean and Harry bragged about what they'd done, and described how they'd gone about it. Feeling vindicated that Dean and Harry now thought the idea was cool, Toby joined in, regaling their friends with the details of their amazing exploit. All of which, he said, explained why it was so easy for the county sheriff's police to find the three of them after the accident.

John: "How did you learn of the accident that happened the next day at that intersection, and which resulted in three deaths?"

Toby: "It was Sunday morning, so of course I was dead-out sleeping. My mom came to my bedroom door and told me Dean called her because I wasn't answering, and it was an emergency. So, I reached for her phone, but she said I should call him back on mine. Then she rolled her eyes and walked away."

John: "What did Dean say when you reached him?"

Toby: "He went nuts. He called me an asshole and lots of other names. He said there'd been a monster crash at the intersection, and that we were all screwed big time. I wasn't following. Then he said, 'You took the stop sign down, you moron. You caused the crash.' So, I said, 'I wasn't even there!' So, he said, 'You're an idiot,' and hung up."

John: "So Dean told you that you caused the crash?"

Toby: "Yeah."

John: "As of today, do *you* believe you have any responsibility for the accident?" (The snarky lawyer objected, but allowed Toby to answer over the objection).

Toby: "Yes. A little."

John: "Just a little?"

Toby: "Yeah. It was broad daylight. So maybe the two vehicles should've seen each other."

John: "Have you gone back to that intersection in the daylight?"

Toby: "Maybe."

John: "Did you notice that the trees to the right of where the driver of the car was located blocked the view to the right, where the truck was coming from?"

Toby: "Maybe. But I wasn't trying to figure out the accident."

John: "Which means you did return to the scene. Right?"

Toby: "Yeah. I guess."

John: "Do you believe it is reasonably likely the accident would not have happened if you hadn't removed the stop sign?"

Toby's lawyer: "Objection. Calls for speculation. I instruct my client not to answer."

John: (turning to Toby's lawyer) "You know very well that's an improper instruction counsel."

"Then let me ask you this, Toby. Once you heard that three people were killed at that intersection the morning after you'd removed the stop sign, what did you do?"

Toby: "I worried I'd be in trouble."

John: "Did there ever come a time when you had a different reaction?"

Toby: "Yes. See, my mom heard right away what we'd done. So, she made me sit at the table while she read to me from the paper about the lives of the three people who got killed."

John: "Did you show any reaction to that?"

Toby: "Yes."

John: "What did you do?"

Toby: "I cried. Then Mom said I better get myself straight with the Lord, because it's not up to humans to take lives."

John: "Did she comment on your legal jeopardy— that you could be held liable either criminally or civilly?"

Toby: "No. She didn't care about that. But she was sure I was a sinner. And she said she was tired to death of it. That was the last time we talked about it."

John: "Have you contacted either of the two survivors of the accident? The woman who was driving the car, or the truck driver?"

Toby: "No way. I didn't have the guts for that. Then once we went in together to get a lawyer" (nodding toward his attorney) "he told us not to talk to anybody about this. You know, taking the stop sign. (laughing without mirth). "A little late for that, but, you know, whatever."

Toby finally glanced at me, biting his lower lip as he did so.

John covered more details, but the word that kept coming to my mind was *feckless*. Every time Toby opened his mouth, my brain said "feckless." I'd wanted to despise the boys who had ruined my life. But what I felt was pity.

I also started to second-guess myself. I wondered whether my decisions were as instrumental as theirs. Planning the leaf-gazing outing. Deciding to take the Blue Ridge Parkway. Choosing to pull off the Parkway at the particular spot I did. Not speeding. Coming to full-and-completes. It all led to my being in that intersection at the exact moment as the truck. And the truck driver also made a series of decisions that all conspired to place him there. I didn't think of it as destiny, or fate, or anything that suggests what happened was pre-ordained. I was convinced that everything is random. But randomness kills people. So why hate Toby any more than hate myself? How much of the fault was mine, rather than his? My stomach started to ache.

Dean Mitchell walked into the room next, tossing back his long, blond hair, a good-looking boy who knew it. He didn't exactly swagger, but he came close. His testimony was generally consistent with Toby's, but Dean was snarky. He admitted to driving without a valid license, but said he couldn't see the relevance of that. He conceded he'd taken his brother's car without permission, and consumed a couple of beers before removing the sign. He said, "Why does that matter?" to each question.

John: "As of today, do you believe you have any responsibility for the accident?"

Dean: (Over objection). "No sir. I mean, there are lots of uncontrolled intersections in the world. Right? And people aren't constantly crashing into each other at those. Us guys just made this controlled intersection into an uncontrolled one." He glanced at me with a self-satisfied smirk plastered over his face. "Not to insult your client, but she should've seen the truck. And the trucker probably should've slowed down and taken a good gander at the intersection."

John: "The truck driver's answers to interrogatories state that he'd driven that route before, so he knew that intersecting traffic had a stop sign. Was it reasonable for him to rely on that?"

Dean's lawyer: "Objection. Calls for speculation. (Turning to Dean) "You may answer over my objection."

Dean: (Leaning back in his chair). "Maybe. But what if somebody just blew that stop sign? People do it all the time. For all we know, your client might've blown the sign, even if we hadn't of removed it."

I almost laughed out loud at his reasoning. At least now I knew how Dean rationalized it. The fact that he didn't seem to have a very analytical mind wasn't his fault, and I didn't hold that against him. But he was so puffed up with his coolness, so seemingly above the fray of the little nuisance case I'd filed, that my first reaction was to want to obliterate him. At the end of the session, he glanced at me one last time as he made his way out of the conference room. I stared hard at him. I wanted him to fear the upcoming trial, a large verdict against him, a lifetime of garnished wages. I wanted him to fear what I could do to him. But that other response nagged at me. Of course, I knew I wouldn't have blown any stop sign—ever. But nasty Dean's comments that I could've been more careful reignited my worry that I was, at least partly, at fault. My stomachache reappeared and my ears began to burn.

The third boy, Harry Phillips, showed up in a coat

and tie. He was chubby, if not technically obese, and looked younger that his fifteen years. Harry's statements were consistent with those of the other boys. He also denied having given any thought to how a missing stop sign might have any bearing on traffic safety. Apparently, they really hadn't considered the consequences of their late-night crime. But Harry had clearly considered them after the accident. John asked him whether he believed he had helped cause the accident.

Harry: "The old couple who died were the same age as my grandparents. And the guy who died wasn't much older than my dad. (Pauses. Eyes glisten with tears. Takes a deep breath to regain composure.) "I don't know whether you could actually say we 'caused' the accident. I mean, Dean and Toby say it was the fault of the two drivers. But we sure didn't help."

John: "What did you do when you heard about it?"

Harry: "I went outside and vomited. That was October. Now, not a day goes by that I don't think about those people."

John: "Because you feel responsible for their deaths?"

Harry: "Not exactly. More like because I feel close to their deaths. We were at the spot where the accident happened just a few hours before the crash."

John: "Are you claiming you were a witness to the existence of the intersection—and nothing more?"

Harry: "Yeah. That's it. Dean says the driver might've blown the stop sign even if it had been standing right there."

John: "And what do you say?"

Harry glanced at me, and I tried to make my face

neutral. I was absolutely certain that Harry knew this was all BS. I would've loved to have known what the kid really thought, rather than what Dean told him to say.

Harry: "I don't know. There's no way to know since the stop sign *wasn't* there."

John: "Because you and Dean and Toby removed it."

Harry: "Exactly."

Chapter 12

There was a half-hour break between the end of Harry's deposition and the beginning of the trucker's. Tooley Freight Lines International and Charlie Bixby were both represented by May. She introduced me to Mr. Bixby, and we shook hands. He opened his mouth to say something, but nothing came out. I gave him a nod and he walked over to take the seat for the deponent, as I took my spectator spot on the side of the table. Charlie was an average looking guy with an old-fashioned buzz haircut, and quite thin. He looked too tall to sit comfortably in the cab of a truck for hours at a time. I couldn't judge his age because his face was deeply lined like he must've worked outdoors at some point. But his hands were wrinkle-free, with elegant piano-player fingers. Something else struck me when we were introduced. It looked to me like his left eye didn't move, as though it were made of glass. John must've noticed it too, because immediately after Mr. Bixby was sworn in, he asked him if he had any issues with his vision.

Charlie: "Yes, sir. I have a glass eye on the left side."

John: "How did that come about?"

Charlie: "I was a youngster at Little League practice. I was looking at a ball I was about to catch when another one struck me in the eye."

John: "Does the fact that you have only one functioning eye hinder your vision, or your peripheral vision, in any way?"

Charlie: "Not that I'm aware of. The baseball accident happened forty-five years ago. So my right eye, which still has 20/20, has compensated. At least, that's how I understand it."

John: "Do you have a valid license to drive a commercial vehicle?"

Charlie: "Yes, sir. A Virginia commercial license. Years ago, I submitted my medical information to the Commissioner, and took a behind-the-wheel test as well, to qualify for a waiver. I have to be tested every so often because my license is based on a waiver."

John: "Have you been involved in any other accidents while driving a truck?"

Charlie: "No, sir."

John then backed up and got Mr. Bixby's personal information: 46 years old, 6 foot 2 inches tall, 160 pounds, divorced, two teenage children, twenty-five years as a long-haul truck driver, fired after the accident. Subsequent to being fired, he'd been working as a handyman.

I found the witness to be a bit more than responsive. He seemed inclined to give just a little more information than the question actually demanded. I knew a jury would appreciate that. I couldn't help myself. I was evaluating every witness that day in terms of their credibility before a jury, just as I did in the cases I handled in which I wasn't the plaintiff.

Somehow, as I had been running through the roster of defendants, pondering how a jury would react to each, John had gotten to the point in the deposition where he was starting to ask about the day of the accident. I have no idea why I hadn't read any of the news articles about the accident. But I hadn't. Still, I don't think anything could've prepared me for what I heard next.

John: "Where were you in the five minutes before the accident?"

Charlie: (Sitting ramrod straight, hands on the table, fingers intertwined) "Travelling due north on Chivens Highway."

John: "How many north-bound lanes were there at that location?"

Charlie: "One north-bound. Also, one south-bound."

John: "In the two minutes before the accident, was there any other north-bound traffic, either ahead of you or behind you?"

Charlie: "No, sir."

John: "Is it correct that the weather was clear and dry?"

Charlie: "Yes, sir."

John: "Your rig was fully loaded, at approximately 80,000 pounds. Correct?"

Charlie: "Yes."

John: "What is the name of the intersecting road you were approaching?"

Charlie: "I was approaching Blackwater Road."

John: "Were you familiar with that intersection?"

Charlie: "I was."

John: "How many times had you passed through that intersection, travelling either north or south on Chivens Highway?"

Charlie: (After pausing to take a sip of water) "Approximately fifty times."

John: "Fifty?"

Charlie: "Yes, sir. It was one of my regular routes."

John: "Was the road you were on level or hilly?"

Charlie: "A little hilly, but not enough to block my view."

John: "Was there any traffic control sign or device in place at that intersection for traffic travelling on Chivens Highway?"

Charlie: "No, sir."

John: "Was there any traffic sign or device for traffic travelling east or west on Blackwater Road?"

Charlie: "Yes, sir."

John: "What was that?"

Charlie: "They had a stop sign. Both for going east and for going west."

John: "How do you know that?"

Charlie: "I've seen the signs. And I've seen vehicles stopped at the signs."

John: "Did you see a stop sign in place for east-bound traffic on Blackwater Road at that intersection on the day of the accident?"

Charlie: "No."

John: "Did you look for one?"

Charlie: "No."

John: "What is the speed limit for north-bound traffic on Chivens Highway, that is to say, your speed limit?"

Charlie: "55."

John: "What speed were you travelling in the two minutes before the accident with Ms. Summerfield's vehicle?"

Charlie: (His hands still folded before him, his fingers tightening) "Between 60 and 62. I never go more than seven above the limit."

John: "Did you reduce your speed at any time before

the truck you were driving struck the car?"

Charlie: "A split second before we hit, I saw her to my left. I slammed on the brakes. I couldn't believe it—that a car travelling at what looked like a reasonable speed would just blow through a stop sign."

John: "When did you first see the car that was involved in the accident?"

Charlie: "Only a second or two before it entered the intersection. See, there were huge trees to my left, blocking my view of the south part of Blackwater Road, and the car had to have been coming up a hill. Lots of hills on that road. As soon as I could see past the trees, I saw the car coming along."

John: "So it's true to say you did not reduce speed at all simply because you were approaching an intersection?"

Charlie: "Correct."

John: "Can you estimate the speed of the car during the time you were able to see it?"

Charlie: "Not precisely. It was such a short time. Maybe doing 45 mph. Not fast."

John: "Did you keep your focus on that car up until the moment of impact?"

Charlie: "Yes. I did. I mean, there was nothing else to watch. As soon as I realized it wasn't going to stop, I stomped down on my brake. But she was already in the intersection."

John: "Did you swerve?"

Charlie: "No time."

John: "Just a 'yes' or 'no' please. Did you swerve?"

Charlie: "No, sir."

John: "Why not?"

Charlie: "No time."

John: "Did you honk?"

Charlie: "No."

John: "Why not?"

Charlie: "No time."

John: "What were you doing in the cab of your truck in the last five minutes before the accident?"

Charlie: "Driving."

John: "Anything else? Was the radio on? CD? Phone?"

Charlie: "No, sir. I like quiet."

John: "Did you sneeze, or cough, or anything else that might've distracted you?"

Charlie: (After pausing to think) "No, sir. I didn't."

John: "And you said you didn't reduce speed at all as you approached the intersection?"

Charlie: "That's right."

John: "So, you didn't touch the brake until you saw the car enter the intersection?"

Charlie: "That's right. I was shocked that the car blew the stop sign. As soon as I saw it, I braked. I had anti-lock brakes, so my foot stayed on the brake pedal. The module took over and acted like a foot pumping the system."

John: "Mr. Bixby, you've used the phrase 'blew the stop sign' a couple of times. Do you now have knowledge that there was no stop sign present at the time of the accident?"

Charlie: "Yes. I learned it had been pulled the night before. I didn't mean any disrespect to your client. It's just that, at the time of the accident, I thought the driver of the car blew the stop sign."

John: "Understood. What exactly happened in the intersection?"

Charlie: "It felt like an explosion. My head flew toward the steering wheel and the air bag slammed into my face. My seat belt grabbed on and locked me against the seat back. As soon as it was over, when I'd come to a stop, I must've climbed out."

John: "The interior of the cab was intact?"

Charlie: "Seemed to be. But I didn't stop to inspect it."

John: "Then what?"

Charlie: (Pausing, then turning his stare inward) "I don't remember getting out of the cab. What I do remember is standing next to my rig looking for the car I'd hit. It seemed to have disappeared. I called 911 on my phone. I think I gave her the intersection. I looked down Chivens to the north. Nothing. I looked east and west down Blackwater. Nothing. I thought I was losing my mind."

John: "What did you do next?"

Charlie: "I started walking north on Chivens. I mean, logically, I must've pushed the car quite a ways. I still couldn't figure out why I couldn't see it. After a while, I saw something off to my right, beyond the ditch, in a field."

John: "What was it?"

Charlie: (Sighing heavily, then taking a moment before speaking) I didn't know. It looked like metal. I figured it was the car, but it definitely wasn't as big as a car."

John: "What did you do when you saw it?"

Charlie: "I headed for the thing. It wasn't making any sense to me. But it was the only thing I could see out of the ordinary."

John: "Did you reach the 'thing,' as you call it?"

Charlie: "Yes. I got up to right near it, and I knew it had to be a car or a part of one. So I walked around it to try to make sense of it."

John: "Then what?"

Charlie: "That's when I realized there was a person in it. I couldn't figure out what body part I was seeing. A leg seemed to be where the head should be. But—"

That's when Mr. Bixby fell apart. Mid-sentence. He started sobbing. I pushed the box of tissues I'd used earlier toward him, but his head was resting on his arms folded on the table and his whole body was shaking. He didn't look up. John told the court reporter we were going to take a break. He turned to May and told her that he and I, the boys' lawyer, and the reporter would leave the room for a while. He asked her to let him know when her client was ready to continue. "No hurry."

When we got out into the hallway, John asked the reporter and the boys' lawyer to wait in the reception area. He and I walked to my office, because it was closer than his. I fell into my desk chair and John took one of the visitor chairs in front of my desk.

I looked at him. "I don't understand, John. Why didn't Mr. Bixby recognize my car as a car?"

"You don't know?"

I shook my head.

"Because it was only half a car. The impact sheared it in two."

"What? You can't be serious." But the look on John's face told me he was.

"And the person he was describing?"

"Your mother."

"Oh, my God!"

"I'm so sorry, Suzanne. I assumed you'd read the

news articles."

I bit my lip, too hard, and bled. I couldn't prevent the tears. I couldn't stop my face from twisting. I thought I was about to hyperventilate. Instead, I cried—hard. John grabbed a box of tissues and set it before me. Once I was able to breathe through my nose normally again, I was still shaking. I said, "So, he must've seen me too."

"Yes. He told the police that both bodies were motionless and covered with blood. He thought you were both dead."

"Did he find the other half of my car?"

"He did. He ran around until he saw it—on the other side of the road, off in the trees. What he described is all in the police report."

I stared at him, unable to talk. I raised my eyebrows.

"Same scenario. But of course, Mac and your father actually were dead."

I gulped, and had trouble continuing. My voice had become a whisper. "What did Mr. Bixby do after that?"

"The sheriff's police found him running full-out between the two halves of your car."

"Trying to help?"

"Or going insane."

"Jesus, John."

"I know."

We remained quiet for a few minutes. I was still shivering and felt a headache coming on. I said, "I'm going home. Get what you need from Mr. Bixby, but make it as quick as you can."

"Of course." He stood to go check on whether May was ready to continue. Just before he walked out of my office, he turned to me and added, "I'm so sorry, Suzanne."

I tried to say thanks, but no words came out. I forced my eyes closed to stem the tears.

As I drove home, I worked to focus on the legal import of what I'd learned from Mr. Bixby to block out the horror of what I'd heard last. He was a nice man and a jury would like him. But he had admitted to speeding in an 80,000-pound vehicle. Of course, I hadn't reduced my speed either. Then again, I was driving within the speed limit, and I wasn't carrying 80,000 pounds. Probably not enough for a jury to find me contributorily negligent. And there was the fact that he has no left eye. A jury would not like that he was driving with impaired vision or that he was speeding.

The distraction only worked for a minute. I pulled over, and forced myself to take long, slow breaths. I have no idea how I reached my driveway, and ended up lying on my couch, shivering under the Alpaca throw. But I stayed there straight through until morning's light.

Chapter 13

On May 25th, Marilee, Polly and I took a series of flights: Charlottesville to Chicago, to Miami, to Santa Cruz, Bolivia, to La Paz, Bolivia, and finally to Oruro. By the time we reached our hotel, we'd been travelling for over thirty hours, and I was realizing how grueling this trip would be. As we'd left the airport building, I thought we had been rerouted to the Arctic. I'd read about the freezing night-time temperatures in the Altiplano, but I was still shocked. According to the cab driver, it was twenty-six degrees Fahrenheit at midnight, when we stepped out of his car at Hotel La Rosa.

Fortunately, the family-owned business accommodated us with a three-person "suite." The owner, Senora Choque, a pleasant, short, rail-thin woman, seemed unperturbed by the lateness of the hour as she accompanied us up a narrow flight of stairs to our digs. It was a small, cramped room with three twin-size beds and a microscopic bathroom. Because the hotel provided heat and hot water, which not all of them did, it suited us just fine. By the time we got settled in, it was past midnight, local time. Although I was sure that no one wanted to get on with our mission more than I did, there was nothing to do but get some sleep and hope to find answers the next day.

Amazingly, we all three slept through our alarms, and didn't wake up for almost twelve hours. Our two small windows looked out over the front entrance, and revealed a brilliant, cloudless sky. Still travel-dazed, we took turns freshening up. We opted for skirts, to appear as respectful as possible at the hospital, then hurried downstairs at twelve-forty to ask where we might get a bite to eat.

Senora Choque told Polly that all the restaurants had closed at 12:30 for siesta, and would re-open at 2:30 p.m. Of course, the hospital doors were open 24/7, but the offices there would also be closed from 12:30 to 2:30 p.m. We stepped outside to temperatures in the mid-fifties, which was a huge relief. Marilee spied a line of people stretched out in front of a food-cart, so at least one vendor wasn't observing siesta. We hurried across the street and joined the queue, not knowing what kind of food the man was peddling. Once we reached the front of the line, the short, dark man wearing a stained white bib-apron and a bowler hat, told Polly that what we were pointing at were called saltenas. Like empanadas, they were filled with chicken in a sweet and sour sauce, and some potatoes and unfamiliar veggies. We were famished, so we each ordered two and returned to our room to gobble them up.

We still had extra time before the hospital offices would open, so we sat on our beds wearing our wool blankets like capes, and gabbed non-stop until time to go. We all spoke faster than usual, and laughed harder than our quips merited, I think because we were so nervous about how things would go at the hospital. I didn't know if the others noticed it, but to me, the joviality felt forced and awkward.

We had read warnings about the dangers of the fake cabs, so we asked Senora Choque to call a legitimate one for us. By 2:45 we were standing at the main entrance to the hospital where I'd been born, a light-colored stucco, three-story building. Being there felt surreal—of great importance, but at the same time meaningless. I hoped my feelings would sort themselves once I got my answers. Marilee asked me to pose for a picture I didn't feel ready for. Nevertheless, I obliged her.

The reception area was small, and the light-blue, fabric-covered furniture was worn but spotless. Polly had my hospital records in hand as she tried to explain to the woman at the information booth what we hoped to learn. The woman seemed agitated, and it occurred to me that she didn't know what to say, or where to direct us. My inquiry probably hadn't come up often.

I pulled Polly aside and suggested she ask for the hospital records department. As she did so, the woman visibly relaxed as she provided directions, which included a lot of gesturing. When Polly appeared to comprehend something, the woman nodded vigorously. As we walked toward the elevator bank, Polly filled us in on the conversation. "The woman kept telling me that nobody there could help us with a problem that happened fifty years ago. She acted very rushed, and really didn't want my lengthy explanation. But your suggestion worked like a charm, Suzanne. She was on firm footing when I said, 'Records.' "

"So that's where we're headed now?" asked Marilee.

"Basement. Room 107."

"Great," I said, without much enthusiasm, since it seemed my anxiety left no room for any other emotion.

The pale-yellow door to 107 was closed. Polly shrugged, stepped up and knocked lightly, then turned the knob and walked in. We saw row after row of tan metal file cabinets, and in a back corner of the huge room, a large man sitting behind a small, gray, metal desk. There was fluorescent lighting, no windows, and the air smelled of stale and ancient documents. The man didn't look up as we snaked our way through the file cabinets.

When we reached him, Polly spoke to him for a minute or so, and pointed at me a couple of times. After he responded, she told us he'd said that all records past twenty-five years old had been destroyed. He looked at me, shrugged, and raised his hands to signify, "There's nothing I can do for you, lady."

I suggested Polly ask him if he had any ideas for what we might try next. After she spoke, he laughed. Then he said, "No," a word I could understand. I broke down sobbing, lowered myself to the floor since there were no chairs around, and cried into my hands. The man must've been concerned because a minute later, he was standing over me with a bottle of water. I was having trouble catching my breath, and felt embarrassed to have fallen apart in front of him. He handed me the water bottle, then returned to his desk as I focused on getting the skinny plastic top off. He asked Polly something, and she moved to stand directly in front of his desk.

She spent the next fifteen minutes telling him everything that had happened to me since the day Mac and my folks and I went for a drive to see the fall colors on the Parkway. Polly used her hands to express herself, and acted some things out. By the time she got to the end, the man had tears shining in his eyes, which he pretended weren't about to stream down his cheeks. Rather than wipe them away, he blinked rapidly. He spoke to Polly, and she interpreted. "He feels your sadness. He'd like to help but has no ideas."

I nodded and pulled myself up from the floor with Marilee's help. I said, "Gracias," and we all shook hands with him. We headed through the forest of cabinets for the door. Just as Polly was about to close it behind us, the man said, "Senora!"

We all stopped in our tracks, did a quick about-face, and hurried back to him. Polly said, "Senor?"

He started speaking rapidly, smiling occasionally, then shrugged his shoulders with his hands upraised, which I took to be, "Who knows?"

Polly explained that it occurred to the man that the only chance I had was to go to the maternity ward and ask around. Perhaps someone there might know an older, retired, nurse, who might remember something.

"It's worth a shot," said Marilee.

"Where do we go?" I asked, and Polly relayed it to the man.

"He says you won't be able to go anywhere in this hospital without him."

"And he's stuck here?" I asked, feeling hopeless the second time in a half hour.

Marilee said, "I don't think he said that. Polly?"

"I'll ask him what he can do."

His response was to lock the top desk drawer, then get up from his seat. I hadn't really focused on him while I was crying. But now I saw that he was shorter than he appeared while sitting. One of those short legs/long torso situations. He was probably five feet tall, and 200 pounds, but he was spry as he hurried us out of 107, locking the door behind us.

He motioned for us to follow, ushered us back into

the elevator, and pushed the button for the third floor. As he led us through the brightly lit hallways, we happened to pass the nursery where little babies, all with hair the exact color as mine, were sleeping. We paused to admire the darling infants. Some made kitten-like mewling sounds, while others screamed for all they were worth with red, wrinkled faces. I had trouble grasping that I'd lain in this very nursery, hearing Spanish chatter in the background, as innocent and helpless as these babes and as clueless about life beyond the next snuggle or warm breast or bottle.

I overheard Marilee whisper to Polly, "I've been thinking about an international adoption."

Polly responded, "How exciting!"

I bit my lip as it hit me that the two of them had been friends for decades, while I'd only known Marilee for the eight years since she joined the law firm. I hoped she would share her news with me soon. Of course, I knew she probably didn't want to detract from our attention to my problem. I filed it away.

The man led us to an office which Polly told us said, "Director of Nursing—Maternity," and knocked on the door. A woman's voice said, "Por favor venga." The man motioned for us to follow him into her office. The space was tidy and orderly, with a wooden desk in the center of the room and a potted palm tree in the corner. Her window looked out over the hospital entrance and was filled with a cloudless cerulean sky. The woman sitting at the desk was elegant looking, dark, slender, and perhaps forty-five years old.

Polly asked if she spoke English, and, thankfully, she did, so we each introduced ourself to her. The woman told us she was Senora Leyna Apaza as she shook hands with each of us. It was then that I realized we hadn't learned the man's name. I looked at Polly, then eyed the man, and she took the hint. I think she apologized for not doing proper introductions sooner. His name was Marco Mamani. Polly addressed him as Senor Mamani.

Marco launched into what I assumed was his version of the events as Polly had laid them out for him. Polly supplemented what he'd said with a good five minutes of animated talking of her own, in English, then handed Leyna my hospital records. Leyna took a moment to review the papers, then looked at each of us, but landed her gaze on me. She said, "So, you were born here. It's not a bad place to be born.'"

I smiled at Leyna. "A very good place, I think." I quickly added, "But I long for the truth about my birth and adoption."

Leyna became businesslike. "Ms. Summerfield, there is no person working here who was also here forty-eight years ago." She paused. "Even if there were, no nurse would remember the details of one of our hundreds of annual births—especially one that took place that long ago." She paused again, glancing down at my records on her desk. When she looked up, she added, "Unless, of course, there had been something very unusual about the birth. Do you have any reason to believe there was anything memorable about yours?"

I swallowed hard. How could I know such a thing? I said, "Well, only that my parents were extremely secretive about it."

Leyna looked at me for a moment, then swiveled her chair to look out the window toward the Andes in the distance.

Polly, Marilee and I glanced at each other, not

knowing if this was our signal to leave. I looked to Marco for a clue, but he stood impassively, his eyes glued to the back of her chair. Leyna swiveled herself back and said, "I will make inquiries."

I swallowed again, then said, "I should tell you that we are here in Bolivia only through Saturday, so if it would be possible to expedite—"

Her head jerked up as though I'd insulted her. "Things like this are not unraveled in seven days. You are lucky if you can find anything in seven weeks. It may take seven months." She paused. "I must say, I find this very American of you."

I was taken aback, and I'm sure it showed.

She shook her head, as though clearing it of something odious. "Your country's efforts to 'eradicate' our culturally significant coca plants are not appreciated down here. Personally, I think it's the sense of entitlement that bothers me the most."

I'd seriously annoyed her, and I could feel my ears redden. "I apologize for my ignorance of what my country has done to offend you. And I wish very much that I could stay for many months. But all three of us must get back to our jobs. So, whatever suggestions you have will be appreciated more than you can know."

Leyna did not look to be completely satisfied with my ignorance or my answer. I appreciated her point. If this were as important to me as I claimed, why would I limit my investigation to seven days? The truth was, my gut told me that if I couldn't find the answer in seven days, I also wouldn't be able to find it in seven months. There was nothing I'd learned so far to suggest I'd ever find it. Leyna pushed a blank piece of paper across her desk to me.

She said, "I'd like your names, your date of birth, Suzanne, and the best cell number for me to reach you. If I come up with anything, I'll let you know." Her words were kind, but her expression was that of someone who just wanted us to leave her office.

After we'd neatly printed our names, Leyna rose to shake hands with each of us, but there was no encouraging smile. Polly told Marco what Leyna had said to us as he escorted us to the elevator. We followed him through the long halls, all of which smelled of cleaning product. When we arrived at the front entrance to the building, I glanced at my watch. The entire visit had taken under an hour.

As we stepped out into the bright sunshine and sixty-five-degree weather, I said, "Crap."

"I know," said Marilee.

Polly said, "What's so frustrating is that our only ball is in Leyna's court." As we walked in the direction of what we took to be a cab stand, Polly pushed me into position so that Marilee could take another couple of pictures. She added, "This time, act like you're happy to have found the hospital where you were born." She struck a pose, one hand pointing at the entrance, and wearing an exaggerated smile.

I laughed, then glanced to see if people were staring. No one seemed to have any interest in us, so I replicated her pose and Marilee clicked a few photos. Unfortunately, that transported me right back to the day I'd last had my picture taken, when a stranger took a shot of me and Mac, and Mom and Dad, with the Blue Ridge Mountains as our backdrop. I slumped to the ground, sobbing.

"Oh, my God," said Marilee. "What is it?"

"Get her head below her knees," said Polly, as she lifted my legs, then shoved her purse under them.

I concentrated on deep, slow breathing. When I'd gathered myself sufficiently to speak, I reminded Marilee that the fall foliage picture had been my last. I remained sprawled on the sidewalk, trying to maintain my controlled breathing as Marilee explained to Polly what had triggered me.

After what felt like an eternity, but was probably fewer than five minutes, I rose, dusted off my skirt, and handed Polly's purse back to her. As I was getting up, I spied a figure in a third-floor window of the hospital building looking toward us. Of course, I couldn't be sure, but I had a strong feeling it was Leyna. "Guys," I said. "I think Leyna's watching us."

"That's creepy," said Marilee.

"It's embarrassing," I said.

Polly said. "Who cares? Let's go back to the hotel and plan our next move."

Chapter 14

A half hour later, we were lounging on our little beds like three girls at a slumber party, trying to come up with a new plan. The sun was pouring in the windows, making rectangular blocks of gold on the hardwood floor. "I've got it!" said Marilee. "We post ads in the local papers for all the towns around here." She nodded, as though to add a period.

"That sounds reasonable," I said. "How do you guys think we should go about it?" I had my back against the headboard and clutched my pillow to my tummy to calm my nerves.

Polly looked at me and said, "It's already done."

"What do you mean?" I asked.

"Well, I was thinking about it a couple of weeks ago, and decided it wouldn't do much good if the ad didn't run until after we'd returned home from Bolivia. So, to be sure it would run starting this past weekend, and every day this week, I went ahead and arranged it back then—two weeks ago."

"You just did it on your own?" asked Marilee. "Why didn't you tell us?"

"I knew you guys couldn't very well do it since you don't speak Spanish. And I thought it would be a nice surprise." She jumped up off the bed and straightened her silky, knee-length knife-pleated skirt. "Hey, why don't we try to find a copy of today's paper to see how the ad looks?" When neither Marilee nor I said anything, Polly pulled off a quick pout, lower lip protruding. "I hope that was okay. You did say not to leave any stone unturned."

Marilee and I looked at each other. I vacillated between irritation that Polly hadn't asked me and gratitude that she'd gone ahead with it. I said, "It was inspired, Polly. Thanks."

Marilee laughed, then eyed Polly. "So, what other stones have you not left unturned?"

Polly raised her eyebrows dramatically and gave us a half smile. "Guess!"

"Honestly, Polly, I have no idea," said Marilee.

Polly turned to me, and I shrugged.

"Duh! I hired a private investigator. We meet with him tomorrow morning to find out what he's been able to learn so far."

"That's terrific!" I said, feeling mildly encouraged but only simulating genuine optimism. "Why didn't I think of that?"

"What's his name?" asked Marilee.

"Senor Angelo Gutierrez."

"And you hired him when?" I asked, amazed at how much preparation she'd put into our quest, and coming down on the side of gratitude rather than annoyance.

"At the same time I placed the newspaper ads a couple of weeks ago. He's great. He may not find anything, but he has the sexiest telephone voice. It'll be fun to meet him."

"Wow. I'm so glad you took the initiative, Polly. I should've thought of both of those things." I felt my forehead wrinkle as I questioned myself on how I could've been so remiss.

"Me, too," said Marilee. "And I don't even have

debilitating grief to blame."

Polly got up on her knees and looked solemnly at me, and then Marilee. "You are both grieving," she said. "Marilee, your dear friend lost her husband, who was also a friend of yours, as well as both her parents. You are grieving, too. And I am without words to express how sorry I am for both of you."

A serious tone, coming from Polly, sometimes made me laugh. This time, however, it felt depressing. I smiled at her, then asked, "There aren't any other surprises, are there?"

"No. That's it." She paused. "So, maybe if the private detective has all the answers, we'll have time to do some sightseeing."

"Absolutely," I said, eager to change the subject from my grief. "Who has studied her guide books?"

"I meant to," said Marilee. "But I got caught up briefing an emergency motion."

Polly leaned down for her phone which was charging on the floor. "I hate carrying those big, heavy guide books, so I put all the highlights on here. Do you want to hear what's on my list?"

"Definitely," Marilee and I said at the same time.

Polly laughed, then sat on the edge of her bed, facing us. "Okay. Here goes: First of all, the things we shouldn't do. One, go on a prison tour."

"Who would do that?" I asked.

"People who haven't read the guide books," said Polly. "Second, we mustn't engage with anyone who claims to be a police officer checking us for drugs."

"Why not?" asked Marilee.

"Because he's an imposter and up to no good."

"Wait," I said, squinting at her. "You're saying that

if a person dressed as a police officer approaches us, we're supposed to ignore him?"

"Yes. Because real cops won't bother tourists. And if ignoring him doesn't work, the book promises the imposter will split if we make a scene."

"What if he doesn't?" asked Marilee.

"Whatever happens, I'm recording it."

"Why?" I asked.

"So I can show it to the embassy staff after you guys are thrown in jail."

"Sounds reasonable," I said. "Is there anything on your list that we might actually like to do—or see?"

"Oh, yeah. I was just getting to that. Would you guys like some background?"

"I always like background," I said, embracing the idea of relaxing and listening to Polly, rather than ruminating on the dead-end I might well be facing.

"Definitely," said Marilee, as she leaned back against her headboard and crossed her ankles atop the wool blanket.

Polly stood and walked around the room as she addressed us like one of her classes. "As we all know, Oruro sits in the Southern Altiplano area of Bolivia. The Andes are basically a two-pronged range." She held out her arms to demonstrate. "There are long plains between them at a terrifically high altitude, 12,150 feet. For perspective, I looked up Peaks of Otter, which is the highest hike I've done near where we live."

Marilee said, "Suzanne and I have hiked there."

"Then you guys know the views are stunning. But it's only one-third the height of where we sit right now, here in Oruro."

"So how high are the surrounding Andes

Mountains?" I asked.

Polly smiled as though pleased with herself for knowing the answer. "Over 20,000 feet. Think of it as five times as tall as the highest point at Peaks of Otter."

"Man!" said Marilee. "That's crazy. It makes me a little dizzy just to think about it."

Polly said, "And, of course, it's the reason I'm getting mild headaches, in spite of the medicine."

"I am, too," said Marilee

I rubbed my temples. "I thought it was just me."

Polly shrugged. "Anyway, the biggest tourist attraction is the salt flats. Well, they're supposed to be visited after a couple of days touring La Paz to acclimatize, but we don't have time to waste, so we need to press on—with or without the headaches."

"But only if Senor Gutierrez answers all of Suzanne's questions," said Marilee.

I sighed. "Or has nothing for me and no idea how to get something."

Polly walked over and knelt beside my bed, took my hand, and said, "Oh, he'll have something, Suzanne. I've been assuming we'll see the salt flats on our next trip." It was kind of her to say, but I was sure we all knew that if we found no answers this trip, there wouldn't be a next one.

"Go ahead, Polly," said Marilee. "Whether we visit them this trip or later, I'd really like to hear about them."

Polly looked at me. Appreciating the distraction from my disappointment, I said, "I would, too. I really would."

Polly rose, gave each of us a big smile, and got herself positioned to present her travelogue. I took the smile as a clue that she had really been hoping to do some touring this trip. She said, "Cool. I'll do it like an info-mercial."

She stood in the small area at the end of my bed and Marilee's, dipped her head down for a moment, then looked up at us with another bright smile. "If you ever find yourself in Bolivia, you must make time to visit that country's crown jewel, Salar de Uyuni—the enormous salt desert. In a land blessed with stunning natural and cultural sites, the salt desert is incomparable. You'd certainly be forgiven if you claimed that one of the other top locales was the unparalleled destination. You'd just be wrong. See them after the salt desert. One of the other 'must-sees' is the steamy Amazon River rainforest, home to an incredible variety of birds, butterflies, monkeys, jaguars, and the celebrated pink river dolphins."

"Seriously?" I asked. "Pink dolphins?"

"Indeed," said Polly. "In fact, they are so pink that early adventurers took them for mermaids."

"That's amazing," said Marilee.

"The best way to see the rainforest is to board a riverboat for a three-day cruise in the heart of the Amazon. But be prepared to sleep in a hammock or on the deck of the boat, and eat dried meat and mashed plantains every night. You'll find it well worth these little inconveniences, though, as over 1,000 different species of birds, and 1,500 of butterflies—rainbows of colors—await you in this, the most biodiverse place on earth."

"On earth? Is that hyperbole?" I asked.

"No," said Polly. "It's true." She nodded, too vigorously, which made me laugh.

"Impressive," said Marilee.

Polly clearly wanted to get back to her spiel. "If I may. Also, don't miss visits into the little villages along the river which provide glimpses into the sleepy charm of traditional Bolivian river life."

"I'm in," said Marilee.

"Me, too," I said.

Polly grimaced. "Guys, you have to consider the other sights." She shook her right forefinger at us to scold us and we both laughed.

"Fine," said Marilee. "Proceed."

"Good. Now, if you are more interested in raucousness than rainforest, head to Oruro for Carnaval." Polly was positively beaming, so I assumed she'd have this preference. "Bolivia's biggest party is hosted there every year and turns that chilly mining town for ten days into an oasis of dance, parades, massive water fights, and at least as much drinking and debauchery as Mardi Gras in New Orleans. But the costumes and dance are pure Bolivian folklore, honoring indigenous dance styles including the wildly popular devil dance. More than 30,000 dancers will keep you entertained as you soak in the relentless sun at 12,000 feet above sea level. So, be sure to pack your sunscreen."

I worried that Polly might take it personally, but went ahead and said, "Sorry. I couldn't do that, even if it were taking place now, during our visit."

"Why ever not?" asked Polly.

"I hate crowds. They suffocate me."

"Me, too," said Marilee. "They make me dizzy. And at this altitude, I'd be on my face in the dusty road the whole time."

Polly squinted at us. "Are you guys serious? I get nothing but energy from the throngs." Her forehead wrinkled. "Wait. That must be hard for you."

I said, "Well, yes. But there are worse things." Polly took the hint and moved on to her next travel destinations.

"Okay, then. Other not-to-be-missed locales are Lake Titicaca and the Isla del Sol. So enchanting that the Incas believed it to be the birthplace of their civilization, at 120 miles long by 50 miles wide, Lake Titicaca in the Altiplano is the highest large lake in the world. But its size, its altitude, and its history all pale in comparison with its sheer beauty. With the Andes as a backdrop, in the spiky-clear air—"

"Spiky?" asked Marilee.

Polly paused a moment, then looked behind her as though a pesky toddler had pulled on her skirt.

Marilee laughed.

"As I was saying, with the Andes as a backdrop, in the spiky-clear air of the Altiplano, the impossibly gem-like waters of the lake will force you to re-think your love affair with the Caribbean." Polly gave us a theatrical kind of wink. "Isla del Sol, the birthplace of the sun, can be accessed by boat from the small, lovely town of Copacabana. On the island itself, see pre-Columbian ruins, breathtaking mountain views, and terraced hills. Again, do not venture to this paradise without sun protection."

I raised my hand like a school-girl. "Are you saying the sun and I were both born in Bolivia?"

Polly smiled and nodded. "Si. Es correcto."

Having been fairly enthralled with what I'd heard so far, I couldn't imagine how the salt flats could surpass it. But since my first meeting with her in my parents' dining room, she'd never failed to deliver. All along, Polly had been using her hands to express herself, as she always did. Now she made a complete 360 degree turn and landed theatrically on one knee with her arms outstretched. "And now, the treasure dreamed up by the gods to test the depths of men's souls. Salar de Uyuni."

She stood and resumed her travel-lecturer stance, but some kind of invisible veil had descended, and her face was transformed. She seemed to glow. I wondered why this woman wasn't on TV or in films. She fluttered her eyes then opened them wide. "Try to imagine! Approximately 35,000 years ago, there was a giant prehistoric lake that covered the majority of southwest Bolivia. When all of the water slowly evaporated, it left behind the largest salt desert in the world.

"The flat, white floor of this desert covers an area the size of Delaware, plus London, plus two times Los Angeles. It is so flat, for so many miles, that the average elevation varies no more than forty inches over that entire area. Scientists the world over use the expanse to calibrate measuring equipment on their satellites because this desert is incredibly large and reliably stable.

"The only building material there is salt. So buildings and furniture are constructed of the bright white sands that make up the desert." She leaned forward and whispered confidentially. "Si. It's true. You and your friends can spend the night in a hotel made entirely of salt, sleep on a salt bed, and sit on a salt chair at a salt table for breakfast."

Polly gave us a discreet, close-mouthed smile. Her eyes darkened with mystery. "Now, envision yourself dropped into this other-worldly space alone, with nothing but a massive expanse of white before your eyes. You pull your sunglasses down over your eyes, which makes it possible for you to take in the scene without the threat of being blinded. You also pull your parka close around you because the chilly air is trying to dissuade you from taking your first step. But you are wearing a hand-made alpaca hat of intricate pattern, with generous ear flaps." She simulated pulling a cap down snuggly. "So you know you are prepared.

"You take a step and hear a crunching sound, as though you are walking on tiny seashells. 'Crunch. Crunch, crunch.' " Polly took tiny steps on her tiptoes as she acted out her narrative. "The sand immediately responds to each step you take. You stop, slowly, more slowly than time, you turn 360 degrees and study the earth below you. Only white. No matter how far you walk today, you will see nothing below you but white. And nothing above you but the brilliant blue, cloudless sky. Only white and blue. So you sit down in that spot and try to understand this new world." Polly eased down to sit on the hardwood floor, cross-legged.

"You gulp the air because your lungs are telling you they are not getting quite enough of it. You take another slower, deeper breath seeking to find the smell. But there is nothing but the faintest hint of sulfur. Because it's barely perceptible, you assume you are imagining it. Suddenly, you notice the taste of salt on your lips. Real salt. For a moment, you wish for something decadent to put it on—popcorn, a sizzling piece of steak, or a hot ear of buttered yellow corn. Silly. You are sitting in a place stranger than the moon. This is no time to think about food." She paused for a couple of seconds to look inward before she raised her head to meet our eyes.

" 'Smaller than a grain of sand on a beach' is a cliché. No. You are more negligible than that. Finally, you stop trying to think of a better analogy and simply exist. Your heart aches with emotion. Your eyes cloud up then release your own salt which merges with the white earth."

Marilee said, "That sounds a little desolate for me."

Polly smiled at her, then whispered, "There is more. Be patient." She stood, the veil came off, and Polly lit up. "On another day, in the middle of the rainy season, you return to the place that haunts you. Only now, a thin layer of rainwater has transformed it. You see not white below you but a crystal-clear mirror image of everything above the soles of your shoes. The clouds are under you, as well as above, which leaves you feeling like a bird in flight. The temperature is in the mid-fifties, so you wear only a light jacket and a feeling of contentment. As much as the dry, white expanse broke your heart, this magical flight among the clouds restores your spirit. You realize that it matters not a whit how tiny your footprint may be. To exist in this world is enough. You can soar with nothing more than that."

Polly smiled and bowed, but there was no applause. I had tears streaming down my cheeks, and Marilee was watching me, looking worried. I clutched my pillow against my heart to keep it from breaking because that was exactly how I saw Mac, and Mom and Dad. I could've taken anything else—any illness, any problem, any setback. If only they could still exist in this world.

Polly rushed up to me and knelt beside my bed. "I'm so sorry, Suzanne. I didn't mean to make you sad."

I finished wiping my cheeks with tissues I got from Marilee. Polly's face looked so wretched, I had to work to keep from laughing. "Oh, Polly, it wasn't you." I sniffled then tossed the tissues into the wastebasket. "I'm fine."

"Terrific infomercial, Polly. Really." Marilee gave her a smile, apparently because it was obvious that she'd earned high marks for her delivery. Then Marilee huffed. "But has it occurred to you guys what's happening here?"

Marilee had my attention. *Were we doing something wrong already?*

She continued, "We're sitting in a tiny hotel room in Oruro, freaking Bolivia, and watching Polly educate us about visiting Bolivia. But we're already here. Why not just step out the door and experience the actual Bolivia?"

"Good point," said Polly, nodding thoughtfully.

I glanced at my watch and saw that it was almost six o'clock, so all the museums were already closed. "What do you suggest?"

Marilee rose and reached down for her boots. "A walk around the town, dinner, then walk some more."

"Brilliant," said Polly.

I smiled as I walked to the corner of the room to grab my shoes, knowing Marilee was right. Not so much because I was desperate to experience the "actual Bolivia." But sitting in that hotel room was probably the least likely thing I could be doing to relax as we awaited rescue by—anybody. There the newspaper ad, Senora Leyna Apaza, and Senor Gutierrez. And not any idea what else we could do while awaiting direction from one of them. We headed out.

Eventually, one of us realized we'd better get back to the hotel for bed if we wanted to be awake for our meeting with our private detective the next morning. I couldn't sleep, even after the exhausting narrated tour of Bolivia, and the walk through the town. I was anxious about sitting down with Senor Gutierrez, who I guessed was our best hope.

The next morning, we walked into Perfecto Oruro, the café where we were to meet him, at 9:45 a.m. The place had a modern, efficient look and feel. The only concession to old world charm was the large mural painted on the back wall. It depicted folks in traditional Bolivian dress—bowler hats, colorful, heavy, full skirts, and elaborate fringed shawls—with the Andes as their backdrop. We grabbed coffees and chose among the tables, all of which were unoccupied. The other customers were in and out for coffees and pastries. Of course, we surveyed each of them, hoping it was he. But all we had to go on was a "sexy voice," and all of the men sounded especially sexy that morning as they ordered their drinks. Ten o'clock came and went. 10:30. Marilee and I were eyeing our watches. At eleven, Polly called Senor Gutierrez's cell, but there was no answer.

I said, "I think we're wasting our time here. Thanks for trying, Polly. But I'm thinking your private investigator wasn't for real."

She smiled. "He's for real. If you'd read your guide books, you'd know that time is ephemeral here. A 'ten o'clock' meeting translates to 'somewhere before noon.'"

"Are you serious?" asked Marilee.

"It's the same in a lot of South and Central America."

"So I'm just being an ugly American—again?" I asked.

"Pretty much." Just as Polly said these words, a short, dark man wearing painter's overalls—or at least overalls spotted with paint—approached our table. He clicked his heels together, which was weird. "Senor Angelo Gutierrez." He smiled and a gold incisor gleamed as it caught the light pouring in the front window. He was a nice-looking man with short black hair and a well-groomed mustache. Polly had been right. His voice was deep and melodic.

After we introduced ourselves, and Angelo took a seat, Polly nodded to his overalls and said what I took to be "Painting today?"

He looked down at his clothing and laughed. "Si. Todos dias."

Polly looked at me and said, "Yes. A painter." She then ordered a coffee for Angelo and another round for the three of us. Once we had all been served, Angelo took a small note pad from his chest pocket and opened it with one crisp motion to the page he wanted. Polly mimicked him by pulling a pad and pen from her purse. Poised to take notes, she must've asked him what he'd learned. After two or three sentences from Angelo, Polly would hold up her hand to pause him, as she caught us up with what he'd said. The gist of it was that he'd spoken yesterday with Senor Marco Mamani of the records department at the hospital.

I said to Polly, "Then why did we bother?"

Angelo listened as Polly told him what I'd said. His response was, "It is one thing, Senora, for me to ask questions. It is something entirely different for you to meet these people in person and show them your pain and desperation. I think you did that."

After Polly's translation, I said, "I'm embarrassed to say that I'm quite sure I did."

"Bueno."

I rubbed my temples to try to relieve the headache

which was starting to pound behind my eyes. Angelo must've noticed because he nodded to me and said, through Polly, "Altitude sickness?"

I said, "Si."

"All of you?"

Polly nodded, then glanced at Marilee who said, "Si."

He responded by sighing and shaking his head as though he understood exactly how we were feeling.

Marilee said, "Polly, ask him what else he's done."

He smiled at Marilee, and I noticed that he looked more handsome when he did so. Polly explained his comments. "He says that he has planted many seeds over the past two weeks. He has made inquiries in the neighborhoods around the hospital, including the more remote areas from which people travel to Oruro for medical services."

"Has any seed sprouted?" I asked.

Angelo nodded as he answered Polly. "I await that."

Polly said, "I'll ask him if he should fertilize these seeds with cash."

She did so then gave us Angelo's response. "This, I think, is a matter of the heart. To offer money would be an insult to honest people. And you do not want to deal with the dishonest ones."

I was nervous that the seeds might not sprout while my friends and I were in Bolivia. I had Polly ask him if there was any way to expedite. His answer was a simple, "No."

Polly smiled at Angelo then asked, "Anything else?"

He responded that he'd seen the ads in the newspaper and thought they couldn't hurt. However, many people would be leery about responding to something like that. He finished his coffee, then told Polly, "I must return to work. I will call you when one of my seeds sprouts." He returned his notepad to his pocket, then bowed to each of us before taking his leave.

Polly cocked her head and squinted dramatically. "Odd. When he introduced himself, he clicked his heels like a German storm trooper. Now he bows like a Japanese businessman."

Marilee said, "I think he likes the movies."

"Well, I'm glad he planted seeds," I said. "He obviously knows the area, and where best to make inquiries. I like him."

"Me, too," said Marilee. "What did you think of him, Polly?"

"I think he knows more than he's telling us."

"Why would he hold anything back?" asked Marilee.

"I don't know. Maybe he's waiting for the buds to shoot farther up."

I leaned forward to finish my third cup of coffee. "Guys, I feel like we should meet with Angelo again tomorrow morning. I think that would help us keep his attention on my case. If he tells us nothing has sprouted, I say we take the rest of Wednesday through Saturday off to do some sight-seeing."

Polly said, "Okay. I'll call him and let him know. And if you're serious about sight-seeing, I'll sign us up for a day-trip to Lake Titicaca. Of course, I'd love for us to be able to do the 3-day salt-flats tour, but there's no way we can be away that long—in case something develops. The lake trip is refundable. Is that okay with you, Suzanne?"

"That sounds good," I said, then gave her a smile so

she'd know I meant it.

"Cool," said Marilee. "But let's head back to the hotel to go over it. If we stay here any longer, they'll start charging us rent."

I said, "I'll leave a big tip." I felt exhausted from the anticipation and then the let-down, but I did enjoy the walk back to the hotel. It was a stunningly bright day, and we wore just the right cloth jackets for the fifty-degree temperature. In the background were the stark, imposingly dramatic Andes demanding our attention. It was impossible not to pause to admire them. They were nothing like the Blue Ridge Mountains of Virginia, which are lush with vegetation and more rounded than pointy. To me, the Blue Ridge Mountains are pure comfort; the Andes are unadulterated majesty.

We grabbed more saltenas around the corner from the hotel and took them up to our room to eat. We sat cross-legged on our beds while Polly made calls about getting us on a tour to the lake.

Chapter 15

On Wednesday morning, we met at the same café with Senor Gutierrez. He surprised us and arrived at the actual time of our appointment, 10:00 a.m. This time, he was wearing khaki slacks and a white long-sleeved shirt, open at the neck. Without the camouflage of the overalls, it was evident he was a trim man, but also muscular—perhaps an athlete. He ordered the coffees and remembered how each of us took ours. I imagined that private investigators must need to be observant to stay in business. He nodded to me as he retrieved the small notebook from his shirt pocket and flipped it open.

Polly said what I guessed to be, "Do you have something for us?"

Angelo glanced at a page of the notebook occasionally as he spoke quickly for several minutes.

Growing impatient, I interrupted and said to Polly, "What?"

She held up her hand to bring Angelo to a pause. She said, "He's regaling me with all the names and neighborhoods of the people he's spoken with. You know, the seeds."

"And?" asked Marilee.

"He hasn't gotten to any 'and' yet."

"Okay," I said. "Let us know when he does."

Polly nodded, then asked Angelo to continue. I watched him closely for any hints that he was saying anything particularly important. He became more animated and spoke faster. Finally, he closed the notebook and shook his head solemnly. I was pretty sure I knew what that meant.

Unfortunately, I was right. Polly looked toward the door of the café for a moment, as if collecting her thoughts. "Angelo says he's talked with everyone he can think of. No one has any memory of Suzanne's birth. He stresses that fifty years is pretty much a lifetime for a lot of the folks who would've been old enough to observe anything in 1970. He also apologizes to have come up empty."

That struck me as unnecessary. I said, "Tell him that no apology is necessary. He can't create facts. Yes. I'm disappointed. But I'm sure he did a thorough job, and I'm grateful for his help. If he drops off his bill at our hotel, I'll be sure to pay him before we check out."

Angelo nodded to me and rose, so I assumed he was leaving. But he pulled a small, tan, fabric bag out of his pants pocket, and sat back down. He placed the sack in the middle of the table and gingerly untied the cloth ribbon to open it. As he held it open-end down above the table, leaves fell out into a messy pile. I eyed Angelo for permission as I reached for one. He smiled and nodded, so I placed a single leaf into the palm of my left hand. It was an opaque green, quite thin, and tapered at both ends.

"Coca?" asked Polly.

"Si."

Marilee pushed her chair away from the table as she looked around the restaurant. So I also surveyed the room, but nobody was paying any attention to us.

"Cocaine?" I asked.

Angelo must've understood because he looked about to laugh. He tried to cover it with a cough. "No, Senora."

I said, "Polly, I don't understand."

She gave me a quick, reassuring smile. "Coca is not the same as cocaine, although a lot of people make the assumption you guys did." She picked up a leaf and studied it as she spoke. "I've read about the leaves. Apparently, chewing them is no more like taking cocaine than eating a poppy-seed muffin is the same as taking heroine. In its leaf form, coca is just a mild stimulant—like coffee."

"So, it's legal?" asked Marilee.

Polly put the question to Angelo, and he said, "Si."

"Why did he bring it?" asked Marilee.

Polly said, "I'll ask him. But what I've read is that it's an appetite suppressant, and also helps with fatigue and pain. But I'm sure he brought it for us because it's well-known as a remedy for altitude sickness."

"It really works?" I asked.

"That's what I recall," said Polly. "I'll ask Angelo about it." Polly spoke a few Spanish words to Angelo, who responded by launching into an uninterrupted couple of minutes of information, accompanied by facial expressions of pain and relief, as well as hand gestures.

Once he finished, Marilee looked at Polly and sighed. "What?"

Polly held the leaf up to the light from the window. "Angelo says that here in Bolivia, a third of the people regularly consume coca, either by chewing it or taking it in a tea called mate. Like coffee, it energizes. But it is also good for pain, especially head pain. Everyone knows it cures altitude sickness. Also, he said the miners used to chew it so they could work long shifts underground without feeling hunger."

Marilee shook her head. "That was so nice of their bosses."

Polly added, "He brought it to help us with our headaches."

"Ah," I said. "That was very kind." I thought about it for a moment. "But, Polly, we're already taking altitude sickness medicine. What if the two interact?"

Marilee jumped in. "Exactly! I'm sure we don't want to risk feeling sicker than we already do." She scooted her chair back another six inches, then added, "I'd rather have a headache than chew coca."

Neither Polly nor I responded. It seemed to me that if coca was no stronger than a cup of coffee, it really shouldn't hurt us. But I knew nothing about what might happen in combination with the medicine we already had in our systems.

Polly must've sensed she and Marilee were at an impasse. She turned to Angelo. "Is all of this for us?"

"Si." He smiled, then demonstrated how to put one leaf at a time into the cheek cavity. He explained the rest to Polly.

"He says we should put a few leaves into our cheeks, then take a little lime juice or soda bicarbonate to help us salivate until we feel the effect of the coca." She leaned back in her chair. "We don't have to chew it like a horse with a mouthful of hay."

Angelo added a couple of sentences.

"Guys, he wants us to take the leaves with us—as a gift. He does not wish to rush us to decide whether we will try it. But he urges us to use it because he thinks it will completely cure our altitude headaches."

Marilee said, "Fine. Suzanne, you have the biggest purse. Why don't you take the pouch. We can talk about it later."

I got all of the leaves back into the bag, and slipped it into my shoulder-bag. I said, 'Muchas gracias, Senor."

He rose and, again, bowed to each of us before shaking our hands. He said something to Polly before he took off.

"What?" said Marilee.

"He said he'll call my mobile if anything comes up that could be helpful. Anything at all."

I took in a long breath and let it out slowly. "You know, guys, I really shouldn't be surprised. After all, my folks covered all their tracks in the states. Why shouldn't time have erased whatever may've been here?"

"Angelo may call," said Polly.

"Yeah," I said.

Marilee put her hand on mine. "What do you want to do now?"

"Go to sleep." I paused to think what my friends might want to do. "Why don't you guys go hunt down some souvenirs? I want to head back to the room for a quick nap. Then I'll be ready to do some sight-seeing this afternoon. Polly, why don't you go ahead and firm up our tickets for the Lake Titicaca tour tomorrow morning?"

"Will do."

"We'll walk with you to the hotel," said Marilee.

"No. Really. I need a little alone time."

"Okay. But we'll cab back to the hotel with you first," said Marilee.

"It's not that far. I'd prefer to walk. But thanks, guys."

Marilee and Polly looked at each other and shrugged. Polly said, "If you're sure."

"Yes. Please."

I walked the seven or eight blocks, indistinguishable terra-cotta buildings lining both sides of the street, alone, in a country where I didn't speak the language. I felt an overwhelming sense of sadness, like a little girl who had lost her mother. And I had. Only I'd lost two mothers, two fathers, and a husband, and I had no way to get any of them back. I adored Marilee and Polly, and wanted them in my life forever, but I also craved family. I wondered how I could ever make peace with life again. I knew I'd never be a whiner. I would tell no one how miserable I felt. Just take it a day at a time, acting like a reasonably happy person, until there were no more days. Then I could rest. Permanent sleep. I also knew I needed to get on with my nap as soon as possible, as I hated feeling sorry for myself, even when I couldn't stop.

I entered through the front door in a bit of a daze, and went up to the reception desk to retrieve my room key. Senora Choque said something to me I didn't understand. I nodded and smiled, then continued up the stairs to my room. I fell onto my bed, atop the blankets, and entered the friendliest place left for me.

By my watch, it was almost two hours later when Marilee and Polly knocked then threw open the door, carrying several small bags of treasures. Marilee also had an envelope in her hand. She said, "Why didn't you call us about receiving a note?"

"What note?"

"Senora Choque said she told you there was a letter for you," said Polly.

I thought for a moment. "She did say something to

me—but I didn't know what." Marilee handed the envelope to me. I ripped it open and looked at a lot of Spanish words. The signature surprised me. I looked up at Marilee then at Polly. "It's from Marco Mamani."

"Marco?" asked Marilee.

Polly snapped her fingers. "The records guy at the hospital."

"I wonder how he knew where we're staying," asked Marilee.

I said, "Of course, I can't be positive. But with Polly's advertisements, and Angelo's one-on-one inquiries, I'm not sure there's anyone in this town who doesn't know."

"Good point," said Marilee.

I handed the note to Polly. She sat on the corner of her bed and read it aloud, slowly and emphatically:

Dear Senora Summerfield,

I mentioned your story to my mother at lunch the day after we met. She took the story to her women's club at church. One of the women there said she remembered a nurse, Edme Parades, who worked for decades at the hospital, always in maternity. The woman promised to ask Edme if she remembers a birth and adoption by a U.S. couple about fifty years ago. The woman found Edme and asked the question. Edme laughed at her and said, 'I have seen thousands of births.' Edme started to walk away, then stopped. She went up to my mother's friend and added, 'But I cannot lie. I do remember one from back then. The woman who delivered the baby was from the United States.'

Polly stopped and looked at me. Marilee and I were sitting on the edges of our beds, eyes riveted to Polly. I said, "Go on, Polly. Please."

Polly looked down at the paper and continued, still in her strong voice:

My mother's friend asked Edme if the reason she remembered this one birth from almost fifty years ago was that the woman was an American. Edme laughed at her again, and said, 'Of course not. We had many foreign women deliver in our hospital.' My mother's friend persisted, but Edme put her finger to her lips, and would say no more. My mother's friend pressed her. But Edme was firm.

I have no reason to believe that the birth Edme recalls was yours. It was the secrecy which reminded me of your situation. I am providing you with Edme's address, as she has no telephone. Good luck with your search, Senora.

Respectfully yours, Marco Mamani
***

No one said anything as we each pondered the meaning of Edme's secret. After a few minutes, I said, "I worry she'll be like Judge Eileen Foster. That she'll know something, but won't tell me."

"From Martinsville," said Marilee.

"Right. I'm afraid Edme may be sworn to secrecy and not the kind of person to break a promise."

Polly considered this, then said, "What if we tell her you have a rare kind of cancer, and you'll die if you don't find the one person who can provide the bone marrow transplant you need to live?"

Marilee and I stared at her. I said, "I can't do that."

"Why not?" said Polly. "It's just a white lie that hurts exactly no one."

"Well, no one except me," I said. "Sorry, I just can't. Any other ideas?"

Marilee studied her hands for a minute or so, and then looked up and said, "I think we need to find out more about this woman, Edme Parades."

"That's a good idea," said Polly. "Shall I call Angelo?"

"Yes," I said. "Tell him we're running out of time. I'll pay him double-time to drop everything and look into Edme's background."

Polly pulled out her cell phone and made the call. After a boatload of Spanish I didn't understand, she gave me a thumbs-up.

The three of us took a long walk to fill the time as we waited for a return call from Angelo. It was a pleasant temperature for a stroll, so we headed east from our hotel and chose streets at random. Most of the buildings we passed were terra cotta or dust covered shades of brown on wood or stone. But the pedestrians were fascinating, wearing clothing like the folks on the wall mural at the restaurant. Everyone, men and women alike, seemed to be wearing a bowler hat. Polly told us that the majority of the people in Oruro are indigenous, and it definitely looked that way to me. That was about all I noticed because I was distracted by trying to will Polly's phone to ring.

We went out to an eight o'clock dinner, early by local standards, and still no call. Finally, as we were getting our showers, Polly's cell chimed. Still dripping wet, and wearing only a towel around her, she answered quickly. She gave me a big smile to confirm it was Angelo. She paced around the small room, completely absorbed in whatever he was telling her. Her eyes grew large near the end of the call and she said, "Excellent" in English. "Muchas gracias y adios!"

"What?" I asked, then held my breath.

Marilee threw her a robe, which Polly gratefully slipped into. She took her regular spot on the corner of her bed. "So, Angelo said that Edme was described to him as bright. I'm pretty sure I heard this right. 'Astute, even shrewd.' She is often short-tempered. Yet her reputation is that she's honest to a fault. So he made the executive decision to approach her directly, and truthfully, with Suzanne's quest. Or, as he put it to Edme, 'Senora Summerfield's heart's desire.' He told her about the auto accident, and the attic, and the three references—everything."

Marilee squinted. "That was a bit beyond what we asked him to do."

Polly said, "Definitely mission creep. But, here's the thing, guys—"

My heart was racing, and my tongue had grown dry. I could hardly manage to interrupt Polly with, "What?"

Polly jumped up, spun around, and landed by leaning down and looking at me face-to-face, while grabbing both my hands. "Edme will meet with you tomorrow."

"Oh my God!" I broke down crying, months' worth of pent-up tears. I slid down onto the hardwood floor, pulled my knees up to my chest, and rocked until I could calm down.

Marilee eased herself onto the floor beside me and patted me on the back. Polly ran to the chest of drawers where we'd laid out our stash to get me a bottle of water.

"You may be getting close to the finish line, sweetie," said Marilee, as she rubbed my back.

Once I'd relaxed enough to speak, I said, "Maybe." I turned to Polly, who knelt on the wood floor directly before me. "Did Edme say you could come with me to be my interpreter?"

"She said just you, Suzanne. She wants her nephew to interpret."

Marilee asked, "Her nephew?"

Polly said, "Yeah. Apparently, he's bilingual."

I thought about it and nodded. "That's fine with me."

Marilee said, "What time is the meeting?"

"Angelo made sure Edme knew the urgency due to our time restriction. She has agreed to meet with you at ten o'clock tomorrow morning. But not at her home. There is a café she's chosen in the small town where she lives."

"How far from here?" I asked.

"Angelo said he can drive you there in an hour. Apparently, Edme retired to a rural area to be near her sisters."

Marilee asked, "Did Angelo say whether Edme has a family?"

"She never married. He described her as a real church-lady-type. Also, she remains very close with her nephews—her sisters' sons."

"Wow," said Marilee "He got a lot of information in a short time."

"It was all from Edme herself. It seems this birth that happened so long ago was meaningful to her personally in some way."

"Anything else?" I asked.

"Yes. She said the reason she wants to meet you in person is to see whether you resemble the birth-mother she holds in her heart."

"God. I hope I do."

Marilee said, "We should research how Bolivian women wore their hair forty-eight years ago, so we can do yours the same way."

"Except that Marco's letter says the woman was an American," said Polly.

"Good point," said Marilee. "So, how did American women wear their hair in the seventies?"

Polly thought for a moment. "Post-Jackie O. Maybe long hair, swept back in the front. Or a feathered pageboy. Or, there's always the iconic seventies straight long hair with center part."

"Only one problem," I said, running my fingers through my hair. "I have short, straight hair, with no feathering possibilities."

"Very true," said Marilee, as she shook her head at Polly's enthusiasm.

Polly ignored her and beamed. "Then all it needs is a center part."

"Seriously, Polly?" I asked.

"Well, if you want to look like your birth-mother, I'd recommend it."

"But what if she just takes after her birth-father?" asked Marilee.

"That," said Polly, "would be unfortunate. But there's not much we can do about it."

Suddenly realizing how late it was, I pulled myself up and said, "If I want to look like a twenty-something in the morning, I should probably start with getting a good night's sleep."

"You can do that?" asked Marilee.

"What? Look like I'm in my twenties? Probably not. But maybe I can get some sleep."

"Fine," said Polly. "Let's all go to bed and pretend

to sleep." We set our alarms before slipping under our blankets.

"Good night, dear friends," I said.

Of course, I got no sleep whatsoever. In the morning, Polly helped me use her makeup to hide the circles under my eyes. When I peered out a window, I saw that Angelo was parked in front of the hotel at 8:45, a small miracle.

He indicated for me to sit in the back seat, and I declined, saying, "You're not my chauffeur, Angelo. I'll sit up front with you." He seemed to understand because he ran around the car to the other side and opened the front passenger door for me. We headed south, and it seemed to me, higher up into the Andes. My head was throbbing from several days of oxygen deprivation, as the pills I was taking were starting to lose their potency. Or if they were working, I hated to think how I'd have felt without them. I thought about the coca leaves in my purse, but then decided my headache was probably mainly from anxiety. When we arrived at the town where our rendezvous was to take place, it seemed to be little more than a dusty intersection. At any rate, there was a café, and it had the right name.

At 10:00, we walked into the empty room. At 10:05, an elderly, brown, stooped woman wearing a bowler hat and a long, purple and red pleated skirt and matching shawl, entered and quickly surveyed the room. She was accompanied by a man, perhaps twenty years younger, who did not look at me as they approached the table. The woman, however, kept her dark eyes glued to me from the moment she entered the café. She walked right up to the table, looked me over, and said something in Spanish. I dared not avert my gaze to look to Angelo for an explanation.

I motioned for her and her nephew to sit, and they pulled out chairs across from me. She abruptly waved Angelo away. He bowed to her before making his exit. The nephew introduced his aunt to me first. Then he said his name was Mario Paredes Torrico. He ordered coffee for each of us, then leaned back in his chair to allow Edme to take the lead in her own time.

She waited until the coffee had been served and she'd taken a sip, which felt like an hour. All along, she continued to study me. I looked back at her deeply wrinkled face and impenetrable stare. I smiled occasionally—to which I received no response. I had never in my life felt so ill-at-ease. The harder I tried not to appear nervous, the more I perspired. I could feel that I was developing a perspiration mustache. I let it alone rather than draw attention to it by patting at it with my napkin, which reminded me of how Marco Mamani had refused to acknowledge his tears, but how obvious they were to us.

Finally, Edme delicately touched her lips with the cloth napkin and then spoke. Mario told me what she said. "I can see that you are the daughter of the woman I remember. Your face is the same, although she had red-brown hair and yours is black."

I was stunned. She had known my mother. My hopes shot up that Edme could help me find her.

Edme continued, "Then again, a child must get something from the father."

I'm sure my eyes widened at the mention of my birth-father, and I realized I was inadvertently raising my eyebrows. Mario said, "She says, no. She knows nothing of the father."

As Edme spoke more quickly, Mario began to relay it rapidly. "There is only one reason that I will tell you what you have come here to learn. Your mother was a kind woman, and very bright. It was she who got my nephew, Mario, out of jail when he was nineteen. He had been arrested at a demonstration against the government. He had no money, so he had no lawyer. He received a long sentence because of his politics. Your mother worked on his case for no charge, found a lawyer who would help him, and got him out of jail after only three months." Mario nodded as he said these things.

"I did not know this woman who Mario told me helped him. But one day, shortly after his release, my nephew pointed her out to me in church."

"She was an American?" I asked through Mario.

"Yes. It was almost a year later that I saw her enter the maternity ward of my hospital, in labor. I knew exactly who she was, but I told no one—ever."

I didn't understand why the fact that this woman did good works needed to be kept a secret. I said this, and asked Mario to speak my words to his aunt.

Edme looked at me and said nothing.

I could hardly breathe as I awaited some unknown bombshell.

Edme continued to look at me as she spoke her next words. By her face, I could tell they were deeply meaningful to her, but I had no idea what she was saying.

Mario looked at me and spoke slowly. "She was a nun."

At first, it didn't register. I said, "What?"

"A sister of a religious order."

"But how? Why?"

He said these words to Edme, and she just shook her

head. She summoned the waiter and requested water. She waited until it was served and she'd taken several swallows to continue. "She did not come to the hospital in religious garb, and none of the other sisters visited her there. Perhaps they'd had a plan. But, you see, the baby came early. So the young woman wore a simple, long-sleeved, light-blue maternity dress. Her shoulder-length hair, reddish-brown in color, was pulled back and tied with a gray scarf.

"As I said, I saw her come into the ward. I was not her attending nurse but I kept my eye on her. The baby went to intensive care due to prematurity, but it was just a precaution. The little girl was not really ill. *You* were not really ill. I had a couple of days off, and when I returned to work, the mother and the baby were gone. I heard that an American man, a lawyer, had come to pick up the baby. His name was unusual, but it was a saint's name. My memory is that it was Bartholomew."

I could feel my eyes grow large at the mention of Darren's father's name, and felt a chill.

"I often wondered what happened to the nun's baby, but I learned that the sister herself was back at her usual activities one month later. I have never told a soul what I know—until today. I decided that the daughter of such a kind and generous mother should know the truth. I want you to know what she did for my family, and for so many others."

"And the father?" I asked.

Edme understood my question. Through Mario, she said, "I always assumed she'd been raped. She was young, in her early twenties, and very pretty. She worked in hard places, and among those in great poverty and despair. And the baby had very dark hair—black. Fair skin, but black hair like a Bolivian. No. I don't know about the man. I only guess."

"What is my mother's name?" I looked to Mario to translate, but Edme had understood.

Edme responded, then Mario said, "Sister Mary Olivia."

"Do you know where she is now?"

Through Mario, she said, "When I retired, I moved out here to the country. I have not kept in touch with the happenings in Oruro. If she still lives, she may be spending her retirement at the convent in Oruro. She was a sister of the order of the Missionaries of St. Lucia."

Edme pushed her chair back, ready to leave. But before she rose, she said, "I hope you find her. If you do, please tell her that the people she helped think of her often, and we keep her in our prayers. We always will."

Chapter 16

Marilee and Polly were waiting for me outside the hotel when Angelo pulled up. He dropped me off because he had other matters to attend to that afternoon. But before he did, he wrote down for me the address for the convent of the Sisters of Saint Lucia.

We three hurried up the stairs and into our room, where we assumed our positions on the beds. Marilee and Polly looked about to burst. I said, "Okay. Since I don't want to keep you in suspense, I'll go to the bottom line first."

"Yes. Do!" said Polly.

I smiled at her, then took a deep breath. "My mother was an American, as we thought." Both women nodded, knowing there was something more, and wanting to hear it soon. "She was also a nun."

Marilee's jaw dropped.

Polly sat motionless for a moment, then jumped up and started pacing as she questioned me. "So, in 1970, your mother was in a Catholic religious order?"

"Yes."

"Here in Oruro?"

"Yes."

"And she got pregnant?"

"Yes."

Polly stopped in her tracks. "Wait. Nuns take vows of chastity."

"They do," said Marilee.

"So, what? An immaculate conception? Making you—"

I couldn't help but laugh. "No, Polly," I said. "Edme assumes it was something far from immaculate."

"She was raped?" asked Marilee.

"It's looking that way." I filled them in on all the details I'd learned from Edme.

Marilee asked, "How do you feel, Suzanne?"

"I'm happy to learn my birth-mother was a good person. The nun thing explains rather well why she gave me up. So that's good news, too."

Polly asked, "What about your father?"

"You mean the fact that I'm probably the daughter of a Bolivian rapist? Of course, it's bad news."

"Anyway, the rapist thing is just speculation," said Polly.

"But logical speculation," said Marilee.

We all sat silently for a few minutes.

Polly broke the quiet by saying, "Shall we visit the convent now, or after siesta?"

I said, "I'd like to avoid being turned away based simply on the hour of our visit. Let's go this afternoon, right after siesta." This time, it would be all three of us.

None of us had visited a convent before. We assumed we should dress especially modestly, which meant that we swapped clothing to achieve looser fits. Polly, who was the smallest, wore one of my dresses. I wore one of Marilee's, and Marilee put a lace shawl she'd bought at the market over hers. As a result, we left the hotel looking unfashionable, but definitely modest. The nuns would probably be better dressed.

We made a plan for how to present ourselves. We

would explain that I was a relative of one of the sisters and hoped to see her on our visit to Bolivia. If we told the truth, we probably wouldn't be believed since apparently the whole pregnancy thing had been kept very hush-hush. Plus, at that point, we didn't even know if my birth-mother was still among the living.

Senora Choque called a cab for us, and it arrived on time at 2:30. We were standing before the door of the convent by 3:00. It was an old building on a narrow side street. The bright sunshine had faded the blue paint on the stone walls of the building. The entrance sat back only a couple of feet from the sidewalk, so there were no plantings in front. But a gray adobe wall extended almost fifteen feet on each side of the building, which suggested to me that the convent must've had grounds on the sides and rear. The wall rose probably six feet from the ground and was clearly intended for privacy. The songs of birds escaped from behind it, and I imagined a lovely, secluded garden with stone benches arranged beneath mature trees for spiritual reflection.

Marilee knocked, but the door looked so heavy I wondered if the sisters would hear it. My question was answered a minute later when a young nun swung the door open and greeted us with a big smile. She wore a knee-length black A-line skirt and a light-weight black cardigan over a white blouse. She had on a black veil, but it was only shoulder-length, and really just hid the back of her head and hair. She looked to be Hispanic, if not Bolivian. Thankfully, she spoke English.

She introduced herself as Sister Loretta Marie, and we gave her our names as we all shook hands. Polly called herself Polycarp to emphasize her Catholicism, I assumed. The young nun invited us into a very small sitting room, which contained four straight-back chairs without seat cushions and a round coffee table in the center. I wondered about the stunning, colorful, woven rug beneath our feet because nuns take a vow of poverty, as well as chastity, and the very un-feminist one—obedience. I assumed it must have been a gift.

I said, "Thank you for inviting us in to speak with you. You see, my friends and I are here in Bolivia on vacation. We're from the U.S. And, well, it occurred to me that I have a relative—a cousin, that is, who, I believe, may live and work at this convent." I'm terrible at telling tales, and I imagined the word "liar" flashing on my forehead. I could feel my face flushing.

Polly glanced at me, shook her head ever-so-slightly, and took over. "Suzanne is nervous because she fears we are imposing on your time. It occurred to her last night that she should've contacted you before our trip." She smiled. Polly was completely believable. "But Marilee and I convinced her that there would be no harm in just stopping by and asking."

Sister Loretta Marie smiled warmly at me, then said, "I can understand your hesitance. But I assure you that your visit is no inconvenience at all. It's delightful to have company. Other than the people we serve, and the vendors at the marketplace, we see few, and almost no Americans. May I offer you something to drink?"

We all declined because we couldn't stand dragging out the suspense by having her leave to prepare refreshments. The young nun said, "What is the name of your cousin?"

Marilee glanced at me, then spoke up. "Suzanne's cousin is Sister Mary Olivia."

"What was her family name before she joined the

order?"

Crap. I had no idea. And no explanation for why I wouldn't know my own cousin's last name.

Again, Polly answered without a moment's hesitation. She leaned forward, and said softly, "I'm sorry to say that Suzanne has heard there were a lot of divorces and remarriages in that family. As a result, she has no idea what last name her cousin went by."

The sister nodded her head. "Yes. I understand. Well, what was her first name?"

None of us had a clue, and I couldn't believe we hadn't thought to prepare for these questions. But Polly made a logical inference and said, "Olivia," as though it were true.

"Ah. So Sister Mary Olivia was called Olivia before she joined us. That's not unusual—keeping our civilian names. Mine was Loretta." The nun actually winked at me.

"Let me start by saying there is no Sister Mary Olivia here now. We're down to just two of us, Sister Edwin Marie, who's been here for two decades, and me. I've only been in Oruro for six months. How long has your cousin been in Bolivia?"

I knew I could answer this one, and said, "Since at least 1970."

She cocked her head slightly and squinted.

I added, "My cousin is twenty years older than me."

"Oh, my," said Sister Loretta Marie. "That was almost fifty years ago."

"Well, she was a young sister here in Oruro at that time. I really don't know if she's even still in Bolivia."

Sister Loretta Marie rose as she said, "Let me just run and grab Sister Edwin Marie. She may know something." She hurried off in the opposite direction we'd come from.

Marilee and Polly and I sat nervously looking at each other. A couple of minutes later, Sister Loretta Marie returned with a much older woman wearing a floor-length skirt, black sweater over a white blouse with a mock turtleneck, and a much longer veil. She looked at each of us before saying, "Hello, ladies. I'm Sister Edwin Marie."

She was white and spoke English without an accent. I took her for an American. As she remained standing and we introduced ourselves to her, the younger nun returned with a fifth chair. Once we were all seated, Sister Edwin Marie said, "Suzanne, please tell me about the cousin you are searching for."

I said, "Well, her name is Sister Mary Olivia. I believe she worked here, in this convent, in 1970 or so. I don't know what happened to her after that. I thought I'd take a stab at finding her while I'm here with my friends."

The older nun nodded, then paused. "I can tell you exactly where she is."

"You can?"

"Certainly. She was here with me in Oruro until about two years ago. Sadly, she took a fall and fractured her hip. We sent her to our convent in Cochabamba to recuperate because it's at a lower altitude, and she was overdue for an altitude leave anyway."

Polly said, "Altitude leave?"

"Yes. Except for the native folks here, the altitude on the Altiplano is tough on people. It is thought helpful to take a break from it periodically. Our normal schedule is that each of us is sent down to Cochabamba or Santa

Cruz every few years."

"She won't be returning to Oruro?" Marilee asked.

"I'm quite sure she won't." Sister Edwin Marie turned her gaze back to me. "You should be very proud of your cousin. She is a legend. She managed the release of a large number of political prisoners, visited the jails, taught sewing and cooking to the girls, and instructed the young ones in reading—in Spanish and English. Really. She changed many lives. I've heard that she decided to spend her retirement in Cochabamba, rather than at our Motherhouse in Wisconsin. It was out of the ordinary for her to decline the relative comfort of our facility near Green Bay. But it was left up to her."

"When did you last see her?" asked Marilee.

"When she moved to Cochabamba. You see, Sister Loretta Marie and I are far too busy to get away. When this mission was first opened in 1968 there were ten sisters living here and serving the poor. But over the years, fewer and fewer young women wanted to join religious orders. Not just ours—all of the orders. So, now we are down to two sisters here."

Polly said, "Can you give us the address for the convent in Cochabamba?"

"I'd be happy to." She smiled. "In fact, I can let them know you're coming, if you like."

Instinctively, I raised my hand. "Oh, no. I'd rather surprise her."

"It will indeed be a surprise. They don't receive many visitors from the states there either."

"Perfect," I said. "Please don't breathe a word that we'll be stopping by."

"I'll honor your wish. Although they would probably bake something special for you if they expected you. I guarantee you they will be thrilled. It's not every day that family travels to Bolivia and looks one of us up." She pulled a small notepad and pencil out of a hidden pocket, and wrote a quick note. As she handed it to me, she said, "Please give all of the sisters in Cochabamba our love." She stood. "I was doing a bit of baking, and I'd better get back to it before it decides not to cooperate. Unless you have other questions for me—"

I said, "Just one. Do you know about anything unusual happening to Sister Mary Olivia around 1970?"

She thought for a moment. "No. Why do you ask?"

"I really don't know," I said. "I just have a vague memory that something out of the ordinary may've happened to my cousin around that time."

"It may well have," said the older nun. "But I'm not privy to whatever it was. Can you be any more specific?"

I said, "We wish I could. But I can't remember what I overheard when I was a little girl. Just that something significant happened."

"That is interesting. But I'm afraid I don't know anything about it. As I said, I didn't arrive here until 1999." As she reached out her hand to me, she said, "Good luck finding your cousin, Suzanne. And Marilee and Polycarp, it was a pleasure meeting you both. I hope you are all enjoying your vacation in Bolivia."

"Yes," said Marilee. "Very much."

Polly said, "I, for one, can't wait to check out Cochabamba. And I expect that our visit to your convent will be the highlight of our trip."

"Bless you, ladies. And thank you for brightening our day by coming to see us."

Chapter 17

The next morning, I woke up bright with gratitude that this would be the day I'd find out about my birth-mother. I made the assumption she was still living based on the fact that Sister Edwin Marie surely would've heard about it if Sister Mary Olivia had passed away. Although I'd nervously pursued her for months, now that I was only hours from her, I mainly felt a sense of calm. It was unlike anything I'd felt since the accident.

Polly had arranged with Senora Choque for a private car to pick us up at 8:00 a.m. for the three hour and fifteen-minute drive northeast to the convent in Cochabamba. I would've requested the longer and more terrifyingly steep scenic route through the mountains for the dramatic views, but something told me I'd regret it if I squandered any minutes. Still, the expressway afforded us plenty of chances to glimpse the barren, rocky terrain of the Altiplano, which eventually gave way to the verdant, hilly, fertile Cochabamba valley. Polly informed us that the guide books refer to Cochabamba as the "city of eternal spring," and "the garden city" in view of the mild temperatures, which align more with Bermuda or Hawaii than the cold, arid Altiplano.

We arrived in Cochabamba a little before noon and grabbed a quick lunch from a sidewalk vendor. By one o'clock, we were standing outside the doors of the convent, which was in a shady, old residential area of the city. The building was a large, terra cotta structure, with a door painted the same light blue hue as the faded walls of the convent in Oruro. I wondered if sky-blue might be the sisters' official color.

We went through the same charade as at the convent in Oruro. Again, the sister who greeted us at the door offered us drinks, which we declined. I claimed to be checking in on an older first cousin believed to be living there. Polly filled the gaps with made-up stuff when words failed me. We had a short meeting with the young nun, but she was notably cautious. Her tight smile, and the clenched fist I saw peeking out of her sleeve made me suspect she was hiding something. She excused herself to retrieve the woman I guessed to be the head nun for that convent. The older woman was plump, with an open face and cheerful disposition. She wore the long, old-fashioned garb, with the full, black veil. When she spoke, it was clear she came from the southern United States. She introduced herself as Sister Mary Catherine, originally from Georgia. "Please forgive the accent. I've been down here for twenty years and I still can't seem to shake it."

After we introduced ourselves, Polly said, "I think your accent is charming. You should try to hold onto it."

Sister Mary Catherine laughed. "Well, charm isn't something we nuns aspire to, but I suppose it couldn't hurt."

I asked, "Did your colleague tell you why we're here?"

She nodded, then took a moment before she spoke, looking only at me. "Ms. Summerfield—"

"Suzanne, please."

"Well, Suzanne, I can't tell you how much I wish

you'd visited eighteen months ago." She simply looked at her lap for a few moments.

Marilee asked, "Has Sister Mary Olivia passed?"

The nun jerked her head up, as though startled by the question. "No. She's still with us."

"Then what did you mean?" I asked.

Sister Mary Catherine looked at me for another moment before she spoke. "I'm afraid she has dementia."

Polly asked, "Alzheimer's?"

"We don't know exactly what's causing her memory loss. Sister Mary Olivia first noticed it a year and a half ago. She found herself getting lost in areas that should've been familiar to her. The disorientation frightened her, and she brought her concern to me. We agreed the best course was to simply monitor it."

"How long had she been with you when she started to have problems?" asked Marilee.

"Only six months. You see, she'd taken a fall and fractured her hip while living at the convent in Oruro. We'd expected to have her with us only for her recovery. Well, that and maybe six months of altitude leave." She thought for a moment, then added, "I have no reason to believe the fracture and the dementia are related."

"How is she doing now?" I asked.

"Not well. She's frail. And she speaks of things that happened many years ago, but can't recall why she is here in Cochabamba—or *that* she is here in Cochabamba."

Polly asked, "Where does she think she is?"

"Oruro. Always Oruro."

"It makes sense," said Marilee. "After all, she was there from her early twenties up to her—"

I took the hint. The dates had to match up for her to

be my mother. I said, "Would you mind telling me how old she is now?"

"You don't know your cousin's age?"

"Not exactly. She was twenty-some-odd years older than me, so we never hung out together."

The nun squinted. "I would think not. After all, Sister Mary Olivia was down here in Bolivia since the time you were probably a very small child."

Polly acted like all of my statements and questions made perfect sense. She said, "Exactly!"

The nun looked sideways at Polly, as though trying to understand her reasoning. She said, "Sister Mary Olivia is seventy. She's been in Bolivia for fifty years."

My heartrate quickened at this additional confirmation. I hesitated only because I felt I'd handled the whole conversation badly. But I had to get on with my next question. "May we visit her?"

"For what purpose?"

I was taken aback by the question. "Well, just to say hello."

"And you don't really expect her to know you?" She smiled warmly, which reminded me that, based on the story I'd given her, I'd been a toddler when she left for Bolivia.

"Oh, heavens no." I paused and looked into her eyes. "Really. I just want to say hello."

"That's perfect then." She rose and motioned for all of us to follow her. As we walked down the cool, terra-cotta tiled hallway, she added, "She does love visitors."

We passed through a heavy door into a bright courtyard, and I saw a nun, sitting alone in a wheelchair on a stone path in a small garden, facing a display of bright, delicate flowers in pinks and blues. Before we approached her, Sister Mary Catherine said, "She will not know you, but she may think she does. The doctor tells us not to contradict her. Just go with the flow. She does have brief moments of clarity, but they are almost always very early in the morning. I would not expect one now."

"How early in the morning?" asked Polly.

"All of the times Sister has been cogent in my presence have been between 5:00 and 6:00 a.m."

I said, "I see." Then I braced myself to meet my mother.

Sister Mary Catherine led us up to the wheelchair, and Marilee and Polly stepped back to allow me to experience the moment. Sister Mary Olivia was asleep, her head hanging down, her chin resting on her chest. Sister Mary Catherine roused her with a tap on the shoulder. "Sister, these ladies from the United States have stopped by to visit you."

Sister Mary Olivia opened her eyes. They were hazel, like mine. Her skin was fair, with only a few wrinkles, and a light sprinkling of faded freckles. I searched her face desperately for similarities to mine. I thought I detected the slightest tilt at the tip at her nose, but I could just as easily have imagined it. She smiled at me and said, "Buenas tardes, Senora."

The head nun said, "These women speak English, Sister. Let's speak with them in English, shall we?"

I introduced myself, and she cocked her head and stared for the slightest moment. She shifted her gaze to Marilee and Polly as they shook her hand and gave her their names. She said, "It's so nice to meet all of you. Where are you from?"

We explained that we were all from Virginia. She

said, "Virginia. Yes."

I said, "We have the loveliest mountains there. They call them the Blue Ridge."

"Ah!" She smiled and clapped her hands together in delight.

I decided to try to get something—anything—out of her. "Where are you from, Sister?"

"Oruro." She said it emphatically, as though she expected a challenge.

"But originally from the States?" I asked.

"No." She looked up and into the distance.

I said, "I believe we are related."

She gave no answer and continued to stare, at nothing, as far as I could tell.

Sister Mary Catherine said, "Sister?" But my mother had left us. It was exactly as though she could neither see nor hear us. Sister Mary Catherine looked at me and said, "Sister is tired. We should let her doze."

As we walked back toward the door we'd come through, Polly said, "I don't think she was dozing."

Sister Mary Catherine stopped in her tracks and spoke to Polly. "Of course not. She'd disappeared into the fog. But on the off-chance that she can hear us and comprehend what we're saying, I always treat the situation with as much respect as I can."

"You are very kind," said Polly.

"Does she ever return to you after a period of time?" asked Marilee.

"Not often." We continued our walk. "The truth is, ladies, you received more acknowledgement than usual."

"Let me ask you something," said Marilee.

"Certainly."

"We're on a rather tight schedule. And I know it

would mean the world to Suzanne to see her cousin at her most cogent. So, would it be possible for us to return tomorrow morning—at 5:00 a.m.—in hopes of connecting with Sister Mary Olivia?"

We had reached the convent building, and Sister Mary Catherine held the door open for us as she pondered Marilee's request. She said, "I would have to miss breakfast with the sisters to attend to it."

I actually took her hand and said softly, "Please."

She glanced down at my hand holding hers, and I worried I'd been overly familiar. But she squeezed my hand before letting hers drop. "I am willing. I'll delay Sister Mary Olivia's breakfast until 6:00 so that you may have an hour to sit with her."

"Thank you so much," I said, pretty dramatically for me. "I can't tell you how much this means to me."

As if to explain the fervency of my request, Polly said, "Yes. Suzanne is very family-oriented."

Marilee half-snorted, but covered it with a cough.

Sister Mary Catherine said, "I hope you understand that there's no guarantee that Sister will make her way out of the fog tomorrow morning. It happens maybe once a week. Certainly not every day."

"We understand," I said. "We'll find a hotel to stay here in Cochabamba tonight. Then we'll be at your front door at 5:00 a.m."

She said, "You'll do no such thing!" It came out exactly like a school teacher's reprimand. She smiled. "We do have a guest room here. Two singles, and I'll pull in the roll-away. The room has its own bath."

"Are you sure?" I asked, surprised by the available extra accommodation but not by the hospitality.

"We would be deeply offended if you went

elsewhere," she said, then gave us a wide smile, which revealed, of all things, dimples. She reached for my hand and gave it another little squeeze.

Marilee, who had always been my most practical friend, had suggested we each stick a toothbrush, a little makeup, and clean underwear in our purses just in case we'd have to spend the night. We had, so we were all set.

It was nearly 1:30 p.m. by the time Sister Mary Catherine showed us to our room. I told her we would spend our afternoon and evening exploring the city, have dinner out, and be back by 10:00 p.m. at the latest, if that would work for her. She said, "That would be perfect."

Apparently, she'd noted our lack of luggage because she brought us three simple white cotton nightgowns and a basket of small assorted shampoos, soaps and toothpastes. We thanked her profusely, as we were spared searching for a shop for those necessities. We were determined not to impose further, so we set out right away to explore Cochabamba.

I'd been feeling a little guilty that my friends weren't getting much tourist fun on the trip, so I resolved to make the most of our time in Cochabamba. I got the others to agree not to discuss anything about Sister Mary Olivia or my adoption mystery until we sat down for dinner. Surprisingly, they not only agreed, but complied. I asked Polly to pull up her list of Cochabamba sights and activities, and then we put them in order to allow us to get as many in as possible. Fortunately, the list included only nine major attractions, so it was easy to whittle that down to our top four, plus a lunch and a dinner spot. Armed with our agreed check-list and our purses, we set out from the convent.

We headed straight for the statue of Cristo de la

Concordia, Christ of Peace, an enormous, gleaming white figure which is actually taller than the famous Christ the Redeemer in Rio de Janeiro. Polly informed us that it wouldn't be safe to walk up the 1,600-step path because chances were good we'd be mugged. I suggested we take a cab up because the line for the cable car, which is called the teleferico, seemed endless. I assumed it would be worth the extra dollars to zip to the top without baking in the sun for an hour or so. I just wanted to get on with taking in the 360-degree view of the city.

That was when it struck me that I was acting like an ugly American—again.

We'd just stepped out of the cab and were headed for the statue. As we walked up to the top of the hill, I said, "Guys. I'm an idiot. I just realized that I've been thinking of this day in Cochabamba as a chance to squeeze in as many sights as possible so you wouldn't feel short-changed about coming to Bolivia with me."

They stopped and looked at me as I continued. "The thing is, on all the vacation trips I've taken before, I was always thrilled with what I saw. Absolutely everything was a revelation in its own way. But today, I feel like I'm hurrying you around, checking off boxes so I won't feel guilty." I paused. "And it doesn't feel very good."

Polly took my hand and pulled me over to a shaded spot. She and Marilee looked at each other. Then Marilee said, "We knew you were worried about us when you had Polly make the list in the hotel room." She gave me a soft smile.

As Polly released my hand, she said, "We think you may be misapprehending the reason we are standing with you on the top of San Pedro Hill, in Cocha-freaking-bamba, Bolivia. We're here to help you solve the mystery of your birth. We're making progress, but I think there's a lot more to discover. Hopefully, Sister Mary Olivia will make it easy for us by emerging from the fog for long enough to tell us her story tomorrow morning."

Marilee said softly, "It's not so much that it's our top priority. It's our only goal for this trip, Suzanne."

Polly sat down on the grass, so Marilee and I did the same. They probably feared I'd collapse again like I did outside the hospital. Polly pulled her knees up and gazed towards the statue. "If I had to put on a blindfold this very minute, and not see one more speck of Bolivia so we could follow up on some lead, I'd do it in a heartbeat."

"Me, too," said Marilee.

They knew exactly how I was feeling. All I could think to say was, "Thanks, guys. You are really generous friends."

"I think 'friends' says it all," said Marilee.

We all stood and faced the mammoth white statue. "Shall we put on blindfolds or take a look at the thing?" asked Polly.

I laughed and we continued on the path around the statue, marveling at the 360-degree panoramic view of the city. We stopped frequently to simply stare. The dramatic snowcapped Andes in the background filled my heart with the same euphoric sensation I'd sometimes experienced in the Blue Ridge—including on the fateful day. I forced myself back to the present.

As we headed for the spot where our cab driver had agreed to wait for us, I said, "Everything you guys said to me is great. And I appreciate it more than I can adequately express. But now that you've cured me of my guilt…" I paused, knowing I was about to embarrass myself. "I do kind of want to see the other sights."

Marilee snorted and Polly laughed at me and at her. Polly asked the cab driver to take us to Palacio Portales, the opulent European-styled palace of the tin baron Simon Patino which was built in 1927. I was thrilled we hadn't opted for the blindfolds because we saw a magnificent array of French, Italian, and Spanish-inspired rooms, furniture, and gardens. It felt like a mini-trip through Versailles, Vatican City, and el Alhambra, all places I'd adored when Mac and I had visited them.

Our lunch spot could not have been more delightful. Thanks to Polly's research, we knew exactly where we wanted to spend the 2:30 to 4:00 p.m. timeslot. We chose it for the parrots and weren't disappointed. The beauties came in all sizes and wore feathers of intense greens, yellows, reds, and even blues in an array of patterns. The variety in their calls surprised me, as many of them sounded almost human. We were seated in a shady spot in a painstakingly landscaped tropical garden.

Marilee looked at Polly and said, "How did you arrange for a bit of the Amazon rainforest to come to us?

"Oh, it's all included in the service."

I smiled, but it was forced. Even after our conversation at the statue, and in spite of my desire to get to know the country of my birth, I couldn't keep my mind on the tourist sights. It was exhausting work yanking it back to the present when it wanted to wander all over my history—what I had thought was my history.

Because we'd agreed not to rush things, we decided to head to the Museo de Historia, and only add Cochabamba's main market, La Cancha, if we had time and energy before our eight o'clock dinner reservation.

The museum was charming in its own way, quite old and generally worn. Each step we took produced a definite creaking sound, which briefly reminded me of the resistance of the pull-down stairs at Mom and Dad's house. I quickly filed that away to consider some other day, and tried to focus on the stuffed birds and animals. We spent an hour or so staring at exhibits, and another half hour zipping through the remaining displays to be sure we'd seen it all. "What do you guys think?" I asked.

"I hope this isn't their only natural history museum," said Polly.

Marilee said, "I hardly think of myself as a museum snob, but—"

I interrupted her. "Yeah." Not wanting to be an ugly American—for the third time—I thought it best that we drop the subject. We exited into the bright sunlight and headed for the market.

"I have no market-snobbery," said Marilee. "They're all intriguing to me. It's not just the wares. It's the vendors and the customers."

"I agree," said Polly "Every city in the world has them. And there's no better place on earth to people-watch." She rubbed her hands together, evidently an avid people-watcher.

Once we arrived, we were all ready for a break. Polly quickly spied an empty bench, sun-dappled from an overhanging tree. What we saw was different from anything we'd come across in Oruro, mainly because of the attire of the passers-by. There were business men in coats and ties, twenty-somethings in jeans or khakis with polos or open-necked dress shirts, as well as many folks in the traditional Bolivian clothing we'd seen in Oruro. But here, those in modern dress far outnumbered the others. We eventually decided to grab a cab to another famous market to see the fruit and vegetable stalls on the shore of Laguna Alalay. We all agreed there is little as gorgeous as carefully arrayed, strikingly vibrant, fruits and veggies, neat as packs of new crayons. The scene we were treated to was even more colorful and vivid than I'd expected. None of us could resist taking pictures, which would never capture the intensity of the experience, but might someday spark a memory.

We didn't want to intrude on the sisters back at the convent, so we freshened up for dinner in the restaurant's restroom—ladies' powder room. Polly had made our dinner reservation at a place she'd chosen from a dozen she'd read about in a foodie's travel book. The outside façade was a corrugated shipping container with fading paint, but once we passed through the door, the vibe was sophistication. Lights enclosed in what looked like filagree pottery made for a quietly elegant, even dreamy, ambiance. But I requested the more private, dimly lit back patio because the conversation we were about to have would be intimate, and more sobbing on my part was a definite possibility.

Once our drinks had been served, I looked at my friends. "So?"

"The main thing I'd like to know is why she wears a silver chain around her neck when it's common knowledge that nuns don't wear jewelry," said Polly.

"She wears a necklace?" I asked and looked to Marilee for confirmation one way or the other.

"I don't know," said Marilee. "I was focused on searching her face for any resemblance to yours."

"And?" I asked.

"Same eye color. Similar shape of nose but

definitely not identical. The truth is, Suzanne, if I didn't know all the stuff I know, I couldn't pick her out of a crowd as your birth-mother."

"Plus," said Polly, "Since she had on the regulation, old-fashioned nun's outfit, we couldn't see her hair or much of her upper forehead."

"It would help if we could see a picture of Sister Mary Olivia in her younger days," said Marilee.

Polly said, "I agree. But it wouldn't be conclusive. Remember how much the picture of your mom on her wedding day looked like you?"

"Yeah." But at that moment I was more interested in Sister than my adoptive mother. I phrased it a different way. "Do you guys think Sister Mary Olivia is my mother?"

Marilee thought for a moment. "Yes. I believe Edme's story."

"What about you, Polly?"

"Oh, she's your birth-mother, all right." She nodded to underline her certainty. "But I still want to know what the deal is with that chain. We should ask Sister Mary Catherine."

Marilee said, "I suppose we could come up with a discreet way to do that."

"How about, 'What's with that chain she's wearing?' " asked Polly.

Marilee groaned, then turned to me. "How are you feeling about her, Suzanne?"

I had to take a moment to think how to describe where I was. "I believe Edme, as well. So I'm convinced I've met my birth-mother. I didn't notice a chain, Polly, but I have no doubt you're right. We'll ask about it tomorrow."

Marilee said, "All understood. But how are you feeling, sweetie?"

She only called me "sweetie" in moments like this, when I'm sure she believed I could easily unravel.

I took a deep breath. "I'm sad she doesn't know me, and that I'll never get a chance to know her. That's a pretty big hit after losing everything, then thinking I might have one parent left. And then finding she is lost in a cloud and can't get out." I dabbed at my eyes with the cocktail napkin from under my drink. I wasn't crying audibly, and strangers probably couldn't even see it in the dim lighting, but I just couldn't stop the tears. I actually felt my aspect flatten as though I'd taken a fast-acting depressant pill. I shook my head and tried to regain my composure. "I'm sorry, guys. Speaking about it, out loud, makes it feel more real. So, in answer to your question, Marilee, I feel—not good. Not good at all."

Marilee put her hand over mine, and it startled me because I didn't see it coming in the dark. She responded by holding tighter, which was fine by me. She said, "But you have some answers. Actually, a lot of answers."

Polly piled on by listing more that I had to be grateful for. "First, you've been inside the hospital where you were born. Second, you've tracked down your birth-mother, which is pretty amazing. Third, you now know why you were given up for adoption, which has to be reassuring. And fourth, and best of all, you got to set eyes on your mother. And you did it all during our abbreviated vacation. So, Senora Leyna Apaza was wrong. It didn't take seven months. You did all of this in under seven days, which is actually incredible."

"Thanks, guys. Everything you say is true. But I'm still feeling disappointed. See, I didn't just want to find my birth-mother. I hoped to develop a relationship with her. When I learned what amazing things she's done, I felt proud to call her mine, even if she couldn't pick me out of a line-up. But now it's clear that she'll never know I've come to find her. And that I'd so love to know her."

Marilee said, "You never know what may happen tomorrow morning."

"I know what will happen to me tomorrow morning," said Polly. "I'll be cursing both of you for the 4:45 buzzing of the alarm clock."

I laughed. Polly was good at lightening the mood.

She went on, "I mean, seriously, she couldn't do her cogent bit at 10:00 a.m.? What kind of person is at her sharpest at 5:00 a.m.? I'll tell you who. Nobody. Absolutely nobody."

"Nevertheless—" said Marilee.

"Yeah. Yeah. I know," said Polly. "But I'm sleeping for our entire three-and-a-half-hour cab ride back to Oruro."

"Fair enough," I said. "And you can crash in our hotel room there before our last dinner in Bolivia tomorrow night. It's a Saturday night. It'll be great!" I was working hard to sound upbeat because I'd been such a fun-suck for most of the trip. "I know you guys are right. We have achieved a lot. Frankly, way more than I thought possible. There will be plenty of time for me to be sad later. Let's just enjoy our second-to-last dinner in Bolivia."

Polly looked dreamy in the candlelight—like she hadn't been paying attention to my little pep talk. She said, "I have a feeling the chain is about you."

"Maybe it is," said Marilee. "But likely we'll never know."

Polly just said, "Hmm." But it was clear to me she'd wrestle the question of the chain all the way to the ground, even if she had to yank it from Sister Mary Olivia's neck. The waiter reappeared to tell us about the house specialties and took our orders.

At 9:45 p.m., we stepped through the front door of the convent, which had been left unlocked, and into complete silence. A hallway light made it easy for us to find our quarters. We took turns washing up, and got out of our things and into the matching white nightgowns. Polly said we looked like three little girls dressing up for our First Communion, which tickled us more than it should have. Something about the situation—sleeping in twin beds in nuns' nightgowns in a convent in Bolivia—got us giggling. We had a hard time stopping. Whenever all of us quieted down, someone would snort a laugh she'd been trying to suppress, and we'd be back at it again. We eventually fell asleep.

Chapter 18

When my 4:30 a.m. alarm went off, I sat bolt upright and took a moment to be clear where I was. I wondered if that's what dementia feels like—only a prolonged state of wondering who and where you are. Then it hit me that, since late-December, my first-moment-awake confusion was always about whether my family had really died, and the idea of merely wondering who and where I was didn't seem so bad.

We dressed quickly, pulled our door closed behind us ever so softly, and realized we needn't have bothered tip-toeing. On our way to the garden, we passed a bright room where a small group of nuns sat at a large, round breakfast table, chatting away as they ate. As we passed through the same door as the afternoon before, we saw Sister Mary Catherine slowly pushing the wheelchair down one of the garden paths. It was obvious that Sister Mary Olivia wasn't sleeping this time because we could see her head moving from one side to the other, apparently looking at the flowers. Sister Mary Catherine parked the wheelchair in a shaded little alcove across from two benches. She motioned for us to come ahead.

Sister Mary Olivia seemed like a different woman as she looked us over upon our approach. Sister Mary Catherine said, "Sister, these three ladies from the States would like to pay you a visit this morning. Is that all right with you?"

Sister Mary Olivia smiled and said, "Of course! You know I love visitors."

"Wonderful. I do have some phone calls to make. So I'll just leave you all to visit, and I'll be back shortly."

I said, "Thank you," as she hurried back into the building.

I sat on one of the small benches and my friends took the other. I introduced myself first and used my full name, Suzanne Reynolds Summerfield, as though that would mean anything to the woman.

Marilee went next, then Polly gave her full Polycarp Kuharski. Sister responded to that by nodding and saying, "For St. Polycarp, disciple of the Apostle St. John."

"Precisely," said Polly.

I was growing optimistic that this would be much easier than I'd thought. But immediately after Polly spoke, Sister Mary Olivia disappeared. Just like that, her mind had returned to the fog. Like a magician. Here one moment. Gone the next.

The panic must've shown on my face.

Marilee said, "Suzanne. It's now 5:05. We've been here five minutes. Relax. We'll get there."

"But how?" I asked.

Polly said, "I have an idea. Why don't I pull that chain up while she's gone, and we'll see if something is hanging on it."

I looked at her like she'd threatened to murder my mother.

She rolled her eyes at me and said, "I was kidding, Suzanne."

"But what if she can hear us?" whispered Marilee.

Polly rolled her eyes again. "Then I hope she

enjoyed my humor."

"But what do I do?" I asked.

Polly said, "I think you keep talking to her. Maybe it will help bring her back. For all we know, your voice may resemble hers at your age."

Marilee nodded. "I think it's a good idea."

I looked at my mother, whose eyes were open but with no evidence she was seeing me. "Sister Mary Olivia, we heard of all the good works you did in Oruro. How you helped so many families—especially with the political imprisonments."

No response.

"We understand you lived there in Oruro from your early twenties until two years ago when you broke your hip."

Nothing.

"I'd love to ask you some questions—when you feel up to it."

Still vacant.

"I believe we may be related. Maybe if you gave my face a good, hard look, you could recognize me."

I was talking to a wall.

When I slowed down, Polly put her hand over one side of her mouth and stage-whispered, "No. Keep going, Suzanne."

I swallowed, then launched back in. "I grew up in Virginia. Actually, I was adopted as an infant."

Nothing.

"If my birth-mother ever wondered if I had a good life, I would want her to know that I did."

Sister Mary Olivia continued to stare.

"My adoptive mother, Betty Bailey Reynolds, was one of the kindest people to have walked the earth. And dad was just as special. No child could ask to be raised by better parents." I hesitated for a moment, then dove in. "The reason I say 'was' is that they passed away a few months ago. Auto accident."

Nothing I said fazed her. But I was amazed I was able to get the story out without breaking down. "So, I'm alone now. You see, my husband was killed too."

No reaction.

"And when I came down here—to Bolivia—I was so hoping to find a relative."

I glanced over at Marilee and Polly on the adjacent bench who were both crying softly as I went on dry-eyed. "Well, you have a lovely convent here. This garden is just delightful." I paused, then blundered on through with anything I could think to say. "You know, Sister Mary Olivia, I always keep a flower garden. I figure I can buy my veggies at the farmers' market. So I plant things that are beautiful and fragrant and make me happy.

"I'm sure I don't have to tell you that every single flower is a piece of artwork. But the funny thing is, the fragrance is where the real power is for me. I find them all memorable. All evocative. In fact, my mother, Betty, always kept a flower garden too. I haven't told anyone this before, but the fragrances of the types of flowers she grew bring her back to me more than anything. When I close my eyes and smell the bearded irises and the lavender, it's almost as though my mother were standing just next to me, smiling softly as she places her fingers ever-so-gently behind a bloom, and studies the intricacies of the colorful patterns."

I prattled on like that until 5:55. Sister Mary Catherine returned, walking briskly. She said, "Did your visit go well?"

I choked up and couldn't respond.

Polly said, "For about two minutes. Since then, Suzanne's been talking to herself."

"I'm so sorry. It's as I told you. Her moments with us are short-lived and unpredictable."

"Yes," said Marilee. "We understand."

Polly said, "Would it be all right with you if Suzanne held Sister's hand for a moment?"

"Certainly. I'll just take a little walk."

I was so grateful to Polly for thinking to make this request because I'd been longing to touch my mother's hand from the moment I laid eyes on her the previous day. I stepped up to the wheelchair and knelt on the stone walkway to be at her level. I took both of her hands in mine. They were cool and surprisingly, soft, even after years of gardening. I squeezed them gently as I said the words I'd been hoping to say since we'd heard Edme's story. "I love you, Mother." I gazed at our hands, together for this one moment in time. I looked up into her beautiful, serene face.

It was then that she spoke. She looked into my eyes and said, "I know who you are. You are our Suzanne." She lifted her hand and touched my cheek.

All I could think to say was, "Oh, Mother."

She reached up around her neck with both hands and deftly unclasped the long silver chain from which hung some type of locket. She smiled as she handed it to me, then said, "This is you."

I had no idea what it was, but I kissed it softly.

She nodded, then said, "Bradley should see you."

I leaned in a bit closer and said, "Who is Bradley?"

Every fiber of my attention was glued to her face as I awaited the answer. But her eyes lost the light and she disappeared again.

I cried like a little girl and begged her to come back to me. But she was gone.

I was still sobbing softly when Sister Mary Catherine returned. Marilee explained that we'd seen the moment of lucidity, and that the Sister had, indeed, recognized her cousin.

I rose, wiped my cheeks with my fingertips, and held out the silver chain. "She gave me this and told me it was me. We don't understand what that means."

"I beg your pardon."

Polly said, "We think it may be meaningful to the family. Can you tell us what it is?"

"I have no idea. Sister would never agree to take it off. May I look more closely?"

I handed it to her, and she turned it over in her hand several times. "This is a style of locket I've seen before here in Bolivia. Such intricate silver work on such a small item. I suspect there's something inside." She looked at me. "Shall we look?"

"Yes," I said. "Please."

She approached my mother and said, "We're going to take a peek inside the locket you gave to your cousin. Just say so if that is not all right with you." Of course, there was no response.

Sister Mary Catherine opened the small, oval item and turned it over until something fell into her hand. It was a silver key, no more than three-quarters of an inch long.

Polly said, "It looks like a key to a little girl's diary."

"Does she have a diary?" asked Marilee.

"No. She certainly does not."

"Does she own anything else with a lock on it?"

asked Polly.

Sister Mary Catherine shook her head. "She doesn't own anything at all. You see, our furniture, our bedding, our clothing—everything—is owned by the community."

"Then what is the key for?" asked Polly.

"I really have no idea." She paused, as she dropped the key back into the locket, and clicked it closed. "But I can tell you that whatever it is, it is probably still in Oruro."

"What makes you think so?" I asked.

"As I mentioned yesterday, when Sister Mary Olivia came to us, she expected to be in Cochabamba for only six to eight months."

"So?" said Polly.

"So, she would've left any personal possessions in Oruro, as she was always eager to return there." She looked at me. "Suzanne, since Sister gave this to you, and you are her first cousin, a good guess is that it pertains to your family. You must keep it. Even if you never learn the meaning of the key, I hope the chain and locket will be reminders of your visit to see Sister."

"Thank you so much. I will treasure it." I held out my hand, and she dropped the piece of jewelry into my palm. I raised the locket and pressed it to my lips for the second time, then clasped the chain behind my neck.

Polly asked, "Do you think there may be someone in Oruro who could help us find whatever the key fits?"

Sister Mary Catherine indicated for us to walk with her, and we headed back down the path to the main building. She said, "I have no way to know, Polly. But Sister Edwin Marie may have an idea. Why don't you give her a call?"

"Thank you. We will," said Polly. "One other thing. Sister Mary Olivia also mentioned the name Bradley to us. Was Sister friends with someone named Bradley?"

Sister Mary Catherine stopped and lowered her eyes in thought before speaking. "Not to my knowledge."

Polly said, "Do you happen to know anyone named Bradley?"

She took a moment, then resumed walking as she responded to Polly. "I do recall there is a man in town who is said to work with the prisoners, the same type of thing Sister Mary Olivia did in Oruro. I know him, this Bradley, only by reputation. I've heard he does his social service work through a government program. But I think he's always been here in Cochabamba, and Sister was always in Oruro. I don't see how their paths would've crossed."

"Is he Bolivian?" asked Marilee.

Sister Mary Catherine turned to smile at her. "I can't say for sure. But the name Bradley sounds American to me."

My heart was racing. "Do you have any idea how we might reach him?"

"I'm sorry. But without a last name, that would be difficult."

"That's all right," said Polly. "We have a friend we can ask to look into it."

Marilee and I both eyed her, wondering who the friend was.

Once we'd all entered the building, she said, "Well, good. I'm so glad you came to see Sister." She clapped her hands together as if to say, "Class dismissed." But she continued, "If you'd like to do more sightseeing, we'd be happy to offer you the guest room for another night."

"Thanks so much," I said. "But we fly home out of Oruro tomorrow morning." I had an idea. "But if you really don't mind, we'd love to stay in our quarters for another hour or so. We have some things to discuss before we head back to Oruro."

"You are more than welcome. I'll have one of the sisters bring you a tray with tea and toast since I know you all skipped breakfast. Then let me know when you are leaving so I can be sure to have the room readied for our next guests. I'll just be in my office down the hall from you."

I took her hand, which, like my mother's, was soft and warm. "You could not have been more kind to us. Thank you. We will not forget you."

She smiled and gave my hand a little squeeze before walking us to our room.

Once we'd closed the door of our little suite and were about to resume our discussion positions on our respective beds, Polly ran up to me and gave me a big hug. Marilee was right behind her. Polly said, "She knew you, Suzanne. She fought her way up through the fog to speak to you. It's so amazing!"

"That's right," said Marilee. "She really is in there. When she joined the living for a moment, she knew exactly who you were."

They were right. I'd found her and she knew me. Of course, we all cried.

Once we'd blown our noses, I sat on the edge of my bed, and the others got in position cross-legged on theirs, like for our Oruro strategy sessions. I said, "I'm thrilled beyond words. She definitely knew me." I paused because I didn't want to come across as ungrateful. "But there were some things that were odd about it."

"No kidding," said Polly.

I laughed. "What I mean is that Sister Mary Olivia used some unusual phrasing. First, she said 'I know who you are.' Right?"

"Right," said Marilee and Polly at the same time.

"But how could she? She hadn't seen me since I was one day old."

Polly said, "Yeah. That is strange."

Marilee shrugged.

"Second, she called me 'Our Suzanne.' But who else's am I? And finally, she said Bradley should see me, but without giving us any clue as to who he is."

Marilee said, "I don't think she was talking about the rapist. It seemed to me she said the name with a level of affection."

"So, a brother, or a friend. Maybe even her father," I said.

"Beats me," said Marilee to Polly. "By the way, what did you mean when you said we have a friend we can ask about this Bradley person?"

"Senor Gutierrez, of course."

I said, "You're right, Polly. Please call him and see if he can get on this right away."

Polly grabbed her phone and stepped over to a corner of the room to call our private investigator.

Marilee and I waited until Polly rejoined us to discuss the last mystery—the locket and key. Polly said, "That was another weird phrase she used, Suzanne. I would've expected something like 'I want you to have this,' or 'This is rightfully yours.' "

"That's right," said Marilee. "What she said was, 'This is you.' "

"What the hell does that even mean?" asked Polly.

I'd been wearing the chain since Sister Mary Catherine gave it to me. I caressed the locket as I spoke. "I don't know. But Sister Mary Catherine made it clear the answer would be in Oruro. So, do you guys think we should head there now?"

Marilee said, "I say we wait to hear what Senor Gutierrez finds. Maybe this Bradley knows something important. And apparently, he may be somewhere here in Cochabamba."

"Right," said Polly. "Somewhere in a city of 1.3 million people."

I said, "Good point. So let's give Angelo until four o'clock, max. If we haven't heard from him by then, we'll head back to the convent in Oruro to ask about the key."

"What can we do in the meanwhile?" asked Polly.

"Why not call Sister Edwin Marie and get a jump on it?" asked Marilee.

Polly bounced up and searched her phone for the sister's number. She paced as she spoke. "Hello, Sister Edwin Marie. This is Polycarp Kuharski." She explained how Sister Mary Olivia had given me the necklace with the key inside the locket, and how we were trying to figure out what it might unlock. Then Polly listened and nodded her head for several minutes, her only utterances being "oh," and "um-hmm," and "I see." Finally, "I understand. Thanks so much for trying to help."

"What?" Marilee asked.

I was holding my breath.

Polly said, "It took her a couple of minutes to think of any possible explanation. Of course, she'd seen the chain, but had decided long ago to allow Sister the gift

Judith Fournie Helms

of a bit of privacy about it. She did not know there was a locket hanging from it."

Marilee asked, "What about the key?"

"That's what took so long. She was trying to think of what it could possibly unlock, especially since the sisters at the convent have no personal possessions."

"What did she come up with?" I asked, maybe a little sharply.

"Nothing."

188

Chapter 19

After we'd enjoyed the hot tea and buttered cinnamon toast one of the sisters brought to us, we headed out to explore the town. I was too nervous to sit still, and the others seemed just as eager to keep moving as we awaited a return call from Angelo. We decided to wander aimlessly so we'd get a feel for the non-touristy parts of the city. If Polly hadn't been able to read the map on her phone, we'd surely have become hopelessly lost.

Fortunately, we did stumble upon a charming, simple, outdoor restaurant for a long lunch, then shamelessly lingered there over coffees until Polly's phone finally rang. It was fifteen minutes before four o'clock. Angelo provided us with an address where we could find Bradley. He explained that Bradley Bowman worked regular hours circulating among the inmates at the three largest prisons in Cochabamba, assisting them with various aspects of their lives. He'd left the priesthood many years before to work as a layperson in social service. That was the extent of information Angelo had been able to gather. But he provided what we needed, the address for the prison where Bradley was working. He would be walking out of the southernmost door of the complex at 5:00 p.m.

We jumped in a cab and arrived at the location thirty minutes early. The breeze was cool, so we warmed ourselves by sitting on a sunny bench just outside the prison gates, and did absolutely nothing but await Bradley.

He walked out alone, carrying only a small briefcase. He met the description we'd been given: his black hair sprinkled with gray, about 5 foot 10 inches in height, average weight, wearing slacks and a blue shirt, open at the collar. His sturdy leather high-top shoes looked like construction boots.

Although I was shaking, I feigned confidence. I rose and approached him. "Senor Bowman?"

He stopped, then stared at me for a couple of seconds before responding. "Si."

"Do you happen to speak English?"

"Yes." He laughed. "I suspected you were English-speaking, but I didn't want to presume."

"My name is Suzanne Summerfield."

"It's nice to meet you Ms. Summerfield. Please do me the honor of calling me Bradley."

"All right. If you'll call me Suzanne." I smiled in an effort to convey that we came as friends, not foes.

The others stepped forward to introduce themselves. When Polly said, "I'm Polycarp Kuharski," Bradley said, "Ah, for the saint."

I looked at him for a moment, then said, "You stared at me. Do you mind telling me why?"

"I'm so sorry, Suzanne." He colored, and it showed on his throat and his ears. "It's just that you reminded me of someone I knew long ago."

"Sister Mary Olivia?"

Bradley took a step back and looked wobbly—as though his knees might buckle.

"Oh, my God," I said. I motioned towards the bench. "You need to sit down."

He hesitated a moment, and Polly said, "Bradley, ahora!"

He startled, then looked at me as he lowered himself slowly, then set his leather briefcase to his right. Neither of us spoke as we studied each other. Apart from the straight, black hair, I couldn't see myself in him. So, I assumed he was my mother's friend. But I did like his face. He had gentle, wide-set green eyes, set off by the wrinkles at the corners. But it was his lopsided grin that most charmed me. He smiled with his mouth closed, one side going up, and the other down. All in all, he was a nice-looking older man. Several years senior, I thought, to my birth-mother.

He took a deep breath, then asked, "How do you know Sister Mary Olivia?"

"It's a long story," I said. "How do you know her?"

He hesitated for a moment, as if debating what, or how much, to say. "I met her when the convent of the Missionary Sisters of St. Lucia opened in Oruro in 1968. She was one of the first sisters to come down from the states to work there."

I watched him for clues, but of what I didn't know.

"I introduced her to the prison system and worked with her—and others—to help the prisoners, who were mainly political. We were able to get many released. For others, we tried to provide support for their families and hope for the men."

Polly said, "Then she was like your student?"

Bradley smiled. "More like my partner. She learned quickly and became quite effective within a very short time."

Marilee asked, "For how long did you work directly with her?"

"Almost two years." He paused. "Up until I moved here."

"So, when did you leave the priesthood?" I asked.

He put his hands on his knees and sighed. "Who are you ladies, really? Why do you know so much about me?" He looked sad and worried.

I said, "I'm sorry, Bradley. I've probably approached this badly. Will you join us at a restaurant? I'll tell you my story. Perhaps you'll want to tell me more of yours."

He nodded, thoughtfully. "Si. I know a quiet café not far from here that will serve us now."

The no-frills restaurant Bradley took us to had a simple concrete floor and offered only four tables. Because of the hour of the day, all but ours remained empty. The wall display was poster-sized pictures of empanadas, and a dish consisting of meat on a bed of rice, topped with a fried egg. Bradley explained that one was called *silpancho*, that it is one of the city's specialties, and that the picture didn't do it justice.

None of us had any interest in food, so we all ordered coffees to justify taking up the table. Once the drinks had been served, Bradley leaned forward, elbows on the table, and looked at me. He gave me a soft half-smile. "Your story?"

I nodded at him "Yes. Where to begin?" I sincerely wanted him to know how a Virginia woman happened to look him up outside a Bolivian prison. He seemed like a nice man. I owed him this before I'd press him for more details about my mother. I forced myself to give a coherent account of the tale I'd now told too many times. Of course, I began with the drive on the Blue Ridge Parkway. I surprised myself at my ability to remain dry-eyed recounting the details of my discovery that I'd been adopted from Bolivia, and my search for the truth at the adoption agency and the lawyer's office. When I explained how we located Edme, and gave her account of the nun who had been raped, Bradley visibly blanched.

Marilee said, "Are you okay?"

He shook his head as if to clear it. "I'm sorry. I think I need some water."

Polly summoned a waiter who quickly brought a glass to Bradley, whom he seemed to know.

Bradley said, "Gracias, Eduardo." He took a long swallow, then looked squarely at me. "Please continue, Suzanne."

The intensity of his stare led me to believe that Bradley had been a close friend of Sister Mary Olivia's, but did not know about the rape, or the pregnancy, or her current condition. I finished with the mystery of the silver key, of which he said he knew nothing. Bradley took a deep breath, then called to Eduardo for three more glasses of water.

Polly laughed. "So you think something in your story will make us go pale, as well?"

Bradley turned to her. "I am fairly certain of it." We three eyed each other. I didn't know where this was going, but my heart was racing. He kept his eyes glued to me.

"I come from Minnesota. Since the time when I was a small boy, I was certain I wanted to live a life of service, and I was drawn to do this work outside of the U.S. At first, it may've been a young man's thirst for adventure. But as the years went by, and I learned about the disproportionate need among the people of Central and South America, it seemed a good choice to prepare to work here." He paused to take a long sip of water.

"I attended secular college—in Minnesota—and was as disinterested in a life of celibacy as any other young man. But as time went by, and I felt called to the priesthood, it made sense to me that, to be as effective as possible in my work, I should forego having a wife and family." He nodded to me, as though to reinforce what he'd said, or because he was nervous.

"After college, I attended seminary in Illinois, and was ordained at the age of twenty-six—in 1966. I was thrilled to be posted to Oruro, and couldn't wait to get to work. Back then, conditions were truly miserable for the poor in Bolivia—especially for the miners, who were unbelievably exploited. They worked underground for inhumanely long hours in appalling conditions. Most died of lung disease before they reached sixty."

Marilee said, "That's so young."

Bradley turned to her and said, "Si. Such a waste.

"Once I was established in Oruro, I also learned of the scourge of the government imprisoning a large number of young men for their political beliefs. Of course, I couldn't stand not to try to help them, so I spent the next two years getting to know the legal system, and partnering with local civil rights lawyers."

"Were you successful?" asked Polly.

"For the most part, si. But it was arduous work because the government lawyers were unrelenting in resistance to us. By the time Sister Mary Olivia's convent opened in 1968, I was eager to recruit the sisters to help me in this effort. The order was receptive to my overture, and Sister Mary Olivia was assigned to work with me to learn whatever she could about how to help these people." He interrupted his narrative to ask me a question. "Suzanne, would you be willing to tell me your birth date?"

I held my breath for a moment, not knowing what his reaction would be. "April 3, 1970."

He took a very deep breath, then said softly, "I didn't know. I'm so sorry. I didn't know."

Apparently, Polly couldn't stand the suspense. She stared at him and demanded, "You didn't know what?"

He glanced at her then turned to me. "Your mother was not raped."

"How do you know that?" I asked.

"I didn't know. I never heard."

"What?" I asked.

Bradley took another deep breath, then responded in a voice both soft and calm. "You are my daughter." He slapped the table and said, "What am I doing? My God! You're my daughter!" He reached over the table and placed his right hand on my cheek, tears streaming down his face.

I was too full of emotion to show any. I said, "Perhaps."

He smiled softly, knowing, I thought, that I needed to hear more of the story. He pulled out a white handkerchief to wipe his face. As he placed it back in his shirt pocket, he said, "I have kept my relationship with Olivia secret for fifty years. I did so because she asked this of me when she chose to remain in her religious life. But for you, Suzanne, I will share everything." He looked at me with a purity of earnestness that made me weak.

"I think I fell in love with her the first time we met. Sister Mary Olivia was fresh out of her novitiate, and chomping at the bit to learn all she could as quickly as possible. To me, she seemed to glow with her passion for justice. You see, she could be a part of a general conversation about some mundane subject. The moment we turned to a social justice issue, her eyes lit up and she became animated with enthusiasm for the cause."

"Wow," said Polly, who appeared to be hanging on his every word, while I'm sure I looked to be in shock.

"Yes, she was a beautiful young woman. But that was not the thing that attracted me to her. As a priest serving in Oruro, I came across countless lovely women in every capacity of my work. I wasn't the least tempted by any of them. I simply saw that part of life as a world separate from mine. I needed to understand sexual passion, but I was better served by not partaking."

"So what did you do?" asked Marilee.

"At first, I felt quite sure Olivia didn't know of my feelings for her. But we spent so much time together, I began to wonder if she felt it too. We'd been working alongside one another for almost two years when I decided that I could serve God just as well as a married man—still committed to social justice, but no longer to celibacy. I pondered for many weeks how I would reveal my thoughts—and my feelings—to Olivia. How I would ask her to enter secular life with me, as my wife."

"Oh, my," said Marilee.

I was simply staring at Bradley and absorbing every word.

"One evening in mid-July, after a long day at the prison, I asked her to take a walk with me. I can tell you, I was pouring sweat, worrying that I might insult her. After hemming and hawing, I told her everything, and begged her to think about a future with me. In the shadow of a large tree, I stood shaking. I leaned in toward her to find out if she was receptive at all to a kiss.

"She was. She told me she had been thinking many of the same things, but had no idea how I felt about her. We went to my lodging and talked for an hour or so before we became physical. It was not my first time, but it was hers. Afterwards, noting the hour, she said she had to hurry back to the convent, lest they worry about her. I did not try to stop her because I believed we would discuss our future together soon and often before arriving at a decision and a plan."

Bradley paused to take a drink of water, then waited another moment or two before continuing. "But the next morning, a letter was hand-delivered to me by one of the boys who worked with us. Olivia said she'd stayed up all night praying and thinking. She said she loved me with every fiber of her being, but that her heart was no longer hers to give. She would seek forgiveness for her lapse, and for the fact that, if she lived to be one hundred, she would never regret it. She concluded by telling me she'd decided to devote her life to God and to the important work her order had sent her to Oruro to do. She asked that I not see her again, as she would not be able to resist the pull if we were together. She said that if I truly loved her, I would respect her sincere wishes. She hoped for me nothing but peace and joy. I remember exactly how she ended her letter, 'Please, I must never see you again. Be strong for my sake, darling Bradley.'"

Marilee said, "Oh, my God."

I was too shocked to speak.

Bradley spoke slowly and quietly, as though the words might choke him. "I was devastated. Yes. She had rejected my proposal. But now I would not be able to enjoy the thrill of simply working beside her each day. But what could I do?

"Of course, I honored her wish. I made sure I did not run into her at our usual places. I secured a transfer to Cochabamba as soon as I could, because there was no way our paths would not cross if I remained in Oruro. But every day I hoped she'd reconsider."

Polly placed her hand over her heart. Marilee had tears streaming down her cheeks.

"I began work in the new city which was similar to what I'd been doing in Oruro. I did rather pine for Olivia, which made me feel like a schoolboy. Other times, my grief at losing her felt adult and normal. Over time, it became clear to me that I was only technically celibate. I was passionately in love with a woman, and I felt confident I would continue to be. Ten years passed without a word from Olivia. But my love for her was every bit as strong as the day I proposed. So, I decided I must leave the priesthood. When all the counseling and petitioning were said and done, it was almost eleven years after I had declared my love for Olivia that I became a civilian.

"Olivia never did reach out to me. Early on, I would fantasize about her walking through my door, with her arms out to me. In more recent years, I've become resigned to the fact that it will never happen. But the truth is, even today, I'm still very much in love with her. Given the chance, I've always known I would marry her in a minute. Still, I've learned that I can live a happy life alone."

Although he said the words "happy life" emphatically, I felt my heart breaking for him.

"From what you've told me, Suzanne, I now

understand that, at some point, Olivia learned we'd conceived a baby. I'm certain she was ordered to reveal the name of the father. But, you see, I didn't leave the priesthood until eleven years later. I'm sure she assumed I would always be a priest, and she didn't want to ruin my position. Don't you see, Suzanne? No one was protecting you from the truth. It was always about Olivia protecting me. I assume it was she who insisted that the adoptive parents promise never to tell anyone. In fact, the agreement to adopt was probably contingent on the secrecy. Remember, nuns take a vow of obedience, so I'm also quite sure she was punished for refusing to divulge my name. What she did was an incredible gesture of love."

"Yes. I see that," said Marilee.

"Right," said Polly. "A gesture of true love."

Bradley continued to look only at me. "Now that I know we had a child together, I must admit to a feeling of profound loss. I had a daughter. A beautiful baby girl. I would've left the priesthood in a heartbeat and raised you as a single father. It does break my heart that I missed out on that." He paused, then took a long breath before continuing. "Do you happen to have a picture of Mac and your adoptive parents with you?"

I wasn't carrying any pictures with me. In fact, the ones I'd had on display at my house were still in the pot-holder drawer. "I'm sorry, but—"

Marilee interrupted with, "The picture on your phone."

"What?"

She raised her eyebrows. "From that day. Do you still have it?"

The heat creeped into my ears. "Well, I-I mean, I

haven't been able to look for it to delete it."

Bradley reached out and placed his hand atop mine. "Please. Do not discomfit yourself. It isn't important."

I thought about it. "It's important to me, Bradley. I'd like you to see them." I opened my phone to *photographs* and handed it to Marilee to find the one. She passed it back to me, and I swallowed hard before glancing at it. I set the phone on the table, facing Bradley, and slid it over to him. "That's us."

He pulled it closer and stared at it for a minute. "A beautiful family, Suzanne. Your parents and Mac—they look like kind people."

I gazed at my hands resting on the table. "They were."

Bradley said, "It's interesting."

I looked up and saw his eyes were glued to the phone. "What is?"

He squinted as he continued to stare at the photo. "It's just that your adoptive mother's smile is like Olivia's—a bit."

I said, "If it resembled my mom's, I'm sure it was lovely."

He pushed my phone back to me then stared at me for a long moment before speaking. "Now, after all this time, nothing would make me happier than to get to know you, Suzanne. Is it possible? Do you have an interest in getting to know me, and the work your mother and I did together?"

I pursed my lips as I nodded my head. I couldn't speak. Anguish was boiling up in my throat. I took a sip of water to help me speak. "Bradley, I'm so sorry."

"For what?"

"For all the love you missed out on."

Bradley squinted hard, but tears made their way out of the corners of his eyes. "Thank you. I've always had romantic love in my life because I never stopped loving Olivia. And I will always believe that her courage in maintaining her secret was proof that she loved me, as well. But a love a father has for a child. Yes. I missed out on that." He slapped his leg. "Oh, I mustn't feel sorry for myself. It isn't too late. I am sitting here with our daughter. This might never have happened. I'm an incredibly lucky man."

He cast his eyes down for a moment. When he looked up, they were moist, and he looked intently at me. "You have to understand. For me, this is rather like a miracle. What I thought I had sacrificed in this world is now bestowed upon me. I love you already, Suzanne. I want you to be assured, you were begotten of true love."

I glanced at Polly, who looked to be completely absorbed in Bradley's words. She said, to no one in particular, "The kind that lasts forever."

Bradley took his eyes off me for a moment, and nodded to her. "Si."

He took my hand and said, "When I look at you, I don't just see the same beautiful face, the same lovely, freckled face. I also see in you the same grace, and beauty, and deep well of kindness that I saw in your mother." He began to weep softly, which made me cry as well. After a moment, he tenderly wiped my face, and then his, with a fresh, folded handkerchief. He looked around the table. "Forgive me, ladies" He gave us one of his endearing smiles. "I have tried to speak from my heart. But the truth is, I am still absorbing this shock, this most pleasant shock."

I said, "I can't tell you how moved I am to have

discovered you, my—" The word felt too strange, and wouldn't come out. "I'm so very happy."

Bradley said, "Would it be possible for you to extend your stay?"

The look on his face was so hopeful that it was painful for me to answer. "I wish I could, Bradley. But Marilee and I are two of only six partners in our law firm. We all agreed long ago that we should all take our vacations, just not two of us out at the same time. It just puts too much stress on the others. Yes, an exception was made for this week due to the unusual circumstances, but—"

"Ah. That makes perfect sense. I understand completely."

Polly glanced at her watch, then told Bradley that we still hoped to unravel the mystery of the silver key.

"Then you must go." He turned to me. "It could be important, Suzanne."

We rose to leave, and Bradley gave me a gentle hug. He pushed me back from him a bit and looked into my eyes. "Hurry back to me, daughter. Please."

I smiled. "That's exactly what I intend to do. As you might imagine, learning about you is a shock on top of a number of others since the accident. I need to process all of it. But I will return soon, Bradley. I promise I will."

Chapter 20

Bradley led us out onto the street and hailed a cab for us. He and I hugged one final time before I jumped in. In his embrace, I felt like a beloved child again, and I realized that experiencing a parent's love might bring me back to life.

Once we were zipping along toward our rendezvous with the car we'd hired for the trip back to Oruro, Marilee said, "How does it feel to suddenly know everything?"

"I think I'm in shock. I have to let all of this sink in."

Marilee said, "The most fascinating part to me is that all of the secrecy was never for you, but to protect Bradley. That's so crazy."

"The most fascinating part for me is that I've found my birth-father."

After a minute, Polly said, "I'm still pretty invested in finding the answer to the remaining unanswered question."

"The key?" I asked.

"I'm pretty sure it's solid silver. The locket is intricately carved. This is no child's toy, guys. And if that much trouble was put into it, it must unlock something valuable."

"Our flight home is tomorrow morning," I said. "It's six o'clock now and we have a three-and-a-half-hour ride to get us back to Oruro. How do you propose we solve this mystery now, while the key is still in Bolivia?" I paused while stroking the locket with my finger. "And I guarantee it's leaving with me because I don't plan to ever take it off."

Polly smiled as though none of this presented a problem. "First, I'll call our driver and insist he meet us in fifteen minutes." She pulled her phone out of her bag and was soon speaking Spanish with her usual enthusiasm. She looked up and said, "Miguel will meet us here in twenty minutes. He just has to settle his bar bill."

Both Marilee and I startled.

"For his lunch, chicas. Geez!" She paused. "And I want to call Sister Edwin Marie again."

"Why?" asked Marilee.

"To prod her some more. I have a feeling there could be something that just hasn't come to mind yet."

"I'd like to be on that call," I said. "Put us on speaker?"

"Sure."

Marilee said, "Let's wait to make the call until we're in the hired car, though. That way we'll have a full, uninterrupted three and a half hours to talk."

"I don't think it'll take more than ten minutes," said Polly. "But I do see your point. I'll sit between you guys so we can all hear and be heard."

Once we transferred to Miguel's warm, cozy car, and were all lined up in the back seat, Polly let her fingers fly over her phone.

We heard, "Sister Edwin Marie speaking."

"Hi, Sister. This is Polycarp Kuharski. I have you on speaker. Suzanne and Marilee are here with me. Is that okay?"

"Certainly."

Polly added, "Is this a good time for you to talk?"

"Absolutely. So, Suzanne, I've been wondering how you're feeling about your meeting with Sister Mary Olivia."

I said, "Hello, Sister. I know Polly told you earlier that my cousin has dementia."

"Yes. I'd heard rumors, but I didn't realize how serious it was."

"Well, when we visited with her on Friday afternoon, she was only lucid with us for a brief minute." I swallowed hard so that I could continue. "Of course, I was disappointed. So we returned very early this morning, and we had better luck. She came out of the fog to speak with us for a few minutes. Well, it was heaven to be able to connect—even for such a short time."

"Yes. That's what I understood from Polly's call, early this morning. I'm so sorry Sister wasn't fully there for you."

"Thanks," I said. "As you know, in her moment of clarity, Sister gave me the chain and locket she was wearing. Sister Mary Catherine opened the locket with us, and a small, silver key fell out."

"Yes. Polly and I discussed that briefly. I'm sorry, but I really don't know what that key could possibly open." She paused. "In fact, once we learned she wouldn't be returning to Oruro, we cleaned out her room and found absolutely nothing beyond the things our convent provided."

"It's Polycarp again. I was just thinking that even people who spend most of their time working for social justice must have a close friend or two."

Marilee interrupted. "You mean another young

nun?"

"Well, another young woman. I'm just wondering if Sister Mary Olivia had a girlfriend—in a non-sexual way."

Marilee's eyes widened as she elbowed Polly, who jerked away and fake-scowled at her.

Sister Edwin Marie said, "Of course, I understand your question. But I didn't arrive in Oruro until 1999, so I have no idea who may've been friends with whom in the early days. But generally, the sisters who come to the Altiplano tended to remain for only a year or two."

Marilee asked, "Is there a way you could check to see if any of them remembers anything?"

"I guess I could contact them, but it would take weeks for me to track them all down and get their responses."

Polly asked, "Why?"

Sister's voice became a bit sharp. "Because I have a lot of work to do every day." It seemed that Polly had managed to irritate our best resource. Our only resource.

I said, "It's Suzanne again. Of course you are terribly busy, Sister. Let me just be sure I understand. From your comments, I gather that Sister Mary Olivia never had a close friendship, to the best of your knowledge. Right?"

Silence.

After a moment or two, I said, "Sister? Are you still there?"

"Sorry. I was just thinking."

I decided against interrupting the flow of her rumination—again—and kept my mouth shut.

After another moment, she said, "There was a woman named Liliana."

"Liliana?" asked Marilee.

"Yes. Liliana Perez. You see, Sister Mary Olivia had helped out the son from one of the miner's families who'd been jailed after a protest. This was decades ago, when she had only been at the convent for a few years. The boy's parents had no money to make a donation to the convent, but wanted to thank Sister Mary Olivia in a tangible way. So they gave the convent their sixteen-year-old daughter, Liliana."

"To become a nun?" I asked.

"No. To spend one long day every Saturday helping Sister Mary Olivia with the gardening."

"And the two young women became friends?" asked Marilee.

"Yes. Understand that no one really ever saw them together because the gardens are behind the buildings. The two women did their work out of view of the rest of us."

Marilee asked, "Do you mean Liliana still worked with Sister Mary Olivia after you came to the convent?"

Sister said, "Yes." She paused. "Something happened two years ago which may be important to understanding this. It was when Sister Mary Olivia went to Cochabamba for her recuperation and altitude leave. Liliana made an appointment to speak with me. She said that the obligation her family had assigned her to fulfill had been satisfied. She had enjoyed working the earth for us, but now, without Sister Mary Olivia to keep her company, she planned to use her Saturdays for other activities."

"That seems fair," said Marilee. "When Liliana was sixteen, she probably thought she'd be indentured for a couple of years, not for almost fifty."

"I'm sure you're right," said Sister Edwin Marie. "It was always the family who insisted this was to happen. The convent appreciated Liliana's help, but never considered her work to be something we were entitled to in any way."

"So how do you know the two women became friends?" I asked.

"It was something Liliana said to me at what was basically her exit interview."

All three of us had our eyes riveted to the phone. "What?" I asked.

"These were Liliana's words: 'We became sisters. We shared our lives, gave each other a tremendous amount of advice, and always encouragement.' Then she added the curious part. She said, 'And I am the one she chose to hold her secrets. I will miss her immensely.' "

"What does that mean?" asked Marilee.

"I had no idea what secrets the woman was talking about, but I'll always remember her enigmatic words. I gave her a small token of appreciation, a rosary that had been blessed by the Pope. I thanked her for all of her hard work with the abundant garden vegetables, and the flowers which brought such joy to us."

We all thought about it in silence for a moment. Then I said, "Interesting wording. She didn't say 'to tell her secrets to.' She said, 'to hold them.' "

"That's exactly right," said Sister Edwin Marie.

Marilee said, "That makes me think Liliana is keeping something for Sister Mary Olivia, and that the silver key may fit that something."

I said, "That's my guess, too." I paused to think. "Sister, can you tell us how to reach Liliana?"

"It's my understanding that she owns a hotel just

outside of town. But I have no idea if she is there now, or, perhaps, travelling. I'm not even sure that she lives there."

"Thanks so much, Sister," I said. "I don't know if this will pan out, but it feels huge to have a lead."

"Well, good," she said. "Best of luck, and God bless you all."

We all said "Thank you" at the same time.

Polly stuck her phone back in the small backpack she used as a purse, which was sitting between her knees on the hump in the floor. Marilee said, "You're right that it's exciting to have a solid lead, Suzanne. But how do we reach a woman that we just learned exists, and on our last night here?"

Polly pulled her phone back out and hit some numbers. As she waited for someone to answer, she looked up and said, "Senor Gutierrez. I'm sure he'll want to do it, Suzanne. Remember, you're paying him double-time at this point." She switched to Spanish as she brought our private investigator up to speed and asked him to find Liliana within the next four hours. She told him we'd be back to Oruro by 9:30 p.m.

Chapter 21

We were riding along in our hired car, all sleeping soundly from the exhaustion that came from sleepless nights, early mornings, and stress. A loud chime from Polly's cellphone wrenched us awake. I glanced at my watch and saw it was 8:30 p.m., only an hour before we would be back at our hotel. I assumed the call was from Angelo and that he'd found Liliana.

Polly scrambled through her backpack to grab her phone. She had the conversation in Spanish, then filled us in as she put her phone away. "He said she wasn't hard to find because everybody who is anybody knows of Liliana Perez."

"Because she owns a hotel?" I asked. "And if that's it, why did it take him two hours to call back?"

"She owns and runs one of the largest upscale hotels in Oruro. Of course, Senor Gutierrez knew that part. But he wanted to confirm that she's still living at the hotel, and that she is in town tonight."

"That's crazy," said Marilee. "She owns a fancy hotel. And, until two years ago, she spent every Saturday toiling in the back garden of a convent. It's just hard to believe."

"Did Angelo have contact information for her?" I asked.

"Yes. He confirmed she's still living at the hotel. He says there is some big benefit shindig there tonight, but he doesn't know if she'll show up. Apparently, she only makes appearances at the galas that groups put on at the hotel for charities that are important to her."

Marilee said, "Interesting. Is there any other tidbit you haven't told us?"

Polly took a moment to think, and finally said, "Just that she's divorced."

"Hmm. So, what's our plan?" I asked.

Marilee said, "Let's see. We'll be back in our room at nine thirty. Then we freshen up and head over to her hotel."

"What do you plan to say to her?" Polly asked me.

"I think I should tell her everything," I said.

"But that would betray the secret," said Marilee.

Polly said, "I don't see it as betrayal. The secrecy was to protect Bradley, who has made it clear he neither wants nor needs protection."

"She may already know," I said. "If they were really close, my mother may have shared the story with her."

Polly said, "Maybe. But my gut tells me Sister Mary Olivia told nobody. And remember what Sister Edwin Marie said. That your mother had been there a few years when Liliana first appeared on the scene. So we know Liliana didn't actually witness the pregnancy."

I felt too tired to think straight. "Help me with this, guys. Do we hurt anyone by telling Liliana the whole story?"

"I can't see any harm in it," said Polly.

"Nor can I," said Marilee.

Polly said, "So we find her. We make her listen to your story. And we show her the key. It's only eight-thirty. We have all evening and all night to locate her and worm the answer out of her."

"Well, we don't actually have all night," I said. "I mean, we can hardly knock on her door at midnight and not expect her to call the police, or just start shooting."

Marilee said, "The first statement out of our mouths—our hook—has to be about how Sister Edwin Marie told us of her friendship with Sister Mary Olivia."

"Right," said Polly. "Then we reel her in." She snuggled her head against my shoulder and said, "Good night."

Because we were all worn to a nub, we made good use of the last hour of the drive to snooze. I guessed that we were all wishing the same thing, that the car ride could go on lulling us into slumber for about six more hours. But we still had work to do—a lot of it.

We dragged ourselves into Hotel La Rosa at 9:15. Senora Choque nodded at us as she said, "Cansadas?" Polly nodded back, then asked her to arrange for a taxi at 9:45 sharp. We tackled the stairs like they were the last few yards of an ironman marathon. As we walked into our room and flung ourselves onto our beds, Polly said, "Guys, we have to re-energize! What does anyone have with calories in it?"

Marilee leaned down over her suitcase, dug through the clothes into a deep side pocket, and produced three energy bars.

"I hate these things," said Polly. "But we need to come back to life. We're going out on the town, ladies! Who wants the first shower?"

It didn't seem like the right time to be underdressed, so we each wore the cocktail dress we'd brought "just in case," and our highest heels. I lost the center-part I'd been wearing to look like I'd stepped out of the '70s, and slicked my hair back with product. Marilee's auburn hair looked great in a high ponytail, and she wore an emerald green dress which made it appear even redder. Polly wore her blonde curls loose down her back and put on a snug, burgundy lace dress with spaghetti-straps. I'd brought only a black sheath—to match the color of my heart.

At 9:40 p.m., we descended the stairs into the lobby to Senora Choque's visible surprise. According to Polly, she said, "You look like three different women."

"Si." I assumed Polly was saying something like, "We are on a mission to see Senora Liliana Perez." When I heard the name, I understood that she was intelligence-gathering. Polly asked Senora Choque another question.

The elderly woman raised her eyebrows, asked Polly a question in return, then regaled her with a couple of minutes of information.

Once we were in the cab, Polly told us what she'd learned. "The first thing she said to me was, 'Do you know a queen?' Then she explained that Liliana Perez is powerful, beautiful, knows all the influential people, and always gets her way. When I asked her how the woman became so successful, she told me Liliana's story.

"Apparently, she was the daughter of a poor miner, and her future looked as bleak as that of any such girl. It was about a year after her quinceanera that she began to change. She married at seventeen but divorced the man when she turned nineteen—which was unheard of at that time. She grew more confident and more assertive every year. Her English became unparalleled. She found a job checking in guests at a decent, small hotel. She excelled in her work and moved up to bigger and finer hotels. Now she owns the new Hotel Liliana, just outside of town. Senora Choque recalled that it opened about two years ago and has exquisite views of the Andes, with a huge window-wall in the lobby, and a view from every guest room.'"

When Polly finished recounting the conversation, I said. "Wait. Did you say she owns the hotel?"

"That's what Senora Choque said."

Marilee said, "But Angelo told you she 'runs it.' "

It all became clear in an instant. "What difference does that make, guys? Don't you see? It was all because of her friendship with my mother. That's how she must have become proficient in English." I couldn't get my sentences out fast enough. "Remember the words Liliana said to Sister Edwin Marie at the exit interview?"

"I do," said Polly. She did an exact imitation of Sister Edwin Marie's voice. "We became sisters. We shared our lives, gave each other a tremendous amount of advice, and always, encouragement. And I am the one she chose to hold her secrets."

"Oh, my God!" said Marilee. "You're right."

"I can't wait to meet her," I said. My right knee bumped up and down from nervousness for the remainder of the cab ride.

The hotel was thirty minutes out of town on a busy street. It was a large, modern stone building. We agreed that it looked dignified, but not terribly imposing. More Marriott than Four Seasons. We were surprised to see that the parking lot was full and a line of taxis and limos snaked around, dropping off well-dressed couples at the main entrance by the minute.

Once our cab made its way to the drop-off spot, a valet in a black suit and tie opened the back door for us and helped each of us out. He said, in English, "You are here for the miners' benefit?"

I started to explain, but Polly stepped in front of me and said, "Si. Of course."

The valet directed us to one of the front doors, where gorgeously dressed people were slowly being admitted into the building after either displaying an invitation or providing a name that must have matched one on the gate-keeper's list.

Once we'd made our way to the front of the line, Polly said, "I'm sorry. We were so excited for this evening that we hurried out without our invitations."

The ticket-taker said, "It is no matter, Senora. I can look you up on the guest list." He looked at her, pen and list at the ready, and raised his eyebrows.

She said, "Senora Polycarp Kuharski," and he blinked twice before reviewing the list. "I'm sorry. But your name is not here. Perhaps the reservations are under the name of one of your friends."

If Marilee or I had known any common Bolivian last names, we might've thrown one his way. But because we didn't, we gave our real names, then feigned surprise that he could not find them.

Polly said, "We don't want to hold up your other guests. Could you just direct us to the head of security so we can get this sorted out?"

"Of course, Senora." He gave her a little bow and waved at a tall, strikingly handsome man standing at one of the interior doors, looking people over. The man led us to a quiet corner. We introduced ourselves, and he said his name was Juan Carlos Flores. He unabashedly looked us over, I thought, appreciatively. I foolishly took it as a good omen. He said, "Forgive me, ladies, but I believe you are not really here for the benefit."

"That's true," I said. "We've come to speak with

Senora Liliana Perez."

"Why?"

"A friend of hers suggested we speak with her."

"What friend?"

"Sister Mary Olivia."

He shook his head. "No. I know of no such friend."

Marilee tried. "Sister Edwin Marie?"

Again, he simply said, "No."

I was growing nervous that he really wasn't going to allow us to meet her. I said, "I believe she will be unhappy with you when she learns that Sister Mary Olivia sent us here, and that you did not even advise her."

His face made it clear he didn't appreciate the attempt at intimidation. However, it did loosen his tongue. "Senora, you are mistaken. Senora Perez is this night hosting her biggest benefit dinner and displaying her fine hotel. Guests are arriving from all over the country. I assure you, she will not wish to be interrupted."

Marilee ventured, "Perhaps afterward?"

Juan Carlos smiled at her the way one does when he is not sad to give more bad news. "No. From here, she and a small group of very important friends leave for ten days on the Amazon River. After she returns from that trip, you may call her secretary. Maybe then you may secure an appointment to see her."

"But our flight back to the States leaves early tomorrow morning," said Marilee.

He smiled again. "Perhaps you should have made the arrangement to see her several weeks ago."

I glanced at Polly, but she was uncharacteristically quiet.

Marilee started to explain my situation to him, but I

said to her, "It's no use."

Juan Carlos bowed slightly, just as the gentleman at the door had done. "Safe travels, Senoras." With that, he motioned for us to follow him to the exit.

Polly reached up and grabbed his arm. I feared he might pull a gun on her for touching him. She launched in with, "Senor, you can see how long the cab line is. It will take quite some time for the driver to get back to the front. May we at least use the ladies' restroom before we head out the door to wait for him?"

He shook his head the tiniest bit, as if to say, "Whatever. Quit bothering me." What he actually said was, "Of course, Senora." He waved down the hallway towards the restrooms.

As we walked, I said to Polly, "My mom always called it the ladies' powder room."

She smiled her tender, understanding smile, but her mind was elsewhere. I saw something else in that grin— something diabolical. Then it hit me. She was planning something.

Once we were in the opulent restroom, I said, "What are you thinking, Polly?"

"Our last stand."

She quickly pulled down her spaghetti straps and tucked them under the dress so it was now strapless. She yanked a ruby-red lipstick out of her evening bag and applied it generously, as one would stage make-up. Then she handed her purse to me and said, "Hold this for me, Suzanne."

Marilee said, "What are you doing?"

Polly ignored the question, and said to her, "I need your rubber band." Marilee obliged her, so now Marilee's hair hung loosely to her shoulders. Polly put her tresses up in a high bun and pulled out tendrils for a romantic-looking up-do.

I said, "What the hell, Polly? You look like you're about to go on stage."

She checked herself in the mirror, then took a deep breath and leaned in to whisper to me, "You must loan me your silver chain and locket."

"No," I said.

"You must."

In that split second of decision, I trusted her. I took it off and clasped it around her neck.

Polly walked out the door.

Marilee and I followed in her wake and gaped at her as she made her way through the crowd. Although petite, she resembled a queen as she strolled right up to the center doors into the party. Marilee and I stood against a wall to view whatever it was she was doing. I was breathing so quickly, I feared I might hyperventilate.

Polly stood, erect and regal, and simply waited for the young men stationed at the doors to open them for her. When one of them hesitated, she broke into the most beautiful song, in a soprano so clear and pure that it gave me chills. The doors opened. Marilee and I slipped into a position that allowed us to see into the ballroom.

She walked down the center aisle of the room between sections of round tables covered in white linen and bedecked with exquisite floral arrangements at which men and beautifully dressed women were seated. Polly expressed the song with her ethereal pale arms as well as with her voice. All of the guests, women and men, paused their conversations, stood, and put their right hands on their hearts. Many raised their left fists. That's when I realized she was singing the Bolivian national anthem.

Juan Carlos ran up to the double doors to see what was happening, but would not dare interrupt his national anthem being sung by an angel.

Polly must have known she could guess which of the women in the receiving line was Liliana, because the moment she finished her song, while the room was reverberating with thunderous applause, she approached an elegant woman in a floor-length pale-yellow gown.

Marilee and I had moved up to the double doors with the crowd of people to watch the spectacle. We were in shock. No one bothered with us, but Juan Carlos and two of his aides rushed up to where Liliana and Polly were talking. Of course, we couldn't hear what was being said. Liliana beckoned Juan Carlos and nodded toward Polly. He escorted her out of the room by a side exit. Lilian then resumed greeting her guests.

My mouth hung open.

Marilee whispered, "Where is he taking Polly?"

We had no idea what to do or where to go, so we remained frozen just next to the double doors trying to think. A few minutes later, Juan Carlos came for us— with two henchmen. He said, "Please follow me," and led us farther into the hotel. We had little choice as his two underlings were walking right behind us. It seemed we'd walked five minutes before he opened a door to a room and said, "Until later."

It was a luxurious suite, and Polly was sitting on the white brocade couch with her shoes off and her feet up. "Come on in," she said.

I said, "What the hell is happening, Polly?"

Just then, there was a loud rap on the door. My heart sank, but Polly, in bare feet, hurried to open it and a young woman in maid's attire pushed in a large cart laden with food and beverages.

As soon as she left, I said again, "What the hell, Polly? Security might've shot you!"

She calmly said, "I thought about that, Suzanne."

Marilee and I were still standing, nervously surveying our surroundings.

Polly said, "Come in and relax, guys. Have a seat, for heaven's sake."

I fell into one overstuffed peach armchair and Marilee the other. Polly looked at me and said, "Of course, I knew they might be pissed. But then I thought, 'I'm a petite person, holding nothing, in a dress that conceals nothing.' I didn't really think they'd shoot a harmless woman singing their national anthem. And they didn't!" She smiled.

I wasn't satisfied. "I have some questions, Polly."

"Shoot." She laughed. "Bad word choice."

"I don't even know where to start," I said.

"I do," said Marilee. "How did you happen to know the Bolivian national anthem?"

I interrupted. "Backing up a bit, I didn't even know you were a singer."

"Fine," said Polly, after taking a bite of one of the green grapes from the bunch she held in her hand. "I'll back it up all the way to college. I studied opera at the University of Texas at Austin. Sensing the dimness of job prospects, I double-majored in opera and Spanish. I went on for my masters in Spanish at Middlebury— because Vermont is such a Spanish-language mecca." She paused to eat another grape. "So, yes, I sing."

"Right," said Marilee. "Has the Bolivian national anthem always been in your repertoire?"

"Of course not. Why would it be?"

"Exactly my point," said Marilee.

"It's just something I do when I take a trip—to get in the mood. Listen, some people study guidebooks. Well, I do that, too. I learn a song. I memorized it about a month before we left. I think it's really beautiful." She sat up straighter with enthusiasm for the piece. "Would you like to hear the words in English?"

We didn't respond. She said, "Well, in English, the title is 'Bolivians, a Most Favorable Destiny.' "

Polly was completely relaxed, as though what she'd done was the most natural thing in the world. Marilee and I must still have looked agitated, because Polly quickly explained how her spectacle had come about. "Listen. I'm really sorry I didn't share my plan. But I didn't think of it until Juan Carlos was making it clear he was giving us the boot."

I said, "We saw you speak to the woman in the pale-yellow dress. Liliana?"

"Yep."

"What did you say to her?" I asked.

Polly raised and lowered her eyebrows dramatically before speaking. "I knew I had only seconds before security would sweep in. So I said, 'I'm a friend of Sister Mary Olivia's.' Liliana gave a small startle, keeping her eyes on mine. I lifted the locket for her to see, and added, 'My friends and I have some questions about this. May we speak after—?' I nodded to the party in full swing around us."

I let out my breath, which I hadn't realized I was holding. "And?"

"And it worked!" Polly rose and walked the four feet to the buffet table, where she took another cluster of grapes.

"She'll see us?" I asked.

She handed the grapes to me and said, "Suzanne, we have fifteen minutes after the soiree and before she leaves for the jungle."

Marilee jumped up and down, which I had never seen her do before. She seemed a little bit slap-happy from all the stress of the past hour, and she pulled me and Polly in for a group hug.

I swallowed hard, not knowing how I could explain everything in fifteen minutes. I said, "What time is it now?"

Marilee pulled her cell phone out of her evening bag and said, "11:15."

"So, maybe around midnight?" I ventured.

"Hardly," said Polly. "The woman who laid out all this food for us came in earlier with a glass of wine and some snacks for me. She told me we'll be lucky if this thing ends by two o'clock in the morning."

"And we have to be at the airport at five o'clock," said Marilee.

"Perfect," said Polly. "We should be back at our hotel by around two forty-five or three o'clock. Then we get ready to head to the airport. An ideal schedule." She laughed, then took a sip of her wine.

"Yeah," I said. "Well, we've already established that you are a crazy lunatic," I said. "But Marilee, can you keep going with no sleep?"

She rose and stepped over to my chair, fell to her knees and took my hands in hers. "Dear friend, I have the rest of my life to sleep."

I started sobbing, as did Marilee and then Polly.

After that, it seemed we all ran out of steam. We

each ate a bit, and then fell soundly asleep, Marilee and I in our respective chairs, and Polly on the couch. It was the kind of sleep I'd been fantasizing about since the accident. Real, dead-to-the-world, dreamless slumber.

Chapter 22

I was jolted awake by a loud banging on the door. Juan Carlos let himself in. He said, "You have fifteen minutes with Senora Perez—no more." We all hurried to regain our focus and scrambled back into our shoes to follow him down the hallway. We were taken to Liliana's suite where two guards stood sentry. Juan Carlos ignored them, knocked, then used his key to admit us. He pointed to a large, opulently furnished living room. "Wait here, please."

We eyed each other, then took seats on one of the long couches. I was now wearing the chain and locket and didn't ever plan to take it off again. I hoped Liliana wouldn't ask me to do so because I wasn't sure how I would respond.

"How do you even tell your story in fifteen minutes?" Polly asked.

"I can do it," I said. I'd learned in presenting arguments in court that some parts needed to be condensed—or even eliminated—so there would be time for more important points to be made without speed-speaking. I planned to say something like, "My parents recently died in a terrible accident. In going through their belongings, I found documents stating that I had been adopted as an infant—something I'd never been told. I was born in a hospital in Oruro. I searched for information back at home, but it became clear that my parents had worked hard to keep the details of my birth a secret. The question that haunts me is: why?

"Here, we learned of a woman from the hospital who remembered my birth almost fifty years ago, of all the hundreds she'd seen. She remembered because my birth-mother was a nun. We have been able to confirm that it was Sister Mary Olivia who gave birth to me when she was twenty-two. We were able to find her and visit with her. We went twice because Sister now has dementia and only comes out of the fog a few times a week—and only very early in the morning. Somehow, she recognized me and said my name, and she mentioned a man, and we were able to find my birth-father. And she gave me a chain and locket and said, 'This is you.' The locket holds a key to something, but we don't know what. We leave Bolivia in a few hours, and we are hoping you are the friend who—here, I would use Liliana's own words—holds her secrets."

I thought again. Even that was too much to digest. I had just started over, further condensing it in my mind, when Liliana elegantly swept into the room, wearing the same yellow gown Marilee and I had glimpsed her in. I was the last to introduce myself to her, and I was so nervous my hands were sweaty and shaking. She reached toward me, took the locket in her hand, then let it drop between my collar bones.

She stood uncomfortably close to me and looked directly into my eyes. "You are Sister's niece?"

I realized she must be seeing my birth-mother in my face. Mimicking Liliana's regal bearing, I pulled back my shoulders. "I am her daughter."

She raised her eyebrows. "I see."

I had no idea what her reaction meant, but I couldn't

help feeling immediate relief when she didn't slap me for what she must've taken as blasphemy about Sister Mary Olivia.

"Please, ladies, take a seat. And tell me why you've taken such an unorthodox approach to getting an appointment with me."

I glanced at my watch and saw that we still had fourteen minutes.

We sat back down, in a row like birds on a telephone wire. I couldn't imagine what first impression she was getting. I had to start speaking, and quickly. "Recently, this past October, my parents were killed in a horrible auto accident—well, with a truck—and my husband died, too."

That was it for me. The tears flowed, my tongue swelled, and I could speak no more words. While I dabbed at my eyes with a tissue that Marilee handed to me, Polly jumped in and told the story, skipping some parts and adding dramatic embellishments, in just a few minutes.

Liliana looked concerned. "Ms. Kuharski—"

"Polly, please."

"Polly, forgive me, but do you always speak so fast?"

Polly laughed and said, "Never. But we were given a hard fifteen minutes." Then she glanced at Juan Carlos, who had stationed himself just inside the closed door.

Liliana laughed. "Such things hardly exist in Bolivia. My boyfriend—" Now she nodded at Juan Carlos. "He is always protecting me and my time. But I would like to know more. And, please, take your time."

Polly started over, and between her and Marilee, they covered absolutely everything. Liliana seemed rapt, but asked no questions. Once Marilee and Polly finished the story, Liliana rose and walked over to me. I stood, not knowing what was about to happen. She hugged me, a gentle, long hug. Then she touched my face ever so gently and returned to her seat. She said, "Now I will tell you my story. I was only sixteen years old when my parents decided I should work every Saturday with Sister Mary Olivia in the gardens behind the convent of the Sisters of St. Lucia. It was to repay her for arranging to have my brother released from jail. Of course, he was a political prisoner, like most of the young men there in those days."

Like Polly, she seemed to be accustomed to story-telling. She spoke with almost unaccented English. Although her voice was light and feminine, it was also resonant and commanded attention. I assumed she'd become an accomplished speaker through her work.

Liliana studied her hands as she spoke. "At first, I resented having to work in the hot sun, ruining my hands, and missing time with my friends." After that, she kept her eyes on me. "But after a few months, I began to see Sister Mary Olivia as a friend. You see, while I was only sixteen, she wasn't that much older—just twenty-three. She was like an older sister, and then as I matured, a friend. I knew things she did not—about the families she served, about courtship and marriage traditions, and about what really went on in our schools and prisons. And, of course, she knew so much that I did not." She nodded to me as though this fact reflected well on Sister Mary Olivia's daughter.

"She left it up to me, and I opted to speak with her only in English. She encouraged this choice because my English was rudimentary, while her Spanish was quite good. Also, we both knew that proficiency in English should help me get a good job."

I was so engrossed in Liliana's story that I calmed down a bit and used every ounce of my energy to focus on each word she spoke.

"Once we became close, she told me she longed to have a private place to keep certain small items she treasured. Of course, she was not permitted the luxury of possessions at the convent. She said the things were of no monetary value. Only sentimental. I told my parents about her wish. One day, my father approached me when I was alone. He said that he and a few of the other fathers whose sons she had helped had made a gift for Sister Mary Olivia. Understanding the need for secrecy, they had put a lock on the gift. Of course, it had to be something that I could carry with me on my Saturday visits so that she could enjoy the items away from the other sisters. Then I would take the package home with me until the next Saturday. There was only one key, and it was for Sister Mary Olivia." She smiled softly, and it was obvious how much she appreciated her father's kindness.

"When he presented the item to me, I was stunned. It was a gorgeous slim, brown leather envelope, probably measuring ten inches by fifteen inches, decorated with engravings of flowers, and with a flap secured in place by a silver lock. Then my father showed me the chain and locket—the one Sister Mary Olivia gave to you, Suzanne. The one you wear."

At that moment, I assumed I would soon see what was contained in the envelope and I prayed it was about me because that would be more proof of my birth-mother's love. I didn't trust myself to get any words out without falling apart again. I swallowed hard, trying to loosen my throat.

Liliana continued, "Of course, I have kept an eye on my old friend since she left Oruro for Cochabamba. Friends of mine look in on her for me. But I did not know that she sometimes comes out of the fog in the early morning. I will stop to see her before heading out on our river trip."

"Did you know of Bradley and the pregnancy?" asked Marilee.

"Not a word that was direct. However, she often spoke of true love, so I assumed she'd been in love before entering the convent. There is more I would like you to know about your mother, Suzanne. She was my closest friend. Yes. But she was also my mentor. She and I planned each of my career moves together. She was an insightful woman, not only bright, but also practical." Liliana turned toward the door and said something in Spanish to Juan Carlos, who then pivoted, walked through the door, and closed it behind him.

Liliana got up to pour herself a glass of red wine and offered to pour for each of us. Only Polly accepted, and Liliana gave her a big smile before returning to her chair and getting settled in. "I was seventeen when I was married to a man who I'd grown up knowing."

This was what Senora Choque had said to Polly, but I hadn't expected Liliana to share it with us. Then it hit me. The story had something to do with my mother.

"For the first few months, he was kind and gentle with me. But he was strongly opposed to me working at the hotels because it made it look as though he was an inadequate provider. I loved my job, but I didn't want to upset him, so I settled in to be a homemaker. I kept our small home immaculate, although there was no money for flowers. I laundered our clothes, washed the dishes, and made the best meals I could on our budget." It was obvious the story was leading somewhere momentous, but Liliana seemed almost serene recounting it.

"He had always liked to drink, but before we were married, I'd never seen him drink to excess. After we lost the extra income I brought in, his mood soured and he began to drink more heavily. In another six months, his drinking had become a serious problem. When he first struck me, I was shocked. Of course, he apologized in the morning and brought me flowers and candies. But it happened over and over again, always followed by gifts in the morning."

I clenched my teeth, and Polly audibly groaned.

"A year and a half later, I became pregnant. I was four months with our child when Pedro kicked me so hard that I lost the baby. As I said, he'd hit me with his fists many times, but he'd never kicked me before. But that time, even before I knew I'd lost the baby, was different. My face bounced off the concrete floor twice, and then it stayed down. The coolness of the hard surface against my cheek was like a glass of cold water thrown at me to rouse me from a deep sleep. I remained on the floor to protect myself and the baby. But my mind was in a new place. I decided that I didn't want to live like that."

"Oh, my," Marilee whispered.

"This time, when Sister Mary Olivia asked about the bruises, I did not lie. She told me I must leave him. She also said that she would help me get a legal divorce. Of course, I was shocked because the Catholic Church doesn't recognize divorce."

Marilee asked, "Did you ask her how she reconciled that?"

"I did. We were close friends by then so I didn't feel constrained by opprobrium. Her answer went something like this: 'We all make mistakes. It is part of the human condition. You made a mistake when you married Pedro. You made a mistake to stay with him after he beat you the first time. The Church also makes mistakes. Its refusal to recognize divorce is one of them.' Sister's permission meant the world to me. I accepted what she said, and never looked back."

"How did your parents take it?" asked Marilee.

Liliana threw her head back and smiled softly. "Not happy. But as long as I did not remarry, I could still receive the sacraments. And it didn't hurt that I was soon able to send them money every month. Today, I am a successful businesswoman and I love my work. I am respected in the community."

"From what I've heard, you are idolized in the community," said Polly.

Liliana nodded to her. "If I had remained with Pedro, I would be a poor, uneducated, beaten housewife. Well, I believe I chose the better course, and I would not have done so without the advice and encouragement of my best friend, your mother, Suzanne."

"Amazing," whispered Marilee.

"Being a feminist, I couldn't be happier for you," said Polly.

"Me, as well," I said. "You have made the life you deserve." I was still concerned about her needing to leave us for the river trip, so I risked irritating her by abruptly changing the subject to ask the question. "Do you still have the leather pouch?"

She studied me for a moment, and I hoped she didn't think I was rushing her story. She said, "My plan was to destroy it upon Sister Mary Olivia's death. But she isn't dead yet, is she?" She gave us a dazzling smile which reminded me of Polly in how theatrical it seemed. She rose and stepped into another room in the suite, closing the door behind her.

My heart raced. Marilee said, "I'm so nervous I think I might have a heart attack."

"Please don't," said Polly. "It would only delay the presentation of the pouch."

Marilee laughed, then said, "Okay. Fine, I'll take deep breaths instead."

A few minutes later, Liliana returned carrying the antique leather pouch with the silver hasp. She walked up to me and gently placed it in my hands as though it were a sacrament. She stood over me, just looking at me holding the treasure, then she walked back toward the door she'd just come through. She said, "Suzanne, what is in the satchel is your business. It is part of the amazing quest you have shared with your friends. I must change now for my trip. I hope that what you find will bring you peace." She was half-way through the door when she turned and looked at Polly. "You have a beautiful voice. I'd like to think that you sing every day."

Polly cocked her head, eyes as bright as ever. "Thank you. I do, actually."

I loved that Liliana's comment was about joy, rather than commerce.

We all rose to thank her, but she waved us back down, smiled again, and exited.

We needed a moment to digest everything that had happened at Hotel Liliana. I broke the silence. "Okay."

Polly said, breathlessly, "Before you open it, think about your birth-mother's words. 'This is you.' "

I nodded. I opened the tiny clasp on the locket and poured the little key into my hand. What I really wanted to do was to take another moment to ponder the choices Sister Mary Olivia had made that had so profoundly affected me. But I feared we wouldn't be allowed to stay long after Liliana's departure. So, again I said, "Okay." I added, "I'm ready." I took a deep breath and inserted the key into the lock, turned it a quarter-turn and heard the faintest "click." The flap was released, and I lifted it slowly. I put my hand inside and felt nothing but pieces of heavy paper. I wrapped my fingers around them, pulled them all out at once, and set them on the coffee table before me. I swallowed hard.

They were photographs of me. Four by sixes, and five by sevens—none larger. They were all in color and in order. On top were the baby pictures, six months, twelve months, eighteen months—every six months. I noticed that my freckles didn't appear until I was two. The pre-school pictures had been taken at my day-care center, the name of which was printed on the bottom. Next were grammar school pictures. So that was what this was all about—a progress report on my life. I tidied the pile and started over in order to examine each picture carefully. Marilee and Polly slid in closer for the viewing and had me scrunched in between them. Polly kept exclaiming about how cute I was.

As I started again, the very first portrait was of me as a baby girl, sitting up holding a small teddy bear. When I set it face-down to move onto the next, I saw words on the back in Mom's small, neat printing. "Our Suzanne at six months."

Polly said. "Bingo. That's why Sister Mary Olivia said, 'Our Suzanne.' Your adoptive mother sent all of these to your birth-mother."

"That was incredibly kind." Marilee looked up at me. "You did tell us that Betty was an especially kind woman."

"Yes," I said.

Seeing this connection between my adoptive mother and my birth-mother overwhelmed me. Tears streamed down my cheeks. Without the tissues Marilee handed me, I wouldn't have been able to continue. And my whole life was right there. "This is you." After the sweet baby poses were the annual school pictures showing my evolution from preschooler to first-grader with a gap between my teeth. It was the very picture on the mug I still used at home. Grammar school in my Catholic school uniform, three years of braces, high school, and finally—one of the few five-by-sevens—high school graduation. In the college and law school graduation pictures, I stood holding red roses in front of university buildings. The remainder of the four-by-sixes were of me posing in whatever outfit I thought looked cool at the time. My favorite wedding picture, the one of me and Mac dancing and laughing at ourselves, was the same image I kept on my hall table. The last picture was one my mother had me pose for in her garden, two years before her death. I still wore the summer dress I had on that day. On the back side of every single one of the photos were the words "Our Suzanne" and the date.

My mouth hung open. Of course, this was how Sister Mary Olivia had recognized me in that brief moment of lucidity. She'd known what I looked like my entire life.

Marilee said, "Do you think your birth-mother and your adoptive mother ever met?"

I was still too stunned to speak.

Polly said, "They probably didn't. Remember, it was Bartholomew, Darren's dad, who came down to pick up Suzanne a few days after her birth. And"—she nodded at me—"Suzanne told us her parents never travelled to South America."

"This is so amazing," said Marilee. She looked off toward the window for a moment. "This is why Sister Mary Olivia was so certain you were you."

Polly glanced at her watch. "Crap. It's 2:15. We'd better head back to the hotel. We need to be at the airport in under three hours, guys." She rang for our taxi, but there was no answer. She said, "We're stranded."

Marilee said to her, "Call your friend, Angelo. I'll bet he'd climb out of his warm bed for double-time pay."

He was at the front entrance to Hotel Liliana in forty-five minutes. In another thirty, we were waking up Senora Choque. It took her fifteen minutes to get herself together and unlock the front door for us. As we passed through, she raised her eyebrows, and Polly told her we'd met with Liliana. Senora Choque smiled and handed us our room key.

"Las cuatro y media de la manana por un taxi?" said Polly.

Senora Choque responded with a long sigh, as though we were her exasperating teenagers. Then she said, "Si," and made a call.

Chapter 23

There was so much new information to digest that we talked non-stop while packing and awaiting the cab's arrival at Hotel LaRosa to take us to the airport. We thanked Senora Choque and handed her an envelope with a nice tip. After the crazy hours we'd kept, she'd certainly earned it. Because Marilee and I knew we had to show up at the office the next day, we couldn't chance missing the flight home. We hurried into the airport and arrived at the check-in counter a full two hours before our flight, passports in hand, carry-on bags and purses in tow. I held Sister Mary Olivia's pouch tight in my hand.

We were glad we had when we saw the line at security, winding around the metal stanchions, probably three or four times. We'd finally made our way to within fifteen feet of the front of the queue when I said, "Oh, shit."

"What?" asked Marilee.

My heart was racing, and my tongue grew thick. I realized we hadn't given it a thought since receiving the pouch from Angelo—probably because the discussion about it felt contentious. But it certainly needed to be back in the conversation now. "In my purse. The fabric bag—"

Marilee's eyes grew larger. "Oh, no."

Polly took a deep breath, then pulled us in toward her as she whispered. "It's illegal to transport coca leaves to the U.S."

I hissed, "I know."

She looked startled, so I added, "Sorry."

"Guys, I don't have time to go to the back of the line to throw this in the trash container," I said.

Marilee stuck her head out of our huddle to look. "Damn. The line's even longer now."

My heart sank. "I had a premonition I'd be arrested on this trip."

"Hush!" said Polly. This time, I startled. She smiled, then added, "I'm thinking."

Marilee whispered to me, "Worst case scenario, you miss the flight. You are not dumb enough to try to take that bag through security, so you won't get arrested."

She meant it to be comforting, but I felt abandoned.

Polly's eyes lit up as she gave me a quick, radiant smile. "It's not a problem." She slipped out of her coat, then her sweater, then her blouse. She was wearing only a pale blue camisole, which might've passed on a beach.

"Suzanne, slip the pouch into my purse."

When I hesitated, she said, "Now!"

She was holding her tote open, so I made the drop. Without another word, she turned and made her way back, as though unthreading the queue we'd just come through. Marilee and I could hear her cheery voice saying, "Excuse me. Pardon me. Lo siento." Occasionally, I heard her say in English, "Silly me. I forgot to dump my water bottle in the trash," followed by a sentence or two in Spanish. I caught glimpses of her blonde ponytail pop into view among the travelers, who were mainly people with dark skin, in dark clothing and hats.

She made it all the way back to the trash container,

and then traced her steps until she re-joined us, in under two minutes. She took her blouse and sweater from Marilee's arm and slipped back into them, then placed her coat over her arm. We still had two people ahead of us in the line.

I could feel my eyes had turned into saucers. "Polly, what the heck?"

She smiled. "I figured, people who might not be paying attention to me leaving would think I was cutting in line when I was on my way back. So, I got nearly naked so nobody would miss the exhibitionist American, running back to get rid of her water bottle."

Marilee said, "Interesting tactic."

Polly nodded. "So I just kept explaining what I was doing." She paused. "I think it worked. People stepped aside for me on my way back."

I said, "But—

Polly sighed dramatically. "I just hope nobody I know is in that line. My cami is practically see-through."

Marilee said, "We noticed that. Weren't you embarrassed?"

Polly nodded. "I was mortified."

"Then you're a hell of an actress," said Marilee.

"Thanks."

I said, "That was very kind—"

Marilee interrupted. "Guys, it's our turn."

The three of us were seated separately on each of the flights that made up the trip from Oruro to Charlottesville in thirty-something hours. Even if we'd been seated together, I doubted we'd have talked since we were all flat-out exhausted. By the time we found each other to go through customs in Miami, they both looked like I felt—about to drop. Thankfully, once we reached home, we didn't have to wait at the luggage carousel because we'd each managed to stuff everything we wanted into a roll-aboard. And, since we'd flown out of Charlottesville before, we knew where to head to grab taxis.

It was 9:00 p.m. local time on a Sunday, and the queue for cabs was short. Every fiber of my being yearned to sit down with my friends over a nice dinner to process what we'd done and what we'd learned. But our level of fatigue made that impossible. We hugged, and cried, and said we'd talk soon.

My own house seemed foreign to me after only a week. The yellow walls were painted a lighter hue than I'd remembered, and the entire space seemed to have doubled in size. But I felt confident I'd re-acclimate in the next couple of days. I mustered the energy to scrub my face in the kitchen sink while the tea kettle rattled and eventually shrieked. When I realized I was out of tea bags, I took a glass of water to the booth to think, and soon nodded off. I awoke to find my face planted on the table.

I forced myself to make it to the couch, pulled my mother's prized alpaca throw, "from Bolivia," over myself, and fell into a deep sleep. I snoozed away, straight through, for ten hours. When I awoke at 8:00, it was to the crack of lightning and the roar of thunder. As I opened my eyes, I wasn't shocked to realize that Mac and my parents were dead. I guess I'd said it so many times by then that the reality had finally penetrated my subconscious mind. I remained on the couch, letting my eyes do the work surveying the room and reacquainting me with my home—for the second time.

I rose and did some stretches, then stepped into the

half-bath to wash my face again and brush my teeth. Back at the kitchen island, I automatically pulled out the tea drawer, forgetting that I'd failed to replenish. I decided to celebrate being home by braving the driving rain for a large black tea with honey and a slice of warm banana bread. First, I called John to remind him I'd be in around noon to work for a half day. He said that was unnecessary, that everything was under control, and that he'd already spoken with Marilee. He insisted that she and I take the day to recover from the jet lag. I was hugely relieved. As much as I wanted to get back to work, my body was telling me it wasn't quite ready.

Still wearing my travelling clothes, black sweats designed to not look like sweats, I grabbed my purse and opened the closet door in search of an umbrella or raincoat. I tried to step in so I could reach the umbrella I saw hanging on the back wall, but my foot struck something. "What the hell?"

When I looked down, I couldn't place the cardboard box at my feet. I assumed it was a delivery I hadn't had time to open and had shoved in the closet. I pulled it out and saw the large black "X" on the top. I remembered it was the box of photo albums I'd stuck in there to get out of the way the day Marilee and Polly helped me clean out my parents' attic.

I lugged the box to the large, square mission coffee table. There was no question it could support the box, and several more. For some reason, I now felt no compunction about paging through their old photos, and decided to make it a little celebration of how far I'd come. So I hurried back to the closet to grab my hooded raincoat and hurried out through the pouring rain to a nearby coffee shop that offered drive-through service.

Back within twenty minutes, I tossed my soaked raincoat over the kitchen counter and unwrapped the bread to set it on a plate. After being away from the luxuries of drive-throughs and having my own thermostat for temperature control, I was feeling mellow to be back in my cocoon. I gazed at the box on the coffee table, then poured my tea into my favorite mug, carried it and the bread to the living room, and set them beside the box.

Pulling open the cardboard on top, I could see there were four volumes, each covered in the same cracked, peeling, red leather. I assumed these were my mom's pre-Suzanne albums, and I knew for certain I'd never seen them before. I'd asked her about her wedding album, but she'd lied, and told me it had been ruined when the basement of their first apartment flooded. Of course, that fib was totally unnecessary because I hadn't been born at the time of the wedding. I shook my head and said out loud, "Mother, whatever were you thinking?"

I grabbed one of the albums from the back of the box to start with. It began with pictures of my parents, looking unbelievably young—maybe nineteen or twenty—playing in the snow. Other pictures showed them sitting side-by-side at restaurants or walking in the woods. One was of them standing at the summit of a mountain. Betty had labelled it, "Ron and me, Peaks of Otter." Their happiness was teleported over space and time, and I beamed at the photograph. I sat back and sipped my tea, feeling a contentment which had eluded me since I awoke in the hospital in December.

The next pages were of my mom's wedding shower, but mainly featured the cake, cute decorations, and piles of gifts. Her wedding day behind-the-scenes photos showed her laughing and seemingly careless as she got herself ready to walk down the aisle. They were all such charming images that I couldn't help wondering why in the world these pictures had been hidden from me. They had nothing to do with my adoption twelve years later. Another puzzle-piece I was missing.

The pictures of the actual wedding were priceless. Mom, looking stunning in a satin, high-necked, ivory gown, and Dad, so handsome in a traditional black tuxedo. The bridesmaids wore Mom's favorite color, pale yellow, a hell of a hue to pull off unless you are a brunette or have a dark complexion. But they'd all managed it, and looked beautiful. It struck me that the fact of Mom's and Dad's existence and loss no longer dragged me into melancholy. I took a long sip of my tea, then turned to the next page. The remainder of the pictures taken on the wedding day were from the reception. Someone seemed to have gotten a picture of the bride, or the bridal couple, with each guest or guest couple. There were six pictures to one side of each page, and they were all filled with faces I didn't know. I was starting to lose interest in all the strangers, when I turned another page. My eyes locked on the first picture. My heart raced and I started to hyperventilate. I quickly got myself down on the floor and put my feet up on the edge of the coffee table. Forcing myself to take long, slow breaths helped after a couple of minutes. I rose, carefully, but didn't return to the photograph that had shocked me. Instead, I ran up the stairs to where my desk sat in a second-floor alcove. I grabbed the top desk drawer and pulled so hard that the thing came all the way out and crashed with a commotion that echoed through the house. I rifled through the junk on the floor until I got my hands on my magnifying glass.

I knew I had to slow down or I'd be lying on the floor with my feet on the coffee table again. I stood perfectly still as I counted off sixty seconds, then slowly took the stairs back down to the living room, magnifying glass in hand. I approached the album cautiously, as though it were about to explode. As I settled myself on the couch and pulled the Bolivian throw over my legs, I took my time the way the bomb squad guy does in the movies. Ever-so-gently, I lifted the book from the table, keeping it turned to the same page, and placed it on my knees.

I raised the magnifying glass to the picture of my mother in her bridal gown, arm-in-arm with a girl maybe ten years old—a child-sized version of Betty. Both beamed at the camera. Beneath the photo, as with all the others, Mom had written the names of the people featured. Under this one, she'd written in her unmistakable hand, "Me with my little sister, Olivia."

"Oh, my God. Oh, my God." I couldn't stop saying it. "Oh, my God." My adoptive mother was my biological aunt. "Oh, my God."

I assumed the other albums were probably pre-wedding day, and I was right. They held Betty's childhood pictures, as well as Olivia's. Although the sisters were ten years apart, it appeared they did a lot together. Olivia at her big sister's birthday parties, Betty at Olivia's. Olivia at Betty's school plays, high school graduation, and college graduation. And they looked like sisters, Olivia a smaller-sized version of beautiful Betty. I kept saying, "Oh, my God," as though those were the only three words I knew.

Thinking about the little, freckle-faced, auburn-haired child being the woman in the wheelchair in Cochabamba felt like blasphemy. It was ridiculous. But it was true. I squinted at the pictures, I shook my head at them, and every time I viewed a new page, my chin dropped again. I struggled to absorb what I was seeing and decided to make sense of it later. I took a full hour to closely examine each photo that included Betty or Olivia. When I closed the back cover of the last of the books, I decided to keep calm and let it all soak in. I leaned back and put my feet up on the coffee table.

So, Betty found a baby to adopt because her little sister, who happened to be a nun, got pregnant. Of course, abortion had to have been out of the question. Maybe. I wondered if Olivia had considered it. After all, Liliana told us how Sister Mary Olivia had dismissed the Church's teachings on divorce. Mom had told me how much she and Dad had been through trying to conceive. Her little sister's misfortune was her own gift from the gods. Evidently, Olivia insisted that Mom and Dad keep quiet about my whole birth-story because she thought she was protecting Bradley. What a soap opera.

I took a sip of lukewarm tea from my mug and let all of the revelations percolate. Percolating didn't last long before I boiled over.

I texted Marilee and Polly. *There's a development. Can you come over? Polly, I understand if you can't get away from work.*

Marilee responded a couple of seconds later. *On my way.*

Polly's text came through a minute later. *I'd forgotten today is a national test day. But no Spanish, so I'm not a proctor. I'm on my way, too. Don't say anything important til I get there!*

I still had no tea bags, so I made a pot of coffee. The whole time I waited for them I was seething, which was strange because I'm not generally a seether. I alternated between pacing the length of my great room, and stopping to stare out the window-wall at the storm. Now that I'd nailed down the whole story, I felt no relief whatsoever. What I felt was fury.

It was 40 minutes before Marilee and Polly showed up at the door—within minutes of each other. As they stepped in and handed me their dripping wet raincoats and umbrellas, Polly said, "Good. I haven't missed anything. What's the news?"

I smiled and pretended to be calm and relaxed. "You guys come and sit with me around the coffee table. I have something to show you."

Marilee said, "Sure. But hugs first. I miss you guys already."

I wasn't thrilled with the delay for the embrace, but pretended there was nothing I'd rather do.

They started to take seats in the armchairs, but I said, "You two sit on the couch. That way you can both see at the same time."

Polly asked, "See what?" I ignored her, wanting to set up the viewing just right.

I'd earlier removed the box of photo albums and placed it behind the rocker. I suppose it had offended me so much, I didn't want it in my sight. As I slid it out again, then leaned over to lift it, Polly said, "That's the box of albums from your mom's attic. Right?"

"Yep." I set it on the coffee table, directly in front of my friends, then served the cups of coffee.

Marilee looked at me and said, "Suzanne, you are

white as a ghost. What the hell did you find in here?"

I was taken aback that my effort to look cool and collected hadn't worked. I gave her a tight smile, then said, "There are four albums, in chronological order. Start with the last. Then you can go back to look at the others later if you want to."

"Okay," said Marilee, warily. She reached into the box and selected the album, then set it on her knees so both she and Polly had a good view.

As they surveyed the first page, Polly said, "This is your adoptive mother, Betty. I remember her from the wedding photo you showed me at her house."

"Yes."

Marilee said, "These must be her albums from before you were born. I mean, she looks so young. And your dad looks like a child."

"Yes."

They were both smiling and taking sips of their coffees as they studied the first few pages. "Ah," said Polly. "Here's another picture with your dad in it. And she's wearing a corsage, so I suppose they were on a date." She looked up at me. "These are precious, Suzanne. Thanks for calling us to come over and enjoy them with you."

I wondered what overabundance of generosity would make her grateful if that were all there were to it.

She smiled and took a sip of her coffee.

"You're welcome."

"Oh, this must be the rehearsal dinner," said Marilee. Apparently, they both thought I'd called them out in the rain, in spite of their major jet lag, just to share my folks' ancient photo albums with them.

"Yes."

"And Betty preparing for her wedding—" said Polly with too much enthusiasm.

Marilee said, "So, you said there's been a development." She raised her eyebrows.

"Yes. Keep reading."

They turned the page to a loud clap of thunder, which made Marilee jump and Polly laugh. I could tell that, all along, they'd been reading the little notes identifying the people in the pictures. Marilee's chin dropped and her eyes widened. She nudged Polly and pointed.

Polly's eyes grew even larger than Marilee's—of course. She said, "What the fuck?"

It was the first time I'd heard her swear and I found it completely appropriate. I rose and handed them my magnifying glass.

"Sister Mary Olivia is your mom's sister?" asked Polly.

"Yes."

"Holy moly," said Marilee.

"Oh, my God," Polly said three times.

"That's exactly what I said when I saw the picture." I rose. "Let me warm up your coffees. You guys, take a look through the other albums. You don't have to study them. It's interesting seeing my birth mother and my adoptive mother as children. Look at their eyes. I get the impression they pretty much adored each other." I assumed what was left of their coffees must be luke-warm, so I brewed a fresh pot. By the time I served the three mugs, they'd piled all of the albums just beside the box.

Polly glanced at the pile, "Sorry, Suzanne. We couldn't concentrate on the other photos since we're both in shock."

"That's okay," I said.

"I don't know what to say," said Marilee. "How does this make you feel, sweetie?"

"Terrible."

"Why terrible?" asked Polly.

I was sitting across from them in an arm chair. But I stood to answer, and paced, with the storm as my backdrop, to answer. "Because it's all bullshit. It was stupid. It was unnecessary." I paused. "And it cost me." My friends watched me cautiously, as though my anger might ignite. "I might've known my birth-mother. I might've known Bradley. Bradley might've known he was a father. Betty and Ron might've been spared the stress of keeping Olivia's big secret. My mother and her little sister might've visited each other." I stared at Polly as though she'd caused it all.

She raised her eyebrows and pretended to cower.

"Sorry, guys. It's just that I have no place for my fury to land."

"Do you want to talk about it?" asked Marilee.

"Of course, it would be fine if you prefer that we rant and rave with you," said Polly.

I laughed. "Polly, if you got to ranting and raving in my house, I'd fear for the rafters. Listen. I really can calm down. But do you see my point?"

"Sure," said Marilee. "I can't disagree with anything you've said. I think the whole mess hurt you and Bradley the most."

"I don't know," said Polly.

"What?" I asked.

"Well, I've been thinking about Bradley. Don't get me wrong. I like him a lot. And I'd be an idiot not to admire his work. But wasn't he more a chump than a victim?"

Marilee studied her. "A chump?"

I said, "Let's stop right here." I stood directly in front of Polly.

She blinked a couple of times, then said, "I'm sorry if that offended you, Suzanne."

"Oh, I'm not offended. I was just wondering if you guys think it's too early for a glass of wine?"

Polly smiled, dramatically lifted her left wrist, and looked at her watch. "Almost ten thirty. Do you have any white?"

Fortunately, there were crackers in my pantry and some good cheeses in my fridge. I took my time laying out the appetizers, wine bottle, and glasses on the coffee table because I needed to cool down to have a meaningful conversation with my friends.

Once I'd served the chardonnay, I sat back down and looked at Polly. "You were saying something about my birth-father being a chump?"

She smiled. "Don't you think? I mean, look. He's passionately in love with an amazing woman, and he only asks her once?"

"She did tell him never to contact her again," said Marilee.

"Exactly!" said Polly. "Because if she saw him again, she wouldn't be able to resist him."

"Fair enough," said Marilee. "That was pretty chumpy." She eyed me for my reaction, but I didn't give her one.

Polly said, "Suzanne, surely you've seen enough romantic comedies to know that the pursuit is ninety percent of the story. Imagine any of your favorites. The film would last about five minutes if, at the first rejection, the protagonist had said, 'Oh, she doesn't want me. I'll just give up.' So, Bradley was a chump. Right?"

"Fine. I concede," I said.

She added in a whisper, "And that's not all."

"More chumpiness?" asked Marilee.

"Judge for yourselves," said Polly. "So, the woman he adores with every fiber of his being is a no-go. But ten years later, he's no longer a priest. Why doesn't he marry some woman who is the second most attractive to him, have a nice family, and experience the love a father has for his children?"

"Chump?" I asked.

"Of course," said Polly. "I get that he was a romantic. But what's wrong with the alternative scenario I've suggested?"

Marilee said, "For one thing, he'd always be pining for the first woman."

Polly cocked her head. "And you guys don't think that happens all the time?"

That stumped me. "It hasn't happened to me. You, Marilee?"

"I haven't even found the first love-of-my-life, much less lost him and settled for someone else. Has it happened to you, Polly?'

She snorted. "I thought it happened to everyone."

I shook my head. "Do you want to share with the class?"

She twisted her mouth before she spoke. "Okay. But I wasn't the lover. I was the lovee. I did send him packing, and he did eventually marry and have children."

Marilee said, "So how do you know he's still pining for you? Looks across a crowded room?"

"He told me."

"Holy smokes!" said Marilee.

"What did he want from you?" I asked, then rolled my eyes.

"Nothing. He wasn't proposing an affair. He wasn't telling me he'd leave his wife if I ever changed my mind. In fact, he told me he'd never do either. He just felt like being honest. So, he told me he was still in love with me."

The guy in Polly's story was starting to irritate me. "For what purpose, Polly?"

"No purpose that I could discern."

"That's just weird," said Marilee.

"I guess," said Polly. "My point is just that Bradley could've had a wife and children, and I think he was acting a bit like a martyr not to."

"That's quite a statement," I said. "I don't think it was such a bad thing that he took his lover at her word and respected her wishes. Maybe he doesn't watch romantic comedies. Also, I can see how it would feel deceptive to him to be in love with one woman and marry another. Say whatever you want about my birth-father. I say he's a man of honor—a pretty rare thing."

Polly grinned at me, and I realized she'd intentionally gotten me to defend Bradley.

Marilee caught on as well. She said to Polly, "Was that story about your old lover who is still in love with you even true?"

Polly sighed and shrugged her shoulders. "Maybe not. But it was offered only for illustrative purposes."

I squinted at her—hard.

Her response was to smile and say, "Good. Now shall we go through whether your birth-mother was a chump to go to such lengths to keep the man she loved from losing his job? I mean, his vocation?" She looked from me to Marilee, and back. "And ladies, I'm pretty confident he would've been booted from the priesthood for getting a young nun pregnant." She paused. "And think of the position Betty and Ron were put in. A sacred promise to keep a secret so their fondest dream, parenthood, could come true."

I pursed my lips as I thought about each of them— Sister Mary Olivia, Bradley, my mother and my father. I looked at Polly. "You're saying there's no reason for me to feel so angry."

"Anger is an emotion. I don't think you can help what you feel. But eventually, what you think will be more important. And I just don't believe you'll come down on the side of thinking them all fools."

Marilee said, "I agree with that. They were just doing the best they could with the cards they were dealt." She paused, then shook her head while a smile crept across her face. "And it's so amazing! Had it not been for the accident, you would never have known anything about all of this."

I nodded. "Probably not. But, of course, I'd rather the accident hadn't happened. And I wouldn't know what I didn't know."

"Shall I put these albums back in the box?" asked Polly.

I shrugged. "Sure."

She picked up one of the albums, checking to be sure it was number one of four. As she placed it gently into the box, she said, "Suzanne, there's a layer of old tissue paper in the bottom. Do you want me to pitch it?"

"I don't care." I paused. "I guess."

She pulled out yellowed paper and balled it up. She said, "Wait. What's this?"

I was studying the rim of my empty wine glass. Without looking up, I asked, "What?"

"It's from the very bottom. An old manilla envelope." She raised it, and we all saw that there were no markings on the outside.

Marilee said, "Probably just there to keep dirt from getting in from the bottom."

I glanced at Polly, who was unclasping it. She peaked in. "There's paper inside."

"Really?" I asked.

Polly handed the envelope to me. "You should open it, Suzanne. It's probably something Betty wrote about the albums."

"Like an index?" asked Marilee.

"Who knows," said Polly.

I slid out the two pages, handwritten in ink. "This isn't Mom's handwriting." I scanned the pages quickly. "It's from Olivia to Betty." I looked up at my friends, as though they could tell me what to expect.

"Seriously?" asked Marilee.

I ignored her question.

Polly asked, "Do you want to read it to yourself first?"

I bit my lip for a moment as I thought. "No. You guys have taken every step with me. I'll read it aloud." I flattened the pages on the coffee table, then held the letter up. "It's dated March 18, 1970. 'Dearest Betty—' " That was it for me. My throat swelled and froze in that state. I handed the papers to Polly.

She took a deep breath before beginning. "'*March 18, 1970. Dearest Betty, Since I received your letters,*

I've done little but ponder your questions. Of course, I've also prayed for guidance. Our baby is due in five weeks. If our blessed little one is to be placed in Bartholomew's arms shortly after birth and delivered to you and Ron as expeditiously as possible, we must come to an agreement.

" 'I will not tell you why things must be as I request. Let me just say that the baby's father has done nothing wrong, does not know of my pregnancy, and must never learn of it. It is better that I not explain further because the more you know, the more likely it is that he will be identified at some time, possibly far into the future. If that were to happen, he would lose all, and many innocent people would suffer his loss.

" 'Therefore, I've come up with three requirements for the adoption to go forward. If you and Ron agree to them, we can go through with our plan that you will raise the baby as yours. (I, however, will always think of the child as ours.) You must agree to: 1. Never tell the child that he or she is adopted. 2. Never tell the child that I exist. 3. Ensure that relatives and friends do not reveal the fact of the adoption or that I exist. I do realize this must seem to be far more caution than is reasonably required. I concede that it is extreme. But my resolve to protect the child's father is not open for further discussion.

" 'Finally, you may wonder how you can possibly comply with my third requirement. Here's my suggestion: Tell family and friends that it is my deep desire to completely separate myself from the distraction of the joy of family and friends so that I can dedicate myself one hundred percent to my mission with the poor.

" 'I hope we will continue to exchange letters and

emails until our child is old enough to have the ability to intercept them. At that point, I encourage you to continue to write to me, but I will not respond. Please know that I will treasure any communication from you. My heart is near to breaking at the idea of surrendering this precious baby. However, I find much solace in knowing there are no people on this earth I trust more to raise the little one than you, my dear, amazing sister, and your beloved Ron. Please let me know if we are in agreement. If not, I have much work to do to come up with another plan.

"'All my love to you and Ron always. Your devoted sister, and mother of our cherished child, Olivia'"

I still couldn't speak. I sobbed, and Marilee knelt by my chair handing me tissues from her seemingly inexhaustible supply. Once I slowed down my weeping enough to allow conversation, Polly said, "Whoa. Olivia didn't really give your parents much choice, did she?"

I shook my head.

Marilee patted my hand and asked, "Does the letter make you feel any better about what Betty and Ron did?"

I nodded—a couple of times. When I could finally form words, I said, "But so unnecessary. I mean, I get Olivia's motivation. But what she said about secrets is so true."

Marilee asked, "You mean that someday someone will untangle the web the person wove?"

"Yeah. Not always. But I have to think that the majority of webs are unraveled. And then all hell can break loose. Lives can be changed." I paused. "And even if the secret remains forever intact, its keepers can be damaged by it. Profoundly."

Polly was uncharacteristically quiet. She stared a hole in her lap. I said, "What's on your mind, Polly?"

She startled, then looked at me. "Sorry. I was just thinking about a secret."

"Would you like to share it?" I asked.

Polly bit her lip. She crossed her legs, elbows on her knees, chin on her fists. "I'm considering it."

"You're among friends," I said, staring encouragement at her.

Polly nodded to me. "Yeah. That's why I'm considering it."

I shut up after that.

After a minute or so, Polly rose and paced between us and the window wall. With the light behind her, she reminded me of one of the ducks in a shooting gallery. She kept walking as she spoke. "Edward and I have been separated for almost a year."

"Wait!" I said. "I thought you were single."

Polly glanced at me for a second and smiled. "Married."

Because I'd been hanging out with Polly for over four months, I couldn't imagine how I didn't know this. I turned to Marilee. "You knew?"

"Of course. Polly and I have been friends for a long time."

My mouth hung open. My shoulders rose in a shrug.

"Listen, Suzanne. When I met you, you'd just suffered an incredibly horrendous loss. You were grieving. You're still grieving. I hadn't been with Edward for eight months."

"So?" I asked.

She resumed pacing. "So, I didn't see any reason to burden you with my little problem."

"Divorce isn't a 'little problem,' Polly. And just because I was—am—barely holding on by a thread some days—"

She stopped and looked at me. "I know. I'm so sorry, Suzanne. I should've told you about it." Polly's misery seemed to deflate her entire body. Her usual stage presence disappeared and her words came out so softly as to be almost inaudible. She stopped to look at me. "I'm really sorry."

"It's okay, Polly," I said.

She looked into the distance and took a long breath which seemed to reinflate her. She resumed walking while she spoke. "We were married for two years. I was happy, and I thought Edward was."

I pointed to the couch beside Marilee. "Don't you want to sit?"

She shook her head. "One night, late, after I'd had a ball with our troupe's improv practice, he'd waited up for me. He said he'd decided he wanted a trial separation."

"Out of the blue?" I asked.

"Completely. He said he'd thought I'd settle down once we were married."

"Settle down?" I asked.

She gave me a sad smile. "Edward said he wanted me to give up the improv and stand-up so I could stay home every evening with him."

"Had he ever asked you to do that?" I asked.

"Never. But about six months before this conversation, he'd stopped coming to my shows."

"Strange," said Marilee.

"Yeah. It was very weird because he always came to my shows and even to most of our rehearsals. And he loved to go out to dinner with the troupe afterwards. He's very handsome and pretty darn funny, himself. So, everyone just loved him." She paused and stared at her hands for a moment. "It wasn't just that, though. The night he confronted me, he also said he was having a hard time dealing with my personality. That maybe I could dial it down and be more like the other women he'd dated."

"Jeez," I said. "That's unbelievable."

"Then he said we'd both changed. He thought we'd grown apart."

"What did you say?" I asked.

"I was shocked. I had trouble analyzing what he was asking for. First, I told him that I hadn't changed. He had. I asked him what was really behind it. He said there was nothing else. None of this made any sense to me. Edward is talented at a lot of things, but he's no actor. It was painted on his face that he wasn't trying to be logical—he was trying to be hurtful. And I didn't want to hear any more of it. So, I told him I'd need to think about it overnight."

"I'm sorry, Polly," was all I could think to say.

Polly gave me a little nod, then kept pacing. "The next morning, I dressed for work and went downstairs to grab breakfast a few minutes after him. Edward had just poured himself a cup of coffee. He looked up at me and said, "Shall we go out to dinner tonight and you can let me know what you're thinking."

I gave him a polite hug, then pushed him back so we could look at each other. I said, "No thanks, Edward. I'll stay in a hotel tonight. Then I'll come by to grab all my stuff on the weekend."

He acted surprised. "So, you won't even consider changing for me?"

"By that point, I felt perfectly calm. 'Of course not.

And I wouldn't dream of asking you to change for me.' I walked out. I haven't spent more than a half-hour at a time with him since then."

"So, you're getting a divorce?" I asked.

"He wants me to sign the papers, but I'll do it at my convenience."

"You don't want out?" I asked.

Polly stopped, then knelt before my chair. Her eyes were huge, but not the least bit clouded. "Oh, yes."

I didn't understand. "Then why not sign the papers and move on?"

She said, "I should. I guess I have to admit to a vindictive streak."

"I've never seen a hint of that," I said.

Marilee spoke up. "Polly, why don't you tell Suzanne the rest of the story?"

Polly let out a little sigh. "It was all a lie. He was with another woman, a colleague at the accounting firm where he works."

I said, "Oh, Polly. I really am sorry. What a jerk."

"Yeah." She grabbed my other hand. "It is what it is. What I feel bad about is keeping my story from you."

I smiled. "You said you didn't want to burden me with it. That's a pretty good explanation."

She nodded sharply. "And that was a big part of the reason. But I also felt pathetic about having such a badly failed marriage."

Marilee said, "It was hardly your fault he had an affair."

She glanced at Marilee. "I know." Then she turned to me. "Suzanne, you and Mac loved each other so long and so well that I was a little embarrassed to admit that my husband hadn't felt that way about me."

I said, "I wouldn't have judged you. I mean, I don't judge you."

Polly said, "I know. And I think I've learned a little bit about keeping secrets in the past few months." She rose and returned to the couch, where she plopped down.

I ran my hand through my hair before speaking. "I've apparently given you the impression that Mac and I adored each other. But the truth is, after the first year, he never gave me an indication of any such thing. I often wondered if he felt any romantic love for me at all—after the first flush of our relationship. Of course, we had the usual thrill of infatuation at the beginning, the euphoric sensation you get when you think you've found your soulmate. But after that, it was more like we were life-partners who also had sex." I took a deep breath. "I'm sure he loved me, in his own way. But it was never the kind of adoration Bradley expressed for Olivia."

Marilee said, "I get that. You know, guys, I've actually been wondering about Bradley."

"What about him?" I said, without understanding why it sounded defensive.

"Well, did he just get stuck in the infatuation stage with Olivia because their relationship ended so precipitously? Or is his love actually of a different character than most people's?"

"It's an interesting point," said Polly. "But we'll never know because Bradley and Olivia will never do the dishes, and pay the bills, and fold the laundry together."

"Yeah," I said, knowing I'd give this a lot more thought. "But let's get back to Polly. I looked at her and asked, "Will you sign the divorce papers soon?"

"I will. It's time to move on."

"Good," I said. "Let us know when it's time to go

out and celebrate that."

She smiled and nodded dramatically. "Absolutely."

I said, "It's odd, but all this talk about marriage is reminding me of how much I miss Mac."

"Of course, you do," said Marilee.

"What I mean is that I've been so focused on my birth story that I haven't been feeling Mac's absence. Now that I'm home, I really miss him." I started blubbering. Both of my friends came over to offer hugs, which were awkward because I was still sitting. Once I'd wiped my cheeks, I said, "Sit down, guys. This is just a part of my new reality. I'm okay. Really. And, Polly, I hope you are really okay, too."

"I'm better than ever." She gave me one of her dazzling smiles, and appeared to be fully back to being herself.

I turned to Marilee. "So, is this a good time for you to share your secret?"

She raised her eyebrows. "What secret?"

"Your international adoption," I said.

Her eyes moved from me to Polly and back. "How did you know?"

"I overheard your comment to Polly when we were looking at the newborns in the hospital in Oruro."

"Why didn't you say something, Suzanne?"

"Honestly, I think I was preoccupied. Why didn't you tell me?"

"Same as Polly. I didn't want to distract from our mission."

I thought for a moment, then nodded. "Yeah. I guess it was pretty intense. But what about before that?"

Marilee laughed. "It was a secret! I wanted to wait until it looked likely it might actually happen before telling anyone. Seriously. When I made that comment to Polly in Oruro, it was the first time I'd breathed a word to anybody."

I thought about it. "Fine. I think I would've done the same thing." I paused. "So, how do your prospects look?"

"I'm not sure. One of the problems with international adoptions is that countries are 'open' one day, then 'closed' the next."

"Why?" asked Polly.

"It seems a lot of it is purely political—whether the country is pissed at the U.S. for some reason."

"Crap," said Polly. "Aren't most countries pissed at us?" Marilee and I shrugged. Polly added, "Where are you looking?"

"China, Russia, Uruguay, and South Africa, at the moment. But the truth is, I've been told I have three strikes against me: my age, the fact that I'm single, and that I work outside the home."

I said, "Oh, dear. But still, this is huge news, Marilee. You have to let us know if there's anything we can do to help."

"You've already done it."

"What?" I asked.

"Your story. I've learned that whatever I do, there won't be any secrets."

I smiled. "Very wise."

"I was just thinking about that," said Polly. "I can tell you, I feel better already now that I've shared mine with you, Suzanne. What in the world makes us think they're ever a good idea, anyway?"

I said, "Or that the truth won't come out."

"And now that your mystery has been unraveled,

Suzanne, what will you do?" asked Marilee.

"I don't have any choice but to go back to work tomorrow. I have to get busy on my wrongful death case—possibly a jury trial—and I owe Judge Foster and Darren updates."

"I meant, about going back to see Bradley," said Marilee.

"Of course I'll go because I promised to. And I want to. I just don't know when. I'll have to give it some thought."

"Don't wait too long," said Polly. "As you know better than anyone, none of us can count on another day."

"I'm aware."

The conversation was slowing down, as was the rain. I said, "I think we're running out of steam. Why don't you guys go home and do what we're all supposed to be doing today, recuperating from our trip?"

As she rose from the couch, Polly said, "Excellent idea."

I'd learned a lot about my new friend over the past few months, and especially the past week. But it wasn't until that day that I really appreciated Polly's wisdom.

We all hugged before they stepped out the door into a light drizzle.

Chapter 24

I spent all morning on Tuesday getting up to speed on my files. I knew that a lot can happen in a lawsuit in a week. One new filing, and you have to drop everything else to attend to the emergency. Fortunately, nothing had changed on my matters, except that every deadline was seven days closer.

Around eleven o'clock, John knocked on my door, which was standing open. "Good time to talk about your case?"

I smiled. "Sure, John. Come on in."

He walked in and stood behind one of the two visitor chairs.

"Is anything happening?" I asked.

"Yeah. Something's happening." He seemed so calm that I didn't think it could be a major problem.

"What? Surely, not a trial date."

"No. Following the depositions, the trucker's insurer took a fresh look at the case."

"And?"

"Last week they made a settlement offer."

"Really?"

"Um-hm."

"I told them you were out of the country, but I'd get back to them this week."

"What's the offer?" I picked up my pen and let it hover over my legal pad.

John adjusted the chair in front of him before he spoke. "You could get more from a jury."

"No doubt." I nodded. "So, what's the low-ball offer?"

"One million."

I dated the page and jotted down the number. "And the limits are one million per person, three per occurrence."

"Right. Of course, it's low. Give some thought to how you want to counter."

I leaned back in my chair. "I know how I want to counter. And it's non-negotiable."

"Non-negotiable?"

"Yes."

"Well, don't keep me in suspense. What is it?" He paused. "Wait. Should I sit down to hear this?"

"You would probably want to *if* I were going to answer your question."

"This is a weird conversation, Suzanne. Why would you think it's a good idea to keep your own lawyer in the dark?"

I smiled. "John, I need to do this my way. I'll type up my demand this afternoon. Then I'd like you to set up a meeting with May, Mr. Bixby, a representative of the truck company he worked for, and the lawyer for the boys. This week, if possible. I'll read my counter to them, then hand out copies. They can either accept it or I'll withdraw it and you'll press the court to set a trial date as soon as possible."

"You're serious? You really won't tell me?"

"Don't I look serious?"

John wrinkled his forehead. "Well, that's different." He sighed heavily. "Okay then. I'll call the other lawyers and see if they can do this Thursday or Friday. Are you available then?"

"If they agree, I'll make myself available."

I'd given some thought to the accident on the flights home—the boys' drunken mischief with my stop sign, the explosion, the trucker running around in the field trying to figure out where my car disappeared to. My parents and Mac, here one moment, gone the next—just like Sister Mary Olivia's sanity. And every image and every thought about that day reinforced my belief in the randomness of it all. There is so little of our fates that we control. Some, surely. But just some. I hoped they would all accept my terms because it was the only resolution that would satisfy me. If not, I'd have no choice but to go through with the trauma of the trial. But it would be a little less traumatic because of Bolivia. Because of how many times I'd had to tell the damn story, I could take one more time.

On Wednesday, John stuck his head in my door and told me that May and her clients weren't available for our meeting until Monday. That was fine with me. I was already prepared, and I didn't plan to give an inch. I smiled. "What time?"

"Ten o'clock. Good for you, Suzanne?"

"Perfect."

"Are you planning to tell me what your non-negotiable demand is?"

"No."

He shook his head. "If you were a regular client, I wouldn't let you get away with that."

"But I'm not a regular client. Am I, John? I'm your partner and your friend."

"So you're saying I should just trust you?"

I just stared at him.

He laughed. "I look forward to hearing it on Monday."

I planned to get in touch with Judge Foster on Saturday morning, and arranged for Darren to meet me for brunch on Sunday. I wasn't sure why I was so driven to bring my adoption mystery to closure, but I was ticking off items on my to-do list like something important depended on it.

Chapter 25

I called retired Judge Eileen Foster at 9:00 on Saturday morning. I wanted to catch her before she'd go out and do whatever she did on Saturdays. I sat at my kitchen island, legal pad and pen at the ready, only because it was a habit I'd developed at work—I wrote everything down. No exceptions. I also had a goblet of water and a box of tissues within reach, just in case I'd get emotional—again. She picked up on the first ring.

"Hello. Eileen Foster speaking."

I intentionally slowed my speech down so I wouldn't resemble the inarticulate, blubbering woman I'd been on my first call with her. "Hi, Judge Foster. This is Suzanne Summerfield."

She said, "What a pleasant surprise. And you must try to remember to call me Eileen."

Great. I'd already made a faux pas. She'd asked me to do that—maybe twice—during our first call. "Of course. How are you, Eileen?"

"Just fine. Absolutely nothing new in my life. I hope you've called to tell me what you've learned about your birth story." I'd forgotten how light and lilting her voice was.

"I have. It's rather a long story. Is this a good time for you?"

"I've been waiting for this call since January, Suzanne. I'd make time for it even if I had an appointment with a president." She paused. "Especially if I had an appointment with a president. You see, I'm not fond of politicians."

"Understandable," I said. "Well, good." I took a deep breath, then dove in. "I'll start with what I didn't learn here in Virginia, then on to Bolivia, where I discovered a lot, then back to Virginia for my biggest shock."

"I can tell this is going to be good," she said. "Hold on while I get over to the couch so I can put my feet up. Bad day for my arthritis."

I smiled to myself. I liked her frankness. "Of course. Please take your time. I have nothing on my calendar for today but speaking with you."

She said, "That's very kind, Suzanne. You're like Betty. Aren't you?"

"I hope so."

A minute later, she said, "Okay. All set. And don't leave out any details. There's nothing I like better than a good mystery story."

I told her every bit of it, with more minutiae than I even knew I remembered. I made sure to pause for questions or comments. But all she said throughout was, "Oh, my," and "Heavens!" and "Oh, dear."

I ended with, "So, that's everything I know. I do plan to return to Bolivia to spend some time with Bradley, but I'm not sure when I'll be able to get there."

"Oh, you must! How extraordinary that you found both of your birth-parents. I'm very sorry to learn of Olivia's dementia. But how wonderful that you still have time to develop a relationship with your father. That's just fantastic news, Suzanne."

"Thank you. It is pretty incredible. So, now I have a

question for you."

"All right."

"Eileen, how much of this did you already know?"

"Let me think." She paused for a moment or two. "Of course, I knew Olivia was Betty's little sister. I knew about Olivia's pregnancy and the agreement that Betty and Ron would adopt the baby and keep Olivia's story a secret."

"What did you know about the circumstances of Olivia's pregnancy?"

"Nobody said how she'd become pregnant. I assumed she'd been raped. I never heard a word about Bradley. I do know that Betty and Olivia corresponded. I recall your mother saying she'd been told not to send money because it never made it all the way to the convent. Betty told me she sent pictures, which I imagined made it all more tolerable for Olivia. I would've guessed Olivia enjoyed the photos, then discarded them. Betty mentioned to me that her sister couldn't keep personal items."

"And Liliana?"

"Never heard of her. Although she sounds like a woman I would like."

"I know. Liliana's story blew me away." I paused to take a sip of water. "But, Eileen, are there things I've missed?"

She cleared her throat, which instantly made me fear another bombshell.

"Nothing about what happened fifty years ago. You've certainly enlightened me about the real story there. But there was something your mother said to me the last time we talked. Since you've cracked the case, so to speak, I feel I can share this without betraying

Betty."

I audibly sucked in my breath.

"It's not really anything shocking, Suzanne."

I laughed. "Right. I'm fine."

"Betty told me that the only person she could think of to ask to remove the boxes from her attic was Mac."

"Mac?" This threw me. Mac wasn't a part of this story. I could feel my heart race.

"Um-hmm. She planned to write to him confidentially—at his office."

"Oh, my."

"Wait. Was she going to tell him about my birth-story?"

"I don't know. She didn't say." She paused, then asked, "Why? Does that bother you?" I detected a hint of a suggestion that I was being foolish.

I couldn't understand how Eileen wouldn't appreciate that it darn-well should bother me. I thought about answering sarcastically, but decided against bridge-burning. "She'd be asking a husband to keep a secret from a wife—whether it was just that he would be moving boxes, or whether he was actually told my birth story. I don't think that's—" I tried to think of the correct word. All I could come up with was, "ethical."

"Not ethical?" Her tone suggested she was considering my word choice, rather than judging it.

"Of course not." The more I thought about it, the angrier I became. "How could she?"

"Listen, Suzanne. Betty did the best she could. She'd gone to extraordinary lengths to honor her sister's fervent wish. How could she just abandon her promise because old age was overtaking her? And who did she know whom she trusted and who was young and strong enough to do the job for her?"

I ignored her defense of my mom. "When do you think she sent the letter?"

"She said she was going to send it, and she sounded certain. So I assume it was shortly after our call."

I said, "Obviously, Mac hadn't done what she asked him to do. I wonder if he intended to."

"I have no idea." She paused, and this time I heard her suck in a breath. "But I hope you won't think badly of Betty. My guess is that she agonized over the best way to honor her agreement with Olivia, and she concluded Mac was best-suited for the job."

"I understand what you're saying," I had no desire to argue the point with her, so I paused, then thanked her profusely for her interest and help.

Now that I had one more, tiny piece of the puzzle, I regretted having called Eileen. I so didn't want to think that Mac had agreed to betray me as one of his last acts on earth.

Chapter 26

The next day, I met Darren Long for brunch at a delightful, upscale restaurant that served only breakfast and lunch, and had a huge following. Fortunately, I had thought to make a reservation. The temperature proved perfect for eating on the brick patio under a canopy of mimosa trees, already rejoicing in full, pale-pink blossoms.

As Darren approached my table, I noticed he'd lost the goatee and gained a tan. I smiled as he sat. "Hi, stranger. You look great!"

He leaned over and gave me a quick peck on the cheek before taking the chair across from me. "Thank you." He looked at the ivy-covered exterior of the restaurant and then homed in on the small, stone fountain a few yards from our table. "What a charming setting."

"Isn't it? A friend told me about it. This is my first time here, as well."

He nodded. "You look lovely, Suzanne. Rested. No more worry lines. You must've found some answers."

"Gee, I didn't even know I'd had wrinkles. Just grateful to hear they've vanished. But before I get into Bolivia, how have you been, Darren?"

"Really great, actually."

I raised my eyebrows.

He leaned toward me as he said softly, "I did meet someone."

"Wonderful. Tell me about—him."

Darren chuckled. "*He* is an architect. From Richmond. We met at the precipice of Peaks of Otter when he kindly offered me a bottle of water. Well, since then, everything has just clicked."

I smiled. "I'm so happy for you. What's his name?"

"Daniel."

He said it so softly, and so lovingly, that I felt envious for a moment. I wondered if anyone would ever say my name like that—or ever had. "I hope I'll get to meet him."

"If you're serious, I can definitely make that happen."

"Within a fortnight, then. And I'll invite Marilee and Polly. I'd love for you to meet them."

"Even better." We placed our drink orders. Then Darren said, "So, did your friends help you solve the mystery?"

I took a breath, knowing I had a whole lot of story to tell. "I couldn't have done it without them, Darren." A minute later, our coffees were served, and we took a moment to review the menus and order our brunches. I scrunched up my face and asked if he really wanted to hear all the details.

Darren leaned toward me, again, elbow on the table, chin resting on his hand. He said, "Suzanne, I wish I could've been with you and your friends. But since I couldn't, I want the whole story, quotes, atmosphere—everything."

I started with a description of Hotel la Rosa and Senora Choque. By the time I got to the meeting with Bradley, our meals were served. As I arrived at the part of the story about the shocker the photo album revealed,

Darren had finished his quiche and was patting his lips with his linen napkin. My quiche was down only a couple of bites, my fruit and muffin untouched. Darren nodded at it. "I hope you plan to take that home."

I smiled. "Absolutely."

He leaned back in his chair. "Good. Suzanne, that's an amazing story. And a birth-father? It's what you were hoping for. Isn't it?"

"In a way. After I lost my parents and Mac, then learned I might have a birth-mother in Bolivia, I was intent on finding her and trying to develop a relationship with her. Then, once I lost her to the fog, I felt seriously bereft. To have discovered Bradley is beyond belief. I plan to return to Bolivia at some point to try to get to know him a bit."

Darren positively beamed at me. "You must! That's all such wonderful news. So, do you feel all the puzzle pieces are now in place?'

"Almost. I learned something yesterday I'd just as soon not have known."

"Oh, dear." He leaned forward, his eyes full of warmth and concern.

"Yeah. It seems my mother wrote to Mac to ask him to haul away the evidence from the boxes in the attic." I filled Darren in on what Eileen had said.

"I think that was an unwise move on your mother's part," said Darren. "Put poor Mac smack dab in a conflict of interest." He shook his head, as though seriously annoyed with Betty.

I took a bite of my fruit salad, then said, "I know. I'm kind of pissed about it."

Darren ran his hand over the area that used to be his goatee. "I don't blame you." He paused, then added,

"She must've thought he was the only one she could turn to—who wasn't you."

"That's what Mom's old friend suggested yesterday. Honestly, I'm more interested in what Mac did with her request."

"Do you think she sent the letter to him at work?"

"Apparently."

"Do you have his effects from his workplace?"

"Yes. A small box. Coffee cup, hand lotion, an electric pencil sharpener and some pictures I'd framed for him. No letter from Betty."

"I suppose you've looked at home."

"At home?"

"Did Mac have a desk or a place he sat to pay bills? That sort of thing?"

I clapped my hands. "I'm so stupid, Darren. I didn't even think of looking in his music room."

Darren raised his eyebrows.

"Mac kept all his papers in there, along with his guitars, the piano, and piles of notebooks and sheet music. But I swore I wouldn't go in there for a year."

"To whom did you swear this?"

"Myself."

"So maybe you could absolve yourself of the commitment?"

"I suppose I could." I rolled my eyes at my hesitation. "Of course I could."

"So?"

I took a moment to think. "I'm ready, Darren."

"Excellent. Would you like to take a few more bites of your meal? Or another cup of coffee?"

I shook my head. "I would, but I have to get home to find out whether Mac passed the test of allegiance."

Darren pursed his lips, then said softly, "Listen, Suzanne. Whatever you find, keep in mind that he's not here to defend himself."

I smiled. "You're a generous person, Darren. I don't know what I'll think. I'm hoping there is nothing to see, and I can just assume Mac would never betray me."

Darren grimaced. "Whatever he might've done, it's not necessarily fair to think of it in those terms."

I started to reply, but decided we were just going around in circles. I nodded to our waiter to get our bill, and when it arrived, Darren promptly grabbed it. He said, "Thanks for filling me in on all of your discoveries. Amazing. I'm so thrilled for you that you were able to get answers. I mean it, Suzanne. My heart is so full for you."

I smiled. "Thanks, Darren."

"When will you visit Bradley?"

"I haven't decided yet. But I'll send you a postcard when I do." I forced myself to remain seated, but was aching to dash home.

Darren, however, wasn't fooled. He said, "And now I can see you are ready to bolt to get to Mac's music room."

I nodded, then said, "I'll text you about getting together with Daniel."

"Please do. And good luck." I stood to leave and Darren hurried to stand to give me a hug. When I picked up my to-go bag, Darren did the same thing as on the last time we parted. He winked at me.

As I drove home, I tried to push out of my head thoughts of my mom's secret communication with my husband, but I was growing more nervous by the minute. I hurried straight through the great room, ran up the stairs, and stood for a moment outside the door to a room I hadn't looked into since the day I came home from the hospital.

I'd never bothered to close the blinds, so the room, which had two walls with windows, was bright and warm. I slipped between two guitars, past the piano, and up to Mac's desk. There it was. Right on top. Mom's letter dated September 25th. There was no envelope, and the stationary was wrinkled, as though it had been handled often.

Dearest Mac,

I hate to write to you at your office, but I have no choice. I must ask you for a favor which you will surely find unusual, and may find unethical.

I couldn't believe my mom had used the very word I did to describe her request. I felt somewhat gratified that she at least recognized how wrong her entreaty was.

I need you to stop by our house and dispose of some boxes Ron and I have had in our attic for decades. You may not mention this little favor to Suzanne, as the boxes concern her, and must be kept from her forever. Please trust me that there is a very good reason for the secrecy.

Ron and I hate to get you involved. We simply don't know anyone else we would trust to do the job, who is also physically able to do it. Please let me know that you will help us out. And of course, please don't call me about this in Suzanne's presence.

Much love, Betty

As much as this piece of paper was precisely what

I'd expected to find, seeing the words in Mom's handwriting gave me chills. I wondered why she hadn't written to me—or called me—instead. She could've told her own daughter that she wanted some boxes discarded and to please not look inside. Why couldn't she have trusted me as much as my husband? I'd never in my life felt so angry with her. But it was more than anger. She was breaking my heart. Even though she was now a box of dust, she was freaking breaking my heart.

I didn't see any sign of a response from Mac. But I did spy a small pile of bills, stamps already affixed, ready for the mail. I couldn't believe I hadn't thought to look at Mac's desk where I knew he kept his outgoing mail. I didn't want to remain in the room where I'd read my mother's letter of betrayal, so I grabbed the mail to go through it downstairs. I began to shuffle through it as I rose to leave the room. There it was. An envelope addressed to Betty Reynolds, stamped, and ready to send.

I eased myself back into the chair slowly because my heart rate was scaring me. I took a deep breath, desperately afraid to read my husband's secret correspondence to my mom. I slid Mac's letter opener into the corner of the envelope and pried it open. It was one page from a yellow legal pad, handwritten in Mac's loopy cursive.

Dear Betty,
I received your letter about the boxes in your attic. I am honored that you trust me with something that obviously means so much to you.

At that point, I was ready to be angry with Mac

forever. Fortunately, I kept reading.

In a lot of ways, I have not been a great husband to your daughter. But I have always been truthful. I don't keep secrets from Suzanne, and I don't believe she keeps them from me. It is inconceivable for me to agree to your request—at least not without Suzanne's blessing.

The problem you've created for me is that I now know something Suzanne would want to hear about. Of course, it isn't possible for me to un-know it. I feel for you, as I assume this is not what you expected to hear. Your secret is obviously sensitive. Perhaps it is painful for you. But I will be sharing your letter with Suzanne.

You may wish to take some time to think about what you will say to your daughter, and I want to be fair about not rushing you. So, I will wait for one month, until October 25th, to show your letter to Suzanne. I'm truly sorry for whatever distress this causes you and Ron. But I did not ask to be put in this position, and I value my faithfulness to your daughter above all else. Frankly, it is one of the few things I've been able to do right by her.

With love,
Mac

My eyes overflowed with tears. This was true love, the kind that Polly said, "Lasts forever." I cursed myself for not fully appreciating Mac when I'd had the chance. I caressed his letter opener, the arms of his chair, and his pen, knowing his fingers had slipped along the same contours only months before. I felt my loss more acutely than I had in all the months that preceded that moment. I was unable to do anything but sit.

After a while, it hit me that Mac's letter meant I

would've learned I'd been adopted even if the accident hadn't happened. I found that thought ironic as well as heart-breaking. I may've been there fifteen minutes. May've been an hour. But I finally got up to head downstairs.

My foot struck something, and I almost slipped on the wool area rug. I leaned over to pick up the standard black and white bound notebook, and I opened it to see if it was music or lyrics, assuming I'd probably heard Mac play the songs.

I hadn't. Only the first page bore writing. There was a title: *Suzanne*. Obviously a work in progress, it was simply a page of phrases and a short bit of music, written for the piano. By that point, I suspected I might not be able to remain standing if I read a single word my darling Mac had written about me. I slid down to the floor and sat, cross-legged, so I wouldn't have too far to fall if I should get light-headed, a fairly likely scenario.

SUZANNE

It was simply a list of phrases in Mac's distinctive, oversized scrawl. He had thoroughly crossed out everything he'd written. I couldn't reliably make out a single letter. At the end of the sheet were the only words I could decipher. "Can't do her justice."

I read it twice. Then I full-out sobbed. My chest heaved and I struggled to catch my breath. My eyes produced more tears than I thought possible, as mucus flowed from my nose. I wiped my face on the sleeve of my blouse and eventually fell into a deep sleep—right there on the floor.

Chapter 27

In the morning, the light poured in through the windows, waking me early, and it took a moment for me to appreciate that it was Monday. Not only did I need to dress for work, I had to prepare myself mentally to make my settlement presentation to May, the truck driver and his company's representative, the insurance company adjuster, and the lawyer for the three boys. I was ready to lay out my demand, but I was concerned that John was going to be unhappy with me.

I thought it best to wear a navy skirt suit, rather than what I normally wore to work, a simple skirt and sweater. Of course, on days I had a court appearance, there was no option but a skirt suit. A few of the elderly, male judges still held it against a female lawyer if she showed up in a dress or a pantsuit, so I never took chances with my clients' prospects, however ridiculous I found the unwritten rule.

I got into the office at eight o'clock, and worked on other matters until John fetched me at around ten. He stepped into my office, pulling the door closed behind him. "They're all in the conference room, Suzanne."

"Great." I put down what I'd been reading, stood, and grabbed my suit jacket from the back of my desk chair.

"So, this is your last chance to share with your lawyer before you present your deal."

"There's no point, John. It is what it is."

He tilted his head down and looked at me over his glasses. "Then I just hope my jaw doesn't drop when you lay it out. I'd hate for the other lawyers to think my client doesn't trust me."

"Well, brace yourself because your jaw may well drop."

He laughed. "Now you're just trying to scare me."

I smiled. "Let's go. Shall we?" I grabbed the small stack of handouts which I would pass out after I'd spoken, while John couldn't seem to stop shaking his head.

It was our largest conference room, with a window-wall overlooking a manicured garden that the business park kept up beautifully. Phlox, petunias, and marigolds nestled under clouds of tall, spindly pink cosmos, a bold array of giant zinnias and delicate orange and black poppies. I glanced at them, as I always did upon entering that room, because whatever battle I was about to engage in with some opposing counsel, I would come to it fresh from a moment of bliss.

I walked ahead of John, and shook the hand of everyone I'd requested be present, before taking the empty seat at the head of the table. Only the truck driver, Mr. Bixby, struck me as especially nervous. His chin quivered before he said, "Hello." Of course, he knew the insurance company for Tooley would pay any settlement or verdict. But he also knew he'd be required to testify if the case went to trial.

I saw that John had already provided everyone with drinks, all waters except May's cup of hot tea. John nodded to me, and I spoke exactly as I'd planned. "Thank you, everyone, for being here. As you all know, I've received a settlement offer of one million dollars on behalf of Tooley Freight Lines and Mr. Bixby. I've had no offer from the misters Thomas, Mitchell, and Phillips, in spite of the compelling evidence against them.

"As a result of the accident of October 13, I lost everything I held most dear, both of my parents, and my beloved husband. The insurance policy for Tooley Freight Lines provides up to three million dollars for my losses." I took a moment to rest my eyes on each person, going around the table. May was watching me impassively, as were her insurance company client, and the representative of Tooley Freight Lines. Mr. Bixby was looking down. The boys' lawyer was feverishly taking notes.

"Today, I will make my non-negotiable settlement demand. You may choose to meet it and put this litigation to rest. But if you do not, I will withdraw it and ask my friend John, here, to push for the earliest possible trial date. Of course, you are free to take notes, but I will be handing out a summary of my demand so there are no misunderstandings."

"How long do we have to decide what we want to do?" May asked quietly.

I smiled at her. "Twenty-four hours. I assure you it will be sufficient time."

She said, "That's unusually short, Suzanne. Why the rush?"

"Let's just say that once you hear my proposal, you may not have a problem with the time frame."

She smiled. "Then by all means, proceed."

"My reasons are my business. My settlement demand is this: Tooley Freight Lines re-hires Charlie Bixby within forty-eight hours of the finalization of the settlement papers. The fact of the accident of October 13 is never used against Mr. Bixby in any manner, for any purpose, at any time. And Tooley Freight Lines and I will enter into a contract guaranteeing that both Mr. Bixby and I receive substantial damages should Tooley ever renege on that agreement."

May said, "I'll have to discuss that with my clients."

"Of course."

She added, "So, is the one million dollars acceptable if we should agree about Mr. Bixby?"

"No. I reject the one-million-dollar offer."

"Well—" She tossed back her coal-black ponytail and stared at me.

"Let me finish, May."

She nodded at me to go ahead.

"No money will change hands in this settlement."

Everyone seemed frozen for a moment. The room went completely silent. Then John jumped up. "Excuse me. I need to meet with my client, with Suzanne, privately." He took my elbow and practically dragged me out of the room. Once we were standing in his office with the door closed, he said, "What the hell are you thinking, Suzanne?" I mean, nice move for poor Mr. Bixby. But you could use that million dollars, and they are totally ready to pay it."

"Calm down, John. First of all, I don't need the money."

"But—"

"Let me finish. Both Mac and my parents were huge believers in life insurance. So I'm just fine. In fact, if I live at all reasonably, I don't need to work another day in my life."

John looked apoplectic, his face beet red. "Even so,

you're throwing away money for no reason. Give it to a charity, for Christ's sake! But don't let the insurance company keep money they're perfectly willing for you to have."

I took a step back and leaned against a wall, my arms folded over my chest, feeling relaxed and confident. "You're not understanding what I'm doing. I'm lifting the weight of guilt from Mr. Bixby's shoulders. You see, he might think my demand that they give him his job back is just charity. But the fact that neither his employer nor their insurer will pay one dime has got to help him accept that he really isn't at fault for the accident."

John was still seething. He raised his voice a notch. "Then, why did you even file the suit?"

I smiled. "Because Marilee was right. The best way to learn exactly what happened was through discovery. You know very well that neither Mr. Bixby nor the three little hoodlums would've talked to me without the legal process to compel them."

"Fine. But how are you justifying letting the boys off the hook?"

"Are you serious?"

John didn't respond but he was working his mouth. So, I said, "They have no money. They have no insurance. And if they are to learn any lesson from being sued and being required to testify, it's already been done." I didn't see how John could legitimately disagree with that. Again, he said nothing.

"I'm really sorry, John."

I could tell he was still pissed. He straightened his already straight tie while he asked, "For which thing?"

"For making you wait until today to hear this. I knew you'd try to talk me out of it."

"Which I just did. But it was a bad call on your part to make me hear it with the others.'

"Yeah. It was. That's why I'm sorry."

John let out his breath, which I took as a sign he was through arguing. "Apology accepted." He paused, shook his head again, then gave me the tiniest smile. "We should return to the room. They're probably all hyperventilating hoping I didn't change your mind."

I laughed. "I'll hand out the copies I prepared so they can relax."

All eyes were on us as John and I entered the room and took our seats. I straightened the pile of handouts. "As I was saying, all of the terms are set out here." I passed out the one-sided sheets of paper.

May took a moment to read it over, then said, "We've all talked in your absence. And I called the top executive at Tooley. Everyone accepts your demand, Suzanne."

I looked squarely at her. "I didn't think you would need twenty-four hours."

She smiled at me and said, "Right."

Poor John still couldn't seem to stop shaking his head. As the others shook our hands and filed out of the room, they were all smiling. Mr. Bixby left last. His eyes glistening with tears, he took my hand and held it for a moment, then said, "You are an unusual woman, Mrs. Summerfield."

"Thank you. And please remember these words for the rest of your life: the accident wasn't your fault." Our eyes locked for a moment, and in that brief second, I thought I'd really convinced him. He smiled, the first time I'd seen that. It was probably just wishful thinking on my part, but after he shook John's hand and headed for the door, Mr. Bixby seemed to hold his shoulders a little higher, and his step seemed to be a bit brisker.

Chapter 28

We'd been back home for ten weeks, and Marilee and Polly and I had enjoyed meeting with Darren and Daniel a couple of times. I received a call at work one early afternoon on a Friday. When I saw who was calling, I yanked my attention from the brief I was studying. "Hi, Polly."

She said, "Suzanne, the headliner at this stand-up club I go to in Merrillville took ill, and I've been slated in her place for ten o'clock tonight. Marilee says she'll be there. Can you come?"

"That's so exciting! I wouldn't miss it for the world. I can pick up Marilee. Should I invite Darren and Daniel?"

"Well, it's super short notice. But sure. Absolutely." I was thrilled to finally have the opportunity to see Polly in what I thought of as her natural habitat—on a stage.

"Wonderful! And break a leg."

"I'll try."

The coffeehouse was in the basement of an old church that had been renovated for performances on a rental basis. It sat at the top of a hill in a nearby town. As Marilee and I stepped through the door at nine o'clock, I saw that the ceiling of the venue was so low that people had left messages, and even footprints, on it. With the beams and brick walls exposed, the place felt snug and intimate. The audience's tables were lit only by candles, while the stage, which sat only a few feet from the tables, had full professional spot lighting. Since the door was standing open, I was able to glance behind us. The line now snaked down the hill.

I looked around and estimated there were seats at tables for about fifty people, but there were also stools at the long bar. Marilee and I grabbed a table and four chairs as another couple indicated to me that they were leaving. I assumed many of the people came to see their friends, since I saw that the audience members kept changing between acts. Marilee and I ordered beers and saved seats for Darren and Daniel, who arrived around nine thirty, and settled in with their own drinks.

By ten o'clock, Marilee and I had seen seven comedians do their things, several landing at least a couple of great lines and receiving loud laughter. Other comedians' jokes were met with near silence. Polite applause accompanied them as they left the microphone, which I assumed had to be mortifying. Marilee looked at me and raised her eyebrows. I smiled and patted her hand. I was eager to see Polly's routine, but not nervous for her. I'd seen enough of Polly to know she'd make it work.

When it was her turn, Polly ran up onto the stage, wearing jeans with holes in them, a snug yellow sweater, and a bowler hat she'd bought in Oruro. She moved like a ball of energy. "Hi! My name is Polycarp Kuharski. Seriously. In my family, you got the name of the saint whose day your birth fell upon. Actually, I was lucky. My nickname is Polly." She smiled one of her radiant ones. "But my brothers are All Souls Kuharski, whom we call Al for short, and Ascension Kuharski. Yep. His nickname is—well, you can guess. So, believe it or not,

I was the lucky one." This joke earned Polly a nice smattering of audience laughter and a couple of guffaws. One person snorted.

"Anyway, my friends and I were recently in Bolivia. True story. I have this hat to prove it. We weren't on vacation to see the Salt Flats. And if you don't know what that is, you're an ignorant loser." She smiled. "I found out while we were there. The truth is, we were on a secret mission. A cinchy assignment. All we had to do was find a person—in a country of 11.8 million people. And this person we were looking for, well, we didn't know her name. Or what she looked like. Or if she was still in Bolivia. Or even if she was still alive." There were several chuckles. I had the strong sense that Polly was warming up, and would have us all rolling on the floor in due course.

"But I'm pretty sure everything would've gone fine if we hadn't been arrested for ignoring everything the policeman said to us. By the way, I'm thinking of suing the travel book author for telling us this was the best approach to take". She held up the book, then threw it to someone in the audience. "Look at page 131. It's true. That was the advice.

"Had it not been for the nice Chinese couple—" Polly whispered, "Spies, actually—" Then she continued in her practiced, projected stage voice, "Who were thrown in the cell with us, we might still be rotting in a dank corner of an ancient adobe building in Cochabamba. Did I mention that the Chinese couple were posing as acrobats, and the woman was a dwarf? No matter. I'll get back to it." For some reason, this comment caused me, alone, to laugh out loud.

"By the way, you've gotta love the names, right?

Titicaca, Cochabamba. Say them fast." She sang the names like a rap song to a couple of suggestive moves, emphasizing the "Titi," the "Caca," and the "bamba." "It sounds like a dirty dance. Right?

"Anyway, back to the Chinese spies—"

And Polly was off and running, her imagination as sharp and boisterous as Polly herself. At that point, the folks at our table weren't the only ones guffawing loudly, but it didn't hurt that Daniel had a booming, infectious laugh. Soon, the entire room was gasping for air, unable to stop laughing.

After seeing Polly mesmerizing her audience at Hotel Liliana with her glorious rendition of the Bolivian national anthem, and now this, it was obvious she was an unusually talented woman. Maybe she worked her butt off practicing, but she gave the impression that it all came naturally, like she was just being Polycarp Kuharski. I took a sip of my beer, hoping some Polly joke wouldn't make me spit it out. It was definitely a risk. I leaned back in my chair and thought about how grateful I was to Marilee for introducing us.

Chapter 29

It was already late July. It had been at the end of May that I'd met my birth-father, and promised I'd return to see him. I hadn't contacted Bradley since then because I didn't want to hear the disappointment in his voice when I would tell him I still did not know when I would be able to visit. For the past two weeks, however, I'd thought of little else. I struggled with how much I wanted to up-end my life. Bradley and I had missed sharing forty-eight years of it so far, and after what had happened to Mac, I didn't take it for granted that I had a lot of time left.

But it wasn't only that. I was feeling the hole in my life that Mac used to fill. It wasn't that I couldn't be content as a single woman. I'd happily been single the majority of the years of my life. It was that time had carved out a place for Mac in everything I did. I'd felt somehow incomplete since I left the hospital. An unrelenting, restless anxiety. Mac's absence seemed to creep into my everyday life even more strongly than I'd felt his presence. I thought of it as loss-sickness, and I needed to do something to treat it. I needed a change.

I sat on the couch exactly where I'd been when I learned that my mother was actually my aunt, and called Marilee and Polly one Friday night. I invited them to join me for an early morning hike on Sunday to the summit of Sharp Top, the most rigorous trail at Peaks of Otter.

Marilee said, "I'll go wherever you want, but that's a strenuous hike, Suzanne. And the temperature is predicted to reach the 90s. What if we do another trail, and save Peaks for the fall?"

"I can't. I have something I need to do there."

"What?"

"The ashes. I need to spread Mac, and Mom and Dad from the top of Sharp Top."

"That's a great idea! But they're not going anywhere. Why don't you spread them in the fall?"

I crossed my ankles atop the coffee table "They may not be going anywhere, Marilee, but I am."

"Oh, my God! You're going back to see Bradley."

"I think so. I want to talk it out with you guys at the summit. Polly already told me she's in."

"She's not worried about heat stroke?"

"She suggested we start the hike at 7:00 a.m. when it's in the mid-60s. By the time we do our thing at the top and get back down around 11:00, it should just be reaching the 80s. So, we won't have to die for me to say my farewells."

"Your last farewells," she said, wistfully.

"My second last. That's another thing I want to talk with you guys about." I pursed my lips. I really didn't want to disclose my plan until we reached the summit.

"Interesting. Of course, I'm in. Why don't you have Polly drive to your house. That way I can pick you both up at 5:30 a.m. This Sunday, right?"

"Yep."

"Okay. I'm stocking my backpack with water bottles.

"Very wise. And thanks, Marilee."

By the time we arrived at the parking lot, there were

already several parked cars, and a couple more disgorging hikers. We quickly applied sunscreen, sprayed ourselves against any early-bird mosquitoes, and slipped into our backpacks. Marilee's may've contained only water bottles, but mine held an assortment of picnic foods—what Mac always referred to as a Hemingway Picnic—a selection of cheeses, hard salami slices, French bread and fresh fruit. In honor of my mom, I'd also baked her flourless chocolate cake, and tucked the pieces into Tupperware, as it would definitely be jostled. It occurred to me that, like Betty, I liked to bother. I carried a second small backpack with the three large baggies of earthly remains. The mortuary folks had thoughtfully bagged the ashes before placing them in the overpriced urns.

Because it was such a steep ascent, we had to take breaks in order to glimpse what was off to our sides. If we didn't keep our eyes glued to where we placed our feet while walking, we could easily have slipped or twisted something. I'd always thought of Sharp Top as the kind of hike where the entire reward is at the top. We didn't chat as we ascended because Marilee and I were too winded, and Polly was too far ahead of us. She hiked up mountains the way she did everything else—a bright flash, more gazelle than mountain goat.

Although it was the coolest part of the day, we were soaked by the time we reached the summit, an hour and a half after we'd begun. We climbed the boulders until we reached the highest point. Miraculously, the few other folks at the top were off having their own refreshments, so we had the spot to ourselves. There is nothing like a 360-degree view, but the expanse we surveyed that morning was stunning. Distant dusty-blue mountains, richly colored valleys, and neatly patterned farm fields, all laid out like a gifted artist had studiously arranged them for the most powerful effect.

We set down our backpacks and just looked without speaking for several minutes. I finally broke the silence by saying, "I have ninety-five percent of Mac, Betty and Ron in baggies in this backpack." As I dug into it to retrieve my family, I added, "I think I'll just wait for the wind to pick up again and then release them."

Polly asked, "Will you say something special?"

"Not this time. Just, 'I love you,' and fling the ashes."

Marilee asked, "What does that mean? 'Not this time.' "

"Later. I'll explain while we have our picnic."

Polly cocked her head as she took this in.

I leaned down and took the first bag, which I'd labelled "Mac" with magic marker on masking tape. The breeze was light but steady. I pushed the inside of the baggie up so that the ashes poured out. As the wind whisked them away, I whispered, "I love you, darling Mac." I repeated the process with Betty and Ron. "I love you, Mom," and "I love you, Dad." Finally, I was able to let them go without tears.

Unfortunately, they didn't all fly out over Virginia. Some ash fell to the rock and had to be nudged off with our hands. I certainly didn't want to leave any bits of my family to be trampled by hundreds of hikers.

With that behind us, we stood gazing at the distant horizons in our moments of silence. After what I deemed a respectable amount of time, I pointed to a near-by flat rock outcropping. We scrambled to it as quickly as we could because we were all ready to sit and relax with a bottle of water. First, though, I passed around the hand sanitizer. I know I would've laughed if Polly had made a joke about it, but if she had the urge, she resisted. I was grateful not to guffaw over eating with bits of Mac, Mom, and Dad clinging to our fingers, although we were all probably thinking the same thing. I laid out the picnic in silence.

Marilee lightly touched my arm. "How are you feeling, sweetie?"

"Sad."

"Of course, you are."

Polly took my hand, looked at me with impossibly concerned eyes, and said, "How can we help?"

I stared at her, appreciating the intensity of her empathy. By that time, I knew it was genuine, but I still marveled at how it seemed to come from the very depths of her being. "I think I was so occupied with my birth-mystery on our trip, and so sleep-deprived, that I didn't dwell on the gaping hole in my life. But now that I'm home, I don't like how constantly missing Mac makes me feel. I thought work might engage me enough that I wouldn't notice the open wound. I still love my job, but it's just not filling the hole. I thought it might. But it isn't. I think of it as loss-sickness, and I feel it all the time."

"So what can you do?" asked Marilee.

"It's time for me to return to Bolivia."

"Do you think that will make you feel it less?" asked Marilee.

"Of course it will," said Polly, brightening like the sun peeking out from behind a cloud. "It will be a whole new world for Suzanne. She'll be so busy absorbing Cochabamba and Bradley's work, she won't have time to feel the loss-sickness."

I looked at Marilee and said, "My hope is that Polly's right."

Marilee said softly, almost in a whisper, "I hope so, too." She paused, then said, "Will you take more than a week?"

I looked out at the glorious expanse and, in spite of everything that had happened, felt the euphoria like I had gazing at the long views the fall day all of my people died. After a minute or so, I said, "Actually, what I've been trying to decide is whether I'll take more than a year."

"Wait!" said Marilee. "You're moving to Bolivia? I mean, can you even do that? Don't you need a green card or something?"

By the relaxed look on Polly's face, I knew she already understood. "Marilee, I'm a Bolivian citizen. They have birthright citizenship, like we do. I could stay there forever if I wanted to."

She looked a little panicked, but she spoke softly. "Do you want to?"

She asked it so earnestly that I assumed she shared my concern about one of her closest friends being 4,000 miles away. I'd been ignoring that worry because I hadn't yet figured out what to do with it. I said, "I have no idea. I'll just see how the first year goes."

"You're a brave woman," said Polly.

"Not hardly. I'll keep my house here—at least for the first year. I'm sure my law partners will want me to return. In other words, I can crawl back home with my tail between my legs anytime I want." I stopped for a moment to think about what I'd said. I admitted to myself that the longer I was away from my job, the harder it would be to get back into it. The law changes every day, as do client needs, as well as firm politics. I wasn't a hundred percent certain my partners would hold my position for more than a year, or even that they could reasonably agree to it without hurting the business.

"But still," said Polly, breathlessly. "You are venturing into a new life, in a far-away country where you don't even speak the language, and with only Bradley to help you. No other friends or family down there."

"Well, I do have my mother, who may slip out of the fog again. I hope she does. I still have questions for her. As to the language, no es correcto. Yo hablo Espanol, un poco."

Polly jumped up. "Oh, my God! You've been studying!"

"Since we returned from Bolivia. But I'd love for you to help me with some grammar questions."

"Quisiera hacerlo." She raised her eyebrows and added, "Comprende?"

"Si. Yo tambien."

Polly leaned over the picnic food to hug me. Marilee jumped up, ran to our side of the food, and knelt to join in the hug. As they both embraced me tightly, I looked out over the expanse that seemed to go on forever, the miles of land over which the breeze was depositing fragments of my beloveds. I started to tear up, but Polly gave me the most comforting look and said, "You will always miss them, Suzanne. But your wonderful birth-father awaits you with an inexhaustible love."

I wiped under my eyes with my fingertips. "I hope so." I was amazed that I was actually able to stop the flow of tears.

We all returned to our picnic positions and resumed

snacking. Marilee said, "I'm thrilled for you, sweetie. Personally, I hope you'll decide to come back home after that because I'll miss you so much."

"Me, too," said Polly. "You're my most interesting friend."

Marilee loudly cleared her throat.

Polly added, "Except for Marilee, of course, who is equally interesting."

I smiled and shook my head.

Marilee said, "By the way, you made a comment about how you wouldn't make a speech about Mac and your folks 'this time.' What were you talking about?"

I put down the piece of French bread I'd been working on. I pursed my lips as I gathered the courage to ask my friends for another huge favor. "Listen, guys. You've done unbelievable things for me already. Holding me up, keeping me moving forward, helping me cope. You've been incredibly generous with your time and with your support in every aspect of my life." I knew I was risking losing credibility by overstating it, but it was important to me that they know I hadn't taken any of it for granted. "You took your vacation time and your own money—" I eyed Polly because I assumed she had a much smaller income than Marilee and I "—to go to Bolivia with me to untangle my past."

"Yeah. We're really generous friends," said Polly, who then laughed.

"As I mentioned before," said Marilee. " 'Friends' says it all."

I nodded, then rearranged myself to sit with my legs straight out before me, ankles crossed. "I know." I hesitated. "Nevertheless, I'm having a hard time mustering the nerve to ask for another, rather large, favor."

"Just ask," said Marilee, as she helped herself to a second, small bunch of grapes.

"Or let me guess," said Polly, who then winked.

I nodded, hopeful that she could put into words what I was struggling with.

"Earlier, you said you had ninety-five percent of Mac, Betty and Ron to release into the breeze. As Marilee noted, you also said you wouldn't give speeches 'this time.' "

I nodded again.

Polly beamed at me. "Obviously, you've saved a small portion of the ashes of each of the three to spread in the Andes. Where, I might add, you plan to say more."

I nodded a third time.

Polly tilted her head in a little bow to acknowledge my endorsement of her theory. Then she said, "And you would like me and Marilee to be there with you and Bradley when you have your dispersal ceremony."

I nodded again, this time deeply, with my hands in a prayer position. "Please."

From the way she was smiling at me, I suspected Polly would go. I looked for Marilee's reaction and saw a big grin. She glanced at Polly. Both of their faces were positively lit up. "Yes," said Marilee.

"Si," said Polly. "Cuando?"

"Thanks guys. I can't believe how you just jumped to my aid—again. As for cuando, not right away."

"Good," said Marilee. "I need to put in a lot of hours before I announce another vacation."

Polly said, "I have none left at all. But maybe we could do it during my spring break, or any time next summer."

"Next summer would be perfect," I said. "I don't plan to head south until the end of August so I can get some work done and whip all my files into shape for transfers to others in the firm for the next year. That means I'll be in Cochabamba until at least the end of August of next year. Maybe we could aim for the best week for you guys in June or July."

"Perfecto," said Polly.

"I'll be counting the days," said Marilee. "Literally. I always count down to vacations."

"When will you tell Bradley?" asked Polly.

"I'll call him tomorrow." I turned to Marilee. "As you know, we have a partnership meeting at noon tomorrow where I can announce it. Of course, I'll tell John ahead of time since he is the managing partner, not to mention a great friend. If there are no insurmountable objections, I'll call Bradley right after the meeting."

"He'll be out of his mind with joy," said Marilee.

"I hope so." I sighed, relieved that my friends were willing to return to Bolivia for me.

"Oh, he'll be thrilled," said Polly. "I think it broke his heart that you had to leave the country two days after you guys met. He'll be beside himself."

"Will you stay with him?" asked Marilee.

I shook my head. "Too much, too soon. I'll rent an apartment near his home—wherever that is. Then I'll just see how things develop." I smiled. "You never know. Maybe I can persuade him to try living in Virginia for a while, whenever I return."

Polly made a little grimace, then said, "I don't think he will while his beloved Olivia is alive."

I felt remiss for not thinking of it. But as I looked back on the power of my mother's few lucid moments with me, I doubted I'd leave Cochabamba either, as long as there was a chance we might connect again. "You're right, Polly. Probably neither of us will." We each took a small bit of the cake on plastic forks, and enjoyed it as we sat silently for a good five minutes admiring the view.

As we packed up the remainder of our picnic, Polly said, "Call me after you speak with Bradley. I can't wait to hear his reaction."

"Better yet, why don't you guys come over for dinner tomorrow night? I'll just make something easy," I said. "Then I can fill you in on the details."

"Let's each bring a dish," said Marilee. "I've got a homemade lasagna I can pull out of my freezer."

"I'll bring a salad and crusty bread," said Polly.

"Thanks. I'll have appetizers and a little dessert." I took a deep breath. "I think I'm counting on this being a little celebration. I hope Bradley reacts the way I think he will."

"Oh, Suzanne," said Polly. "Just remember the look on his face when he asked you to stay. Tomorrow night will definitely be a celebration."

Marilee smiled, then said, "I'd bet my life on it, and as you know, I haven't got a gambler's bone in my body."

"Thanks, guys."

We hoisted our backpacks onto our shoulders and made it back down to the car in half the time of the ascent.

Once Marilee dropped us at my house, and Polly was pulling away, I took a moment to watch her car disappear into the distance. I didn't want to be overly-optimistic, but I felt no loss-sickness at all. I let myself in through the front door, made a cup of tea, and sat in the booth to start creating checklists for my move to South America.

Everything went as I'd hoped the next day. Waiting for Marilee and Polly to arrive for dinner, I was so excited that I couldn't sit still. I compulsively paced the length of my great room until I was saved by the doorbell.

After Marilee had placed the lasagna and bread in the oven, I laid out appetizers and wine on the living room coffee table. Once we each had a glass of chardonnay in hand, I filled them in on my call with Bradley. "We had a nice conversation about how we are each doing—before I got to the important part. I told him how I'd learned that my adoptive mother was my biological aunt. Bradley said he knew Olivia had an older sister named Betty who was married to Ron. He remembered their names because they're both alliterative, like his: Betty Bailey and Ron Reynolds. That was when it hit me that we might've realized Betty was Olivia's sister while we were talking with Bradley in Cochabamba."

"You're right," said Marilee, setting down her wine glass. "If we'd only thought to ask him if he knew whether Olivia had siblings." She shook her head slowly.

Polly whistled. "Wow. If I hadn't been so invested in the mystery of the locket, we might've spent more time getting details from your father." She clasped her hands together and said quietly, "Sorry."

I laughed. "Polly, meeting Liliana was huge. It doesn't matter when I found out that Betty and Olivia were sisters. I'm just happy to know. It explains so much."

"Good!" said Polly. "So, how did he react when you

told him you'd be visiting him in Cochabamba?"

"He said the words I'd hoped he'd say. He really wants me to come."

Chapter 30

Bradley pulled into short-term parking and found a spot right away. We were early, but we were determined to be at the meeting point, the baggage pick-up area, before Marilee and Polly arrived. Bradley took my arm as the two of us hurried into the terminal. I couldn't help wondering if passers-by saw a father and daughter.

It had been almost a year since I'd seen my friends, although we'd kept in close touch through frequent FaceTime calls. I lived in a sweet, two-bedroom apartment that I'd decorated with gorgeous, locally-made fabrics and intricately patterned woven rugs. The large front windows overlooked a park, and the side windows faced a charming, old, stone Andean Baroque-style church. It wasn't far from Bradley's simple, neat studio. I assumed his appreciation for the austere life of a priest had followed him into his lay existence. I, however, found real comfort in lovely surroundings.

Bradley had left his government job three months after my arrival to start a non-profit that could work under fewer constraints, although he kept his good relationships with the prison administrators. I was working with him toward having a staff large enough so we could visit all of the prisons, teaching and mentoring, on a daily basis. I spent most of my time in the office, but was also training to collaborate at the courthouse with the attorneys, both the volunteers and those we retained, to help us gain the release of the hundreds of people who didn't remotely belong behind bars. I found it hard to believe how much I'd learned since I'd moved to Bolivia—basic Spanish, about Bradley's work, and about myself.

I glimpsed Polly first. She must have spied us in the distance, because she was sprinting toward us, her roll-aboard flying behind her. It actually looked to be airborne a couple of times. Marilee was right behind her, also running. Thankfully, they were just as attentive to Bradley as to me. While Marilee spun me around in a hug, Polly clung to Bradley like he was her oldest and dearest friend. Then they switched partners.

I said, "So, you're glad to see us?"

Polly guffawed as though I'd landed a world-class zinger, which made all of us laugh.

Bradley said, "I must say, I've never in my life been greeted with such enthusiasm. Senoras, your being here is a gift from the gods."

Polly dramatically raised her eyebrows and tilted her head. "Gods?"

"Right. I meant to say, 'From God.' "

We laughed again because we were all giddy with the moment. Marilee and Polly were beyond exhausted, having flown for over 25 hours, and I was just as delirious at seeing my closest friends. Bradley was so thrilled for me that he was ebullient, as well.

We beamed, and talked, and laughed as we made our way to Bradley's car. As he drove through the Saturday morning Cochabamba traffic, we women yakked non-stop, barely pausing to breathe. After we'd covered the travails of their super-short connections, and the terrifying turbulence, I asked the question I was most concerned with, "Did you have any trouble getting the ashes through customs?"

Marilee snorted and Polly guffawed.

"I'll take that as a yes."

Polly said, "Here's what happened."

I knew I'd better not take a sip from my water bottle, lest it end up on Bradley's dashboard.

"Of course, we had researched how to take cremains on an international flight."

"Cremains?" Bradley asked.

Marilee said, "Catchy, isn't it? 'Cremation remains' is now efficiently shortened to 'cremains.' "

"As you know," said Polly, "we have only a thimble-full of ashes for each of them. The instructions said we should put them in sift-proof containers, and then seal them in plastic baggies." I turned in my seat to watch Polly, in the back seat, acting all this out.

Marilee said, "The problem was that all of the containers were way too large for the small quantity left of your relatives, Suzanne."

"And," said Polly, "we assumed you didn't want Mac and Betty and Ron all mixed together into one of the readily available larger containers."

"Good assumption," I said.

"Right," said Polly. "So I eventually found three containers on the web that looked like hollowed-out lipstick tubes. I hope that's okay."

I nodded, "It's fine. As long as you got them all here—in separate tubes."

Polly sighed. "Good. We were hoping it wouldn't bother you that your dad and Mac are in these feminine-looking containers."

"It's really fine. What do you think these lipstick

containers are really designed for?"

"Smuggling," said Polly without missing a beat.

I just shook my head.

Marilee said, "You know how thorough I am, Suzanne."

"Yep."

"So, I also got an affidavit from the mortuary owner attesting to what the contents are."

"Attesting?"

Marilee laughed. "Remember the blue-ribbon rule from law school?"

I nodded. "That the more official a document looks, the more credibility is ascribed to it. So?"

"So I had him notarize the affidavits. Then I affixed a blue ribbon."

"Brilliant," I said without meaning it. I assumed any investigation would be more about what the dust was composed of. "Wait. How will I know which lipstick tube is whose remains?"

"Easy," said Polly. "Mac is in the purple one, your dad is in the maroon, and your mom is in the soft pink."

"I can remember that." I was nervous about how bad their experience may've been. "What went wrong, guys?"

Polly bit her lip before speaking. "I'm very environmentally conscious."

"Good for you," I said.

"Thanks. I re-use baggies."

"Laudable," I said.

"And I might've re-used one that had had my pot stash in it."

Bradley must've been following all of this because he suddenly coughed. I said, "What?"

"It was an innocent mistake, Suzanne."

"What happened?"

"It was in La Paz, where we went through customs. Everything was going swimmingly. We cleared in probably twenty minutes, and our bags weren't searched at all. As we headed for our final gate, a German Shepherd across the hallway from us started going crazy, moaning, and pulling at his leash. A beefy soldier approached us with the dog in tow. This part was very stressful, Suzanne, because the dog was suddenly on top of my backpack, where Mac and Betty and Ron were innocently hanging out in lipstick tubes. I tried to explain to the guy, but he wouldn't listen to a word I said."

"In Spanish?"

"Si."

"Oh, my," said Bradley.

"He led us to a small interrogation room," said Marilee. "We assumed they might throw us in jail without a trace."

"Oh, my God," I said.

"We were told to sit at a table and watch while two male police officers emptied my backpack," said Polly. The dog stood patiently while the baggies with Betty and Ron were placed on a tray. Then Mac's baggie was lifted out. The dog went nuts again, growling, pawing at the ground, and straining against his leash. Finally, the soldier he was working with led him out of the room. The dog was still barking, and I swear, craning his neck to get a good look at me, the drug smuggler. That's when it hit me that there was a logical explanation."

"One of the officers held up Mac's baggie and asked me what was in it. I told him that the lipstick tube inside held the ashes for our dear friend's husband, which she wanted to release over their beautiful Andes Mountains. And I said that I'd used the baggie in the past to hold a small quantity of marijuana, but that I hadn't brought any with me on the trip."

Marilee said, "Even though they were all speaking Spanish, I understood how they responded because the officers looked at each other and both rolled their eyes. But Polly persisted."

"Right. I took the notarized affidavits with the blue ribbons out of my backpack."

"But they were in English," I said.

Marilee said, "Didn't I just remind you of how thorough I am?"

"So?" I asked.

"I'd had Polly prepare an identical affidavit in Spanish."

"Who in the world did you get in Charlottesville to notarize a document she couldn't read?"

Marilee looked at me like I was the one who was senile, rather than my mother. "Your secretary, of course."

Bradley said only, "My, my."

"The affidavit did the trick?" I asked.

"Not quite," said Polly. "They took Mac's tube and baggie to their forensic lab at the airport and came back a half-hour later."

"What did they say?"

"Nothing," said Marilee.

Polly said, "They handed Mac back to me and escorted us to our gate. They'd already returned Betty and Ron. We boarded and fell into our seats only a few minutes before the plane started rolling down the runway."

311

I thought about asking Polly whether any of her story was true. But Marilee had done half the talking, and there was no way she would've made up such a scenario. "Wow." I paused. "Well, thanks for getting them here for me. I really appreciate it."

Polly said, "About that."

"What?"

Marilee leaned forward and placed her hand on my shoulder. "Polly and I have been talking about it—why you didn't just bring the ashes with you a year ago when you made the trip."

They were on to me, but I played innocent. I turned to stare out my window. "Why do you think I didn't?"

Polly said, "We think it was your insurance that we'd come for a visit. I mean, we all know the ashes couldn't have been mailed with any expectation you'd ever receive them."

I said, "Like I told you guys, I'd forgotten to research how to properly prepare them for an international flight."

"One problem with that," said Marilee. "It's not believable. No way you would've forgotten anything that important."

I continued to look at the passing sights as I spoke. "Fine. Maybe that was my motivation, but it was subconscious."

They maintained their silence until I cracked. I turned to my left and craned my neck until I could see both of them. "Okay. It might've been conscious." I was hoping they didn't feel manipulated. "Is it okay?"

They both laughed. "Of course it is," said Polly. "Frankly, we were both honored that you entrusted the ashes to us. Regrettably, we almost screwed it up with my pot baggie. We would've felt terrible if five percent of Mac had been lost forever."

There was something about the percentage reference that got us all guffawing again. Of course, my friends knew full well that I still grieved for Mac. But sometimes grief can be mixed with humor, with no one doubting the love that lies beneath. Still, I did wonder what Bradley must think of my friends, and the way I acted when I was with them.

My guest bedroom had two twins, so Marilee and Polly crashed there for a few hours before we gathered at my kitchen table to discuss plans for their week. Bradley had gone back to work, but agreed to take the rest of the week off to lead us around to all the locations I wanted to share with Marilee and Polly. But there were two things we needed to do before the sight-seeing.

While we chatted, I served a cheese board with a Bolivian cheese bread called *Cunape*, and fresh fruit, with large ceramic mugs of hot tea. "First of all, Bradley and I would like to take you out to dinner tonight at our favorite restaurant, just south of downtown. And I planned an itinerary for the week, but we can change anything if something else suits you better."

Marilee leaned back in her chair, her fingers wrapped around her mug. "You have it typed up, don't you?"

"Of course."

"You haven't changed then," she said as she rolled her eyes comically.

"I can't wait to see it," said Polly as she rubbed her hands together as though preparing for a feast.

I retrieved my folder from the desk that was tucked in a corner of the kitchen and handed out the copies.

Polly scanned it and said, "Dinner at 8:00 p.m. We have a reservation?"

"Si."

"Excellent. I can't wait to spend some time getting to know Bradley."

I leaned in, and waited until they'd both looked up from their itineraries. "I talk about you guys so much that Bradley says he feels like he already knows you."

"I guess that means he knows your version of us," said Polly.

"I guess."

"Good. You think I'm much funnier than I actually am." Polly smiled then burst out laughing.

Marilee said, "But we don't know him at all—"

Polly said, "Except for his life story, of course."

"I know," I said. "That's why I'm so happy he'll be spending the week with us." I paused. "You're going to love him."

Marilee put her hand atop mine, and said, "There's no doubt about it, sweetie."

"He certainly made a great first impression when we stalked him outside the prison, and had coffee with him at that empty restaurant," said Polly.

I smiled, then lifted up my copy of the itinerary to suggest I was ready to move on. "So, tomorrow is Sunday. We'll get the two must-do items out of the way."

"There's nothing on your schedule for tomorrow," said Marilee. "What are the must-dos?"

I watched them carefully for any sign that what I was about to say wasn't their idea of a vacation. "Bradley and I visit Sister Mary Olivia every Sunday at 5:00 a.m."

"We're up for that," said Polly with too much enthusiasm, which made me think there was nothing she'd rather not do.

"I don't see any point in your visiting Sister Mary Olivia again. I think it should just be Bradley and me. But I do want to make sure you guys don't feel like I'm abandoning you. I'll be back by 6:45 at the latest."

"6:45 in the morning?" asked Marilee.

"Right."

She released a huge sigh, "In that case, take your time. Polly and I will be sound asleep."

"Good."

Polly said, "You've told us about the few little things your birth-mother has said when she's lucid. How often does she make it out of the fog to connect with you or Bradley?"

"Sadly, not often." I closed my eyes as I tried to calculate the frequency. "Maybe one time out of six visits."

"That must be frustrating," said Marilee.

"I think it's exciting," said Polly. "It's like gambling. You know it probably won't happen—but it could. You watch Sister Mary Olivia like a hawk. If you notice the light start to return to her eyes, you move quickly to ask a question about something you burn to know. Or to tell her something you desperately want her to take with her to wherever it is she goes when she leaves you."

"You're both right." I shook my head to clear it of Olivia so that we could move on. "Anyway, you can guess what the second 'must-do' is."

"The spreading of the ashes," said Marilee.

I rose to boil more tea water. "Right. I'd like to do it tomorrow afternoon. Bradley will lead us on the hike. Do you remember when we first saw him, how we thought he was wearing construction boots?"

"Sure," said Polly.

"They're his hiking boots. He wears them all the time, and he hikes the mountains whenever he gets the chance."

"Good," said Polly. "I don't want to take off into the Andes with no guide. We could end up like the Bolivian soccer team that had to turn to cannibalism."

"Weren't they Uruguayan rugby players, and didn't their plane crash?" asked Marilee.

"Nevertheless, they were lost in the Andes."

I laughed. "We won't have to resort to eating each other. I'll bring snacks."

"Even better," said Polly.

I shook my head, which I realized I did a lot when I was with her. "Once Mac and Betty and Ron are drifting over the Andes, I can relax and enjoy our vacation week together."

"Makes sense," said Marilee.

Polly smiled sympathetically and patted my hand as she added, "We want you to be relaxed."

"Thanks. The plan is that on Monday morning, we take a short flight to Uyuni where we start our three-day tour of the salt flats, including one night in a salt hotel."

"Everything's made out of salt. Right?" asked Marilee.

"Exactly. Then early on Thursday morning, we fly up to La Paz, and rent a car to drive to Puno. From there, a boat ride on Lake Titicaca to Isla del Sol, where we have reservations for two nights on the island and a catamaran dinner cruise on the lake."

They were both following along on their written itineraries.

"We fly back to Cochabamba on Saturday morning, and explore some off-the-beaten-path parts of Bradley's city all day. We'll have a final dinner together, then your flight home is early on Sunday."

Polly looked up at me and slowly released a smile that soon lit up her face. "Excelente! Perfecto!"

Marilee said, "This sounds just lovely, Suzanne—the top sites Polly laid out for us on our last trip. And this—" she pointed at the itinerary. "—was a lot of work. All the reservations, and flights, and rental cars." She put the papers back down on the table. "Thanks so much."

"It's just such a big country," I said. "I'm afraid all the flights and car rides will take a chunk out of our time."

"I look at all of it as seeing Bolivia," said Polly. "People-watching at the airport, and scenery watching on the car trips. It's all exploring, Suzanne. It's all getting to know the country of your birth. Really, it's just perfect."

She convinced me enough that I quit worrying about my itinerary. "Thanks, Polly. And there's one thing I know for certain—we'll have a ball."

Marilee raised her mug of tea, and we toasted, "To friends."

Polly asked, "What time will Bradley pick us up for dinner tonight?"

"He wants to leave early, so he can drive us around some sights first. So, let's be ready at six o'clock. And feel free to dress up, or wear jeans. The restaurant makes everyone feel welcome."

"In that case, let's dress," said Polly. "I doubt we'll be wearing anything but jeans for the other days."

"Sounds good to me," said Marilee. She took a very

deep breath, then leaned in and looked from me to Polly and back. "I have an announcement to make."

Polly's eyes grew huge. "An adoption?"

Marilee cocked her head and said, "A *possibility* of an adoption."

"Oh, my God," I said. "Which country?"

Marilee looked at me and then at Polly. "Our country."

"I thought you were working on an international adoption," I said.

Marilee smiled. "I was. But it's been made clear to me that I won't be approved due to my advanced age." She rolled her eyes.

"You're only forty-two, Marilee," I said.

"But they'd prefer I were under forty."

"Wouldn't we all?" I said. "So, tell us all about it."

"Well, I'd been working on the international adoption with a woman named Edith who has a small general practice in Charlottesville and specializes in adoptions. One night she called me to tell me about a freshman at the University of Virginia who is pregnant, and determined to have the baby and place it for adoption."

"And this student chose you to adopt her baby?" asked Polly, her eyes widening.

"Not immediately," said Marilee. "You see, Edith had told me most of her birth-mothers—and there are precious few of them these days—choose based on albums each prospective adoptive couple puts together. Pictures of the adoptive parent or parents, siblings, home, pets, family friends—that sort of thing. Apparently, most birth-mothers select young families where the woman plans to stay at home with the child."

"Bummer," said Polly.

"Yes," said Marilee. "But this UVA student asked Edith to recommend someone she trusts, preferably a woman with a career."

"And Edith recommended you," I said.

"She did. But the student still had some concerns about my age and being single. And she wanted to hear my child-care plan." Marilee used both hands to pull her cardigan close.

"Did you meet her?" I asked.

"Um-hm. Lovely young woman. Very serious about her academics. In fact, she plans to become a pediatric oncologist—after facing the loss of her little sister to cancer when the child was only three."

"That's heartbreaking," said Polly.

"Yes, it is," I said, but I didn't want to linger on anything that sad. "So, what did you tell her your child-care plan is?"

"Four months maternity leave/sabbatical, then a nanny at my house."

"And?" I asked.

"She chose me! The truth is, we hit it off from the first. She wants an open adoption, and plans to stop by to visit the baby once a quarter—as a friend—until the child is old enough to understand their connection. She asked if that would be okay with me, and I told her I wouldn't do it any other way, which seemed to cinch it." Marilee put her hand over mine. "And, Suzanne, I doubt I would've been so enthusiastic about the open approach had it not been for you."

"Oh, my God!" said Polly. "You're going to be a mommy!"

We all rose for a long, tearful hug. Then Marilee

pulled out her chair to sit back down, so we did, as well. "I hope it works out. The baby is due in four months, but I won't believe it until a judge signs the final order of adoption."

"But you're pretty sure it will happen?" asked Polly.

"Pretty sure. But I've read that about fifty percent of birth-mothers who sincerely plan to place a child for adoption change their minds after the birth."

I thought for a moment. "I can see how that might happen."

Marilee smiled. "Me, too. That's why I told the student I'm working with that I would understand perfectly if this happened with her."

"What did she say?" I asked.

Marilee bit her lip before responding. "It was like what I'd said had been magic words. She said that my statement just made her more certain she'd chosen the right woman to adopt her precious infant."

"Oh, my God. That's wonderful," said Polly. "Say, I was just wondering about the birth-father. Is he on board?"

"He is. I haven't met him, but he made it clear to his partner and to Edith that he'll support his girlfriend, however she wants to handle the pregnancy."

"This is so amazing!" said Polly.

"Fingers crossed," said Marilee. She then turned to Polly. "And Suzanne picked up some champagne for us to celebrate *your* news."

"You mean that I'm a free agent again?" asked Polly.

Marilee nodded, her eyebrows raised.

As I opened the refrigerator, I asked Polly, "Is this okay with you? Are you feeling like celebrating that your divorce has been finalized?"

Polly laughed as she threw her head back. "I thought you'd never ask. Absolutely, Suzanne."

I retrieved the bottle I'd hidden in my fridge and three champagne flutes.

Polly said, "It does feel like freedom to me. You know—a second chance to find a relationship that's honest. I don't expect to find anyone like Bradley, with a heart so consumed with me that he'd never consider another—even if I rejected him. But just someone I genuinely care about who sincerely cares about me. That's what I'll be keeping my eyes peeled for. And, above all, no damn secrets."

I poured, and we clinked our glasses to Marilee's toast, "To no damn secrets!"

After we'd each taken a sip, Marilee set her glass down and looked at me. "Do you have an announcement to make as to whether you'll stay down here another year?"

Polly wrinkled her forehead. "It hasn't even been a year yet. Do you have to decide now?"

I smiled at her. "It's for our law firm. I have until October 1st to decide if I'm returning to the office for the new year."

"And if you aren't?"

"Then the firm will need to replace me."

Polly looked from me to Marilee, then landed her concerned frown on me. "Are you okay with that ultimatum?"

I smiled. "Oh, yes. It's more than fair. Our firm is just so small, Polly. If I decide not to return, they really do have to bring in another partner to supervise my associates and be there for my clients. John, our managing partner, has been incredibly supportive."

Marilee was lightly tapping her fingernails on the tabletop. She said, "What will you do, Suzanne?"

I smiled at both of them, then took a sip of wine. "Listen. I love you guys. I'll make sure we visit every year. If you can't make the trip south—and you won't be able to with a new baby, Marilee—I'll head north."

"You're staying," said Polly.

"I love it here." They said nothing, just stared at me, wide-eyed, so I continued. "The climate is heaven. The Andes restore me every time I set eyes on them. I have friends here, mainly people from work. They're really good people, guys. And working at Bradley's non-profit is more challenging and meaningful than anything I've done before. Our mission changes lives—sometimes saves them. All this makes me feel more alive than I've felt in a very long time.

"But most of all, I have Bradley. He's such an extraordinary man. I'm proud as hell he's my birth-father. And his unconditional love for me lightens the load of my grief so much that I feel happy to be alive again. I have no more desire to sleep away my existence."

Marilee sighed, then patted my hand. "Then I'm happy for you."

"Me, too," said Polly. "So, how does that feel, exactly. What you said about your grief."

"I've been thinking about it a lot, Polly. It's as though a large box had been dropped on me and I could barely stand under its weight. I couldn't get up off my knees to move forward. Then a very strong man came along and lifted one end. I immediately felt the release of the weight." I paused and swallowed hard to keep from crying. "I'm still carrying the box, and always will be. But his assistance makes it possible for me to stand, to walk, even to stop and do a little dance sometimes."

Polly reached both of her arms over the table to take my hands in hers. "His love has saved you," she said.

"Si."

She squeezed my hands before releasing them.

Marilee asked, "Have you told Bradley you've decided to stay?"

I leaned in and whispered, "Actually, I'm going to surprise him."

"When?" asked Polly.

"I've been telling him I'll be here at least through New Year's Day. So, on Christmas morning, when we visit Sister Mary Olivia, I'll make my announcement to both of them."

"But she won't understand," said Marilee.

I nodded. "Probably not. But I think it will mean more to Bradley if I do it that way. To him, we're a kind of family. And Christmas would be such a beautiful day to make my news a kind of gift."

Polly spoke breathlessly. "He'll be so thrilled."

Marilee smiled, her eyes clouded with tears, as she shook her head ever so slightly. "This is so amazing, Suzanne."

We all rose at the same time and hugged and cried.

Chapter 31

At 5:55 p.m., Marilee, Polly and I walked through my apartment building doorway into a gorgeous, balmy, Bolivian night. We had on our cocktail dresses and wore heels. I'd thought to let Bradley know, so he wore a sport coat and tie when he picked us up. Same boots, though. I suspected they were the only pair of shoes he had. At least he was ready to start a mountain hike on a moment's notice.

Bradley seemed excited to give us a little car-tour of some of the interesting sites and landmarks of Cochabamba. He provided a quick background on each site, all of which had Spanish names, of course. Polly and I were laughing at Marilee, who was mutilating the pronunciations as she tried to commit them to memory. In fact, we were laughing so hard that we almost missed a beautiful building just south of town.

Polly yelled, "Bradley, stop!"

He pulled to the curb, and said, "What? What have I done?"

"Lo siento, Bradley. But that the building we just passed—"

He took a deep breath to relax, then said, "Si. A new hotel. It opened only a month ago."

Marilee and I were both craning our necks to look back to see what had seized Polly's attention.

She said, "It looked like it said Hotel Liliana."

"Si. It is owned by your old friend, Liliana Perez."

Marilee asked, "Do you know her, Bradley?"

He laughed. "No. We don't travel in the same social circles."

Polly said, "Hey, why don't we stop in and say hi?"

"Seriously?" I asked.

"What can it hurt?" asked Polly. "Anyway, if we do happen to run into her, you and Bradley can talk with her about how her best friend is doing."

"She's probably not even here," said Marilee. "But maybe we can just leave her a hello note."

"Okay. We won't look too creepy if we just congratulate her on the new hotel." I turned to my father. "Please come in with us to see the reception area. Based on her other hotel, it's probably beautiful."

He said, "And you'll simply leave a message for her?"

I crossed my middle finger over my pointer in the promise sign, then placed my hand on my heart.

Bradley smiled and shook his head, then backed up to get properly parked. We all walked up the stone sidewalk and into the second Hotel Liliana. Like the first, it was elegantly appointed, with giant vases of fresh flowers atop highly polished tables. I approached the concierge and explained that we wanted to leave a message of greeting for Senora Perez. The gentleman kindly provided me with several pieces of hotel stationery and a pen bearing the hotel's name. I stood at a corner of the marble reception counter to pen our message. I'd almost finished it and planned that we'd each sign it. Glancing over my shoulder, I saw that the others were wandering around, admiring the architecture and the décor.

A soft voice behind me said, "Hello, Suzanne."

I turned, and saw none other than Liliana Perez, looking elegant in a heavy, emerald green satin cocktail dress and matching heels. Juan Carlos stood ten feet behind her. I had forgotten just how beautiful a couple they were. He said nothing, and his handsome face remained non-committal.

"Senora Perez! I was just writing you a little note."

She smiled. "Why?"

"I live here now—in Cochabamba."

"Ah, to be near your mother."

"Yes. And to be near my father, Bradley Bowman." I turned to look at him and saw that he was watching us, but from too far away to hear.

Liliana said, "The Bradley who Sister Mary Olivia mentioned to you?"

"Si." I nodded toward him.

She smiled, then said, "Will you introduce us, please?"

I sputtered, "Yes. Absolutely." I motioned for Bradley to join us, and he hurried to me. He nodded and smiled his lopsided smile at Liliana. I said, "Senora Liliana Perez, this is my father, Senor Bradley Bowman." He nodded again, which I thought was charming. "And Bradley, this is Senora Liliana Perez, the owner of this gorgeous hotel."

He took her hand to shake and said, "Senora Perez, it is my great honor to meet you. Of course, I have heard of you and your fabulous hotels—and also of the benefit galas you host to help the poor. You are a person of great generosity."

As he released her hand, she smiled and said, "I have not done nearly as much as you and your beloved

Olivia."

Bradley smiled softly, then nodded. He seemed at a loss for how to answer the compliment without getting another. We were saved from the awkward moment when Polly and Marilee returned from the restroom, saw who we were speaking with, and hurried to join us.

Liliana addressed Polly first. "It seems odd for you to appear at my hotel and not be singing the national anthem, Polly."

Polly beamed. "Your new hotel is gorgeous. Congratulations." She drew out her words dramatically.

"Thank you. And Marilee, how nice to see you again." She continued in a soft, confidential tone. "I hope you ladies will excuse us for a moment. I would like to speak with Senor Bowman and Suzanne privately for a moment."

"Of course," said Marilee and Polly at the same time, after which Marilee laughed and shook her head in mock—or real—embarrassment.

Liliana led us to a little alcove where two small, off-white brocade couches faced each other. After indicating for me and Bradley to sit, she took her place across from us. "I'm sure you have dinner plans, so I won't keep you long."

I nodded. "When we glimpsed your hotel from the car, we just had to see it."

Liliana nodded and smiled. "Juan Carlos and I are also on our way out, so I also have only a few minutes. First, how do you find Sister Mary Olivia?"

Bradley said, "She is a lovely woman still. Her great gift to me is that she has remembered me—only two times. But she spoke to me of our love, which, of course, broke my heart."

I admired how forthcoming he was with this woman, who was essentially a stranger to him. I said, "We go to visit her every Sunday morning at five o'clock. She'll come out of her mind's prison perhaps one time out of six to remember one of us. We adore her either way, but those moments are precious." I paused. "In fact, we'll be seeing her tomorrow morning. She may not connect with us, but even if she doesn't, we'll be honored to hold her hand for a while."

"Ah. I am so happy you see her regularly. I spend most of my time at my hotel in Oruro. But I visit Olivia any time I am in Cochabamba—always on a Saturday morning, like in the old days."

"Has she remembered you?" asked Bradley.

"Once. About two weeks ago, in fact. She knew exactly who I was, although she thought we were in Oruro. It was such a thrill to be with my best friend again, even though it lasted just a few minutes."

I placed both of my hands over my heart. "That's wonderful. I couldn't be happier for you."

"Thank you." She turned to Bradley. "Senor Bowman, I know of your non-profit. You continue the work you introduced Sister Mary Olivia to."

Juan Carlos cleared his throat, and Liliana laughed. She looked at her partner and said, sharply, "Un momento!"

It was interesting to me that he laughed heartily at the scolding. Perhaps he was more down-to-earth than I'd thought when we'd met the last time.

"Yes," said Bradley. "It is the same approach. I try only to increase the scale so we can serve more prisoners."

She gazed intently at Bradley. "It is noble work. I

host one benefit every year at each hotel to support a local charity. My first gala here in Cochabamba will be in eleven months' time. Guests will fly in from all over the country—and many of them have very deep pockets." She paused to let this sink in. "I would like to sit down with you and Suzanne to discuss whether the first benefit here could be for your non-profit."

Bradley seemed stunned. After a moment, he said, "Thank you. I would welcome such a discussion."

I was beaming, so Marilee and Polly must've figured out that something good was happening. They were both smiling at me.

Liliana said, "I have only one condition."

"Ah," said Bradley. "Is it one I have control over?"

Liliana closed her eyes for a second in thought. "I really don't know. But the condition is that Polly sing for my guests, including, I must add, her lovely version of our national anthem."

Bradley looked at me. "What do you think, Suzanne?"

"I don't think we could stop her if we wanted to."

Liliana laughed. "Good. I'll have my secretary set up a lunch meeting. For now, I must be going. Juan Carlos is a sweet lamb, but he's a very hungry lamb."

We shook hands with her. Then as she passed Marilee and Polly, they did the same. In a moment, she was out the door and Juan Carlos was helping her into a chauffeured limousine.

Bradley was literally scratching his head, and I was laughing at him for it. At dinner, Bradley and I explained what Liliana had offered to do for the non-profit. I put my hands into a prayer position—again—as I added the information about the one condition. Polly said, "You couldn't stop me if you tried."

Marilee said, "This is so amazing—and it's only Day One of our trip."

Chapter 32

Unfortunately, Sister Mary Olivia did not make her way to the here-and-now that Sunday morning. Nevertheless, Bradley and I had the opportunity to hold her hand and tell her we loved her, and that was valuable to us—if not to her.

As promised, Marilee and Polly were sound asleep when I got back to my apartment. I didn't disturb their slumber until 10:00 a.m., as we'd agreed the night before. Then we needed to get ready for our trip to the Andes to release Mac, Betty, and Ron from the lipstick tubes. Bradley had described a hike for us which would start at 14,400 feet above sea level and end at 16,500 feet—Tunari, the highest peak in the area. He explained that the problem with it was that Marilee and Polly had not had time yet to acclimatize, so what would normally be a two and a half to three-hour ascent could take up to four hours to be safe. The descent would be half that time, but it was still a difficult hike. My friends insisted that they were in good shape and that only the highest peak would do.

It took two hours to drive from downtown Cochabamba to the trailhead. As we began the ascent, Bradley informed us that we would notice the difficulty breathing more and more as we reached higher elevations. He also said that our hearts would race, which might make us think they were about to explode. But he assured us, they wouldn't actually do that.

At the beginning, the hike wasn't as hideous as I'd feared, but it still required more oxygen than we seemed to have. As a result, there was no conversation on the way up. The terrain was gravel-covered rocks mixed in with all sizes and shapes of boulders, all in grays, browns, and blacks, depending on how the intense sun was hitting them.

When we came upon a pristine mountain lake, the stunning clear blue color was so incongruent with its surroundings, it was like finding a rose bush in full bloom in the middle of an asphalt parking lot. Unfortunately, we couldn't delay to admire it and still complete the hike before dark. We were treated to a second lake, as delightful as the first. But I will always remember it as the point just before the demands of the ascent changed dramatically—and not in a good way. The path virtually disappeared. Were it not for Bradley, we would've been left to guess which huge boulder might be the best choice for survival. If there was no conversation before, now we could hear plenty from each other—all gasping sounds. That was when I had to focus on Bradley's promise my heart wouldn't actually explode.

When we finally reached the summit, we women threw ourselves on the first relatively flat rock at the top and took a break to breathe, then to sip a little water. Bradley walked around, taking in the phenomenal view. He licked his finger and held it up to test for the prevailing wind, which would carry the ashes of my family over peaks and valleys of the stunning, craggy landscape.

Once we could all breathe semi-regularly again, I

nodded to Marilee that I was ready to begin. The others stood together and gave me some space at the precipice to conduct my memorial. Marilee handed me the purple lipstick tube containing Mac first. Bradley stepped up to show me how to turn it just right to release the dust into the wind, rather than over my jacket. He stepped back to the witness position.

I took a very deep breath, then said, "It is my strongly held belief that words about death are inherently inadequate. Perhaps a moment of silence would be a better choice. But I don't want to risk doing a disservice to my family by not trying to put my thoughts into words— however lame my effort will be.

"Mac was a good man and an honest man, who died too soon. He dedicated his work life to helping the less fortunate. He spent his leisure time creating beauty. He was my partner, my friend, my beloved, and my anchor. I will love him and miss him all the days of my life. His ashes rest in the Blue Ridge Mountains he adored. Now, his ashes will also become a part of the Bolivian Andes, which is fitting because he will be near to me. But the truth is, it is wherever I am, and wherever I may travel, that he will live—in my heart."

I'd told Marilee that I wanted to release Betty last, so she handed me Ron in the maroon lipstick holder. She stepped back with the others to watch and listen.

"My father, Ron, worked long hours teaching, and did it out of optimism about his students and his absolute belief in their potential. So too, he believed in me. He helped me, he guided me, and then he set me free to be an adult. He was a loving father until the end. Ron knew that I started my life-journey in Bolivia and carried on with it in Virginia. So it is fitting that he will rest here, as well as in the Blue Ridge Mountains. He will live on in all those who knew him, and always in my heart."

We took a moment to watch Ron's ashes sail up and away, over the valley below.

Finally, Marilee handed me the pale pink lipstick holder with my mother Betty inside. I held it up for a moment or so, trying to summon the strength to speak the words I'd planned. I addressed her in the second person, and felt exactly as though we were having one of our chats at the kitchen table—where we'd had dozens of intimate conversations.

"Mom, I'm sorry I doubted you, believing you were unfair to me—and to your sister. I've given it a lot of thought since Polly tried to straighten me out, and since we found Olivia's letter to you. I've come to believe that you, like Olivia, sacrificed much for me—and for Bradley. Everything you did flowed from the purest intentions. I do still think people suffered unnecessarily. But I appreciate that you meant only to honor Olivia's most fervent request, so that your baby girl would lie safely and securely in your arms, blossom into young womanhood in your home, and carry on into adulthood with her friendship with you intact. And this is important, Mom. I forgive myself for doubting you. Somehow, it's all come full-circle. I stand here at the summit of Tunari, the highest point in central Bolivia, with my father as my witness, releasing you into the country from which you received me. I will love you, and Dad, and Mac forever." With that, I tipped the container and released Betty into the breeze. I took a good five minutes to just stand there, looking over the impossibly moving landscape, embracing everything I was feeling.

Then I was finished. I smiled at the others and said,

"Snacks before we head down?"

They understood, and let it be as I'd left it. Each of them gave me a tender hug, but we said no more about my loss.

We rehydrated, and chowed down on bland energy bars. We took dozens of pictures, none of which would do justice to what lay before our eyes.

The descent was, indeed, much easier, and neither my lungs nor my heart made any serious complaints. As we reached the trailhead, we dove into the logistics for the next day's journey to Salar de Uyuni. Polly cracked so many jokes that we were all in tears as we climbed back into Bradley's car. But unlike the tears I'd wiped from my cheeks for the past twenty months, these marked unadulterated joy. These were the drops of my own salt which I planned to mingle with nature's the next day, with my father and my friends by my side.

A word about the author…

Judith Fournie Helms grew up in southern Illinois, and attended college and law school in Chicago. She became a founding partner of a law firm based in Chicago with offices on both coasts, and was recognized by her peers as a "Super Lawyer" and a "Leading Lawyer." Retired from the practice of law, Judith writes novels and short stories at her home in Virginia where she lives with her husband. She is also the author of the 2018 novel 'The Toronto Embryo,' the 2021 novel 'Grudge Tiger,' and the 2025 novel 'Statures of No Limitations.' www.judithhelms.com

Thank you for purchasing
this publication of The Wild Rose Press, Inc.

For questions or more information
contact us at
info@thewildrosepress.com.

The Wild Rose Press, Inc.
www.thewildrosepress.com